Alpha Revealed

by

Brenda Sparks

Alpha Council Chronicles, Book 5

Alpha Revealed

Contact Information: info@thewildrosepress.com

Cover Art by *Rae Monet, Inc. Design*

The Wild Rose Press, Inc.
PO Box 708
Adams Basin, NY 14410-0708
Visit us at www.thewildrosepress.com

Publishing History
First Black Rose Edition, 2020
Print ISBN 978-1-5092-2917-8
Digital ISBN 978-1-5092-2918-5

Alpha Council Chronicles, Book 5
Published in the United States of America

Acknowledgments

First and foremost, my deep appreciation
goes out to my readers. I love you guys!

~

I must give a special shout out to Kim,
whose bug phobia has provided
ample amusement and inspiration.

~

Heartfelt gratitude to my heartmate and son—
I couldn't write without their love and support.

~

And last but most certainly not least,
I owe my sincere gratitude to my fabulous editor,
Callie Lynn Wolfe,
and the wonderful staff at The Wild Rose Press
for helping me share the Alphas with the world.

She lifted one arm in his direction. He raised a hand to still her movement. “Don’t…touch me.”

Well, damned if that didn’t smart. He didn’t want her to touch him, even to offer him a little comfort. My, how things changed. He certainly hadn’t minded her touch the night of her brother’s wedding.

Fine. If he doesn’t want me touching him, so be it.

Natasha turned around, sending her harlequin-colored pigtails twirling about her face and retrieved the bag of blood from the floor. Without looking in his direction, she stalked through the room and sat in the only padded chair. She punctured the bag with her fangs and drank, glaring at him over the top of the bag.

The blood seeped into her cells, nourishing both her and the baby. The baby moved as she continued to down the bag quickly. Her hunger pangs eased a little with each gulp of the life-sustaining liquid.

Vlad slowly straightened to his full height. The expression on his face, a cross between disdain and pain, softened her eyes. With an awkward gait, he gingerly moved in her direction.

“We need to talk,” he barked, his voice still rough with pain.

She just bet they did. No doubt, Vlad would tell her to leave. It was there on his face. He obviously didn’t want her in his home, and she didn’t blame him.

She had run out after they made love, avoided him for months, and now she had injured his manhood. If the tables were reversed, she probably wouldn’t want him around either.

Praise for Brenda Sparks

"Brenda Sparks weaves stories that are filled with sensuality, mystery, drama, and awesome vampire action. They keep you on the edge of your seat and never fail to deliver a satisfying conclusion."

~DW Adler, author

~*~

"Ms. Sparks takes you on a journey that'll have you turning pages just to find out what happens."

~Rhea Regale, author

~*~

"I loved the world building in (Brenda's) story."

~Harlie Williams, author

Prologue

As the world detonated around him and the flashes of light exploded before his eyes, he transported, albeit briefly, to one of countless battles. For centuries much too long to remember, he had fought. One battle blurred into the next, with another on the horizon. So many battlefields. So much death. Destruction and brutality littered every front-line. And he was always in the midst of it. Merciless and ruthless.

Vladimir Starikovich had executed many enemies over hundreds of centuries. Killed again and again until blood and death were forever stamped upon his being. There was no other way of life for him. He had become pure predator, a bringer of death.

His life was dark, dangerous. No place for light or love. It made for a lonely existence, for he could not share his burdens with another.

This night though no battle needed to be fought. This night held only peace and happiness while he stood observing the fireworks overhead at the reception of his friends' wedding. Unlike him, they were free to find their one true love, their heartmates. He wanted to be happy for them, and in some ways, he was. But he'd never be able to find that kind of true happiness with another.

A hard sigh pushed from his lips. He treasured love. Knew what it was to have loved and lost. And though the exile from caring for another may be self-imposed, it nonetheless was a heavy burden for him to bear.

His only companions were the animals with which he communicated, similar to the one he now scratched. Vlad looked down at the canine beside him, pushing into its mind to send the nervous dog a soothing feeling of warmth to calm its agitation at the loud fireworks. Their eyes met when Vlad rested his hand on the Irish wolfhound's large head. Connor settled under his touch.

"That was amazing. You have a way with animals."

The soft, feminine voice startled the warrior, pulling his attention from the mind of the dog. Her presence surrounded him, taking the chill from the night. Her enticing scent wafted over him. Without conscious thought, he took it deep into his lungs, enjoying the outdoorsy aroma. *Gardenias.* The delicious aroma masked the sulfur from the fireworks, filling him from the inside out.

"I didn't realize anyone was watching," Vlad said, never taking his eyes from the hound for fear he would be lost if he looked into her eyes.

"I was. That was really impressive. He calmed immediately under your touch."

Steeling himself against her beauty, his eyes slowly lifted to hers, pinning her with his intimidating stare as if to warn her away. "My touch can do much."

A shiver flowed through her body as his dark tone washed over her. Her gaze captured in his, she moved forward. A small movement, barely noticeable. He would have missed it had he not been so acutely aware of her presence.

It had always been like that around her. Natasha Peterhof affected him as no other. Sister of his friend the great Nicholai Peterhof, she'd been born Russian royalty. The siblings had been brought into the vampiric world centuries ago by their cousin Demetri.

Vlad and Demetri were part of an elite fighting group called the Alpha Council, then once trained to fight, Nicholai joined their ranks. Theirs was a comradery born on the battlefield. The males he fought with, battled with for centuries, were as close as brothers—like family to him when he had none left. As such, everyone they held dear Vlad gladly took into his keeping.

Natasha was no exception.

No. Actually, she was a *big* exception. Natasha drew him to her in a way that terrified him. When she came near, his entire being focused solely on her. He forced himself to stay away, putting as much physical distance as possible between them. Tonight, that had been exceptionally difficult. They sat near each other during the wedding. At the reception, she had been placed so close to his seat all evening he'd nearly drowned in her delicious scent.

She called to him, his inner beast warring with him in her presence. His control around her was tenuous at best, and on a night like tonight, when she appeared exceptionally gorgeous in the black dress she had chosen, the control was slipping.

He was sorely tempted to throw her over his shoulder and take her to his lair to do all kinds of deliciously salacious things to her. Vlad's gaze roamed her body, burning over her like a brand.

She looked away just as his eyes reached her

beautiful face. His gaze followed hers to notice Demetri staring in their direction. The sight of his fellow warrior gave him the kick in the gut he needed.

His feet moved, taking him steadily in the opposite direction of his desire while leading the canine away from the ruckus of the wedding. With each long stride, his breath came a little easier, and his self-control reined in his inner beast. He pushed past Marcus' butler, Payton.

"Excuse me, sir," the elderly valet said, spinning away from Vlad's muscular body with practiced ease.

"My apologies," the Alpha mumbled, making his escape through the kitchen door. Inside he released the hound, and the two parted in opposite directions.

He bound up the stairs three at a time. Spotting the nearest door, he entered quickly and closed it behind him. He leaned against it, his breath pushing from his lungs as he fought to ease the physical response of his body. Lust pulsed steadily in his veins. He knew it would recede if he could just be away from the object of his desire.

For centuries he'd practiced avoiding Natasha. He could not allow himself to indulge in the comfort she offered. She wanted him. She made that clear long ago, but he dared not risk a relationship. It was not safe. Of course, there was also her brother to consider, as well as, her cousin.

"She is most definitely off limits," he reminded himself.

A soft knock on the door made him jump away from the wood as if it was aflame. *Natasha!* Her sweet scent drifted into his lungs, her presence weaving its way through his mind. He took a deep steadying breath, drawing her deeper within.

Big mistake and one too late to undo.

The door opened to reveal her supple frame, hugged lovingly by the simple black dress she wore. A strand of gray pearls circled her neck, drawing his gaze to the pulse beating just below her creamy skin.

Vlad's heart raced in his chest like a thoroughbred at a derby. Fates above, why had she come to him? He longed to be with her, caress every inch. Vlad's self-control wavered as Natasha slipped into the room and closed the door behind her.

He was a man alone in the world. It must be that way. Yet, the woman standing before him made him want to turn his back on all he knew as right and decent. He wanted to take her, mark her as his.

Natasha was impetuous, high-spirited. She drove him mad with hunger for her spirit. It was as dangerous for her as him.

What exactly beguiled him? She was stubborn. Pushed him. Drew him to her until he wanted to possess her. She was pure temptation, and the realization she had him warring with himself frustrated him.

"What are you doing here?" He barked from between clenched teeth. Vlad's hands fisted by his side as much to keep him from reaching out to touch her as in ire.

Her eyes went wide, like a doe staring at a bear. "I—I wanted to see you."

Unable to take his eyes from her beating pulse, he licked his lips. "Where's your usual choker?"

Tasha's hand covered her throat, hiding the temptation from his sight. "I wouldn't wear that to a wedding."

His mind created a vision of her wearing only the collar around her delicate neck, its skull and crossbones pattern circling the black leather. It brought all kinds of sinful thoughts to the imagination. His inner beast awakened, stirred for her. The slip in his control infuriated him further. He tried to swallow his rising lust. It stuck in his throat.

"Coming up here was a mistake." Natasha started to push from the door as if to leave.

He landed in front of her before she could blink, his hands framing her against the door. Her tongue darted out between her lips to moisten them. Vlad's gut tightened. "Why did you come?"

Her eyes darkened in response to his rough voice.

"I-I just…"

He ran one finger down her bare arm. The slight contact sent a rush of lightning through his bloodstream, sizzling bright like the fireworks outside.

"I thought…"

Vlad dipped his head, so his deep Siberian accent purred in her ear. "You thought what?"

Her throat worked to swallow before she replied. He moved closer, keeping only a handbreadth between them. Her warmth surrounded him, pushing at his self-control.

"Just forget it," Natasha whispered.

"Forget *it* or forget *me*?" His heart raced awaiting her answer.

"I tried. I can't forget you," she confessed.

In perfect synchronicity to the grand finale outside, Vladimir's self-control shattered. Desire exploded through his veins, sending a rush of fiery blood to his shaft.

He closed the small gap between them, pushing her against the door as he took her lips in a heated kiss that bespoke a promise of what was to come.

Chapter 1

Natasha stood before the mirror, her eyes tracking the movement of the brush through her hair. The bristles wove their way through the multicolored strands, the lighting shimmering over the purple and blue hues. The colored locks played hide-and-seek with her naturally black hair, weaving between until it became difficult to see the bold striping. The muted colors reminded her of six months ago when she chose to tone down the normally loud volume of her hair for a special occasion.

Her brother's wedding…Natasha smiled at the memory. A double wedding, actually, for her brother, Nicholai, and a friend of theirs named Marcus. Both men were fortunate enough to find their heartmates after centuries of existence.

For their kind, each male and female had one true love, someone who completed them, the other half of their souls. A heartmate. Her brother had been lucky enough to finally find that special person, and Natasha could not be happier for Nicholai and Juliette.

She enjoyed herself at the event.

Perhaps too much, she now readily admitted to herself.

Overjoyed, she indulged in a little too much of the vodka that had poured freely through an ice fountain at the reception. It gave her the courage she needed to flirt with a male who she'd had a crush on for centuries.

Natasha gave an inelegant snort. *And didn't that just turn out super.*

She pushed away from the vanity, taking the brush with her as she moved into her bedroom. Needing a distraction, she noted the features in the room. She loved the beachy room with its white walls, nautically themed paintings, and ocean-blue bedspread. The large steamer trunk that served as a hope chest at the end of the bed added to the oceanic feel.

She enjoyed it here in Australia. Found it to be a peaceful place to spend the fall months since it was warm here. It gave her more time to be outside, to do things like snorkel the reefs and go zip-lining through the trees. She loved adventure and enjoyed living life, experiencing new things. But her newest adventure made her weary.

She crossed to the bed and lay down, her hand automatically finding the rounded swell of her unborn child. Natasha closed her eyes, taking in the rush of the ocean coming through the open window. The rolling waves were a soothing contrast to the chaotic thoughts in her mind. She let out a deep, wistful sigh.

The sound of the doorbell opened her eyes. Natasha pushed from the bed, pulling the tight T-shirt over her slight baby bump as she walked through the home to answer the door.

A wide smile graced her face when she opened the door and found Harleigh. Great name for a fun girl. Appropriate too since the woman loved motorcycles. Her parents had done a fantastic job in the picking-a-name department. Natasha wondered briefly if she would do as well.

"Hey, girl." The woman with hair every bit as colorful as Natasha's held up a large fish by its tail. "Look what I caught today. Guess what's for dinner?"

Natasha chuckled. "Good lord, that thing is huge. Did you bring an army to help us eat it?"

"We could always invite your baby daddy." Harleigh pushed past her and smacked the fish down on the kitchen counter.

"Are you really going to go there again?" Natasha pulled a knife from the butcher block.

"I can't believe you haven't told him you're pregnant, Tasha. Every man deserves to know he has an offspring in the world."

"I didn't make the decision lightly. I still feel the same way I did five months ago when I discovered I was going to have this baby. I don't want Vlad to feel like he is saddled with a baby and a wife. If he knew about the child, he would demand we marry so he could take care of us."

Harleigh took the knife from Natasha, then cut the tail and head of the fish off in two clean whacks. "So, he's old-school?"

"Very old-school." *Medieval-school really,* Natasha thought, leaning against the counter. "I don't want to trap him into marrying me."

It was more than just not wanting to trap Vlad in a marriage. She didn't want Vlad to know about the baby because she wanted him to be free to find his heartmate. If they were married, he would be faithful to her. His honor would allow no less. He would never find his true love—*if* she was waiting out there for him somewhere.

Natasha shook off the melancholy trying to worm

its way into her heart. She didn't mind raising the baby alone and saw it as another adventure. One she would gladly take on, especially once she got her energy back.

"How did you two meet, anyway?"

A heavy sigh pushed through Natasha's painted lips as the memories pushed in.

"It was a long time ago. Vladimir drew me to him the moment our eyes first met. His black eyes held an intensity that made my knees weak. When Nicholai introduced us, he clasped my hand in a firm grip and brought it to his lips for a kiss. I fainted dead away."

Harleigh laughed. "Not exactly the first impression you want to make on a hot guy."

Natasha rolled her eyes. "It gets worse. I woke to find my brother looming over me and Vlad nowhere in sight. Since then, I've rarely seen the guy."

"Until the wedding." Harleigh wagged her brows.

For over a century, he seemed to be avoiding her and did an excellent job of it until the night of her brother's wedding. Emboldened by the alcohol, Natasha had followed him into the house, cornered him, and finally gotten a taste of what she'd wanted all these years.

And what a taste it had been!

Natasha's tongue darted between her lips at the memory. "Yeah," she sighed wistfully. "Until the wedding."

She still felt the heat of his skin against hers, smelled his scent which possessed the power to drive her wild with need. Remembering the feel of his coarse goatee on her face, her hand covered her lips.

He had taken her to heaven, pushing her body to the brink of ecstasy again and again. Even the next day she had wanted more of him. In fact, she still did. The draw to him had only grown since they were together, not diminished as she hoped.

Natasha shook off the memory.

"But what's done is done. I've made my decision to raise the baby alone. Vlad doesn't need to be saddled with a family."

Her voice sounded wistful even to her own ears, and she hoped Harleigh hadn't noticed the tone.

"Sounds like you might want to be married to him, though."

Harleigh never missed a thing. It could be very annoying.

Tasha shook her head in irritation. "Look, it doesn't matter how I feel about the guy. He deserves the right to live his life. He shouldn't have to pay for our mistake."

Harleigh stopped scaling the fish to look at her friend. "But you should?"

Her hand flew to her stomach, the protective gesture automatic. "I'm not paying. I already love this baby. From the first time I felt him move, I knew I would do anything to protect him, to love him. I already treasure him, and I can't wait for the day when I finally get to hold him in my arms."

Harleigh nodded as she resumed her work on the fish. "But Vlad wouldn't feel the same?" It seemed more of a question than a statement.

"I honestly don't know how Vlad would feel about the baby. It's not like we ever spoke of our future."

I never gave him the chance.

She had run, leaving the warmth of his bed without so much as a thanks or see-ya-later. When she snuck away that night, she intended to resume her life, but reality had other plans. She still felt as sharply as she did six months ago, and she wanted him with a desperation that scared her. She had hoped putting some distance between them would have lessened the pull.

It didn't.

Natasha pulled a cast-iron skillet from under the sink.

"Then how do you know he doesn't want you and the baby?" Harleigh scooped the fish onto a plate.

"I just know. He isn't the kind of guy who would want to be forced into a relationship." Natasha shook the pan at her friend. "Come on, no more talk about Vladimir tonight. Let's get this fish frying so we can eat. I'm starving."

"No surprise there. You're always hungry now that you're eating for two," Harleigh quipped. "I swear I don't know how you don't gain weight given the way you eat. From the back, you'd never know you were pregnant. Even from the front, it isn't really noticeable."

Natasha followed her friend outside and watched her build a bonfire on the beach. Tasha placed a metal grill over the roaring fire, then put the skillet on top before she settled down in the sand to observe Harleigh put some oil and the fish in the pan.

"Seriously, Natasha, I don't know how you can look so thin when you are six months pregnant. Most people would be big by now. Are you sure about the date?"

"Quite sure." Natasha rubbed her small belly.

Typically, vampires barely showed a pregnancy.

Often it wasn't until the eighth month that a pregnancy became obvious to others. Their doctors believed it had something to do with their high metabolism, but Tasha didn't care why. Here in Australia, away from her family and their preternatural hearing and sight, she could keep the pregnancy a secret.

And I want to keep it that way. Natasha's gaze roamed over the gentle waves.

If her brother found out the baby belonged to Vlad, he would lose his mind. He thought himself her parent, had acted in the role of her protector ever since their father died when they were children. His care and concern for her had a way of making her feel smothered. The last thing she needed was for him to find out about the baby.

Natasha blew out a sigh, the sound lost to the ocean, as she considered telling Nicholai about the baby. She would have to eventually. At some point, her son would be born. She smiled at the thought. But just because he was born, didn't mean she had to confess the paternity of the babe.

"Why are you smiling?" asked Harleigh.

"Oh, nothing. I'm just thinking about the baby."

"I should have known." Harleigh's gaze fell to the fish. Her nose crinkled. "Smells like it's starting to burn. Where is the spatula?"

"I thought you brought it."

"Nope."

"Guess it's inside then." Natasha pushed up.

Harleigh laid a stilling hand on her forearm. "You sit, Mama. I'll go get it."

Her friend bound up the dune, her small pigtails, one mostly red the other a yellowish-orange, bouncing in the wind. Alone, Natasha lay down in the sand, reveling in the salty air on her skin. It made her tingle like Vladimir's touch had done.

She mentally shook herself. Best not to go down that road. She didn't need to think about how Vlad made her feel again. She'd thought of little else since she left him that night. Everything reminded her of him. The softness of the sheets on her bed, the scratch of the sand on her skin so like his goatee, everything seemed to remind her of the male she left behind. She tried hard to forget about him, knowing it did no good to remember their time together. It only made her miss him.

And she did miss him. Missed the sound of his whiskey voice with its deep Siberian accent. Missed the feel of his arms, even though she had only spent a few hours in them. She had it bad for the man, and no amount of time or distance seemed to help the ache in her heart.

Tears pushed at the backs of her eyes. She was tough. She didn't cry.

Must be the hormones, she thought rubbing her eyes with the back of one hand.

A howl in the distance drew her attention. A look of confusion furrowed her brows as Harleigh rushed to her side, spatula in one hand and a potholder in the other. "Did you hear that?"

"Hear what?" asked Harleigh as another howl called into the air.

Natasha did not miss the tension in her friend's shoulders. "That. It sounds like a wolf, but that's impossible."

Harleigh flipped the fish and waited for the sizzling

sound to die down before she replied. "You know there are no wolves in Australia." She gave an insouciant shrug. "Probably just a dingo or dog."

"I've never heard a dog sound like that." A shiver went down Tasha's spine, the hairs on her neck rising.

"I'm sure it's nothing." Harleigh prodded the fish. "Look, the fish is about done."

"Let's eat inside tonight." Natasha rose and brushed the sand from her jeans.

A cool breeze blew, bringing with it the stench of wet wolf. Her face snapped into the wind, and she turned her back to Harleigh. Though not well-practiced in the ability, she pushed her senses in the direction of the smell, over the sandy ground, through the seagrass to push out as far as they would reach. She focused all her concentration toward the odor.

Natasha sensed crabs burrowing under the sand, the birds settled peacefully in their nests. She felt a couple walk down the beach and something…else. She guided her senses, opening herself fully to all they communicated.

A void, a blank spot. Small, but there. Down the beach and moving toward them.

Panic pushed her into action. Her brother warned her about sensing voids because a blank spot might indicate a demon was near.

Demons were attacking their breed. In fact, her cousin, Demetri, had recently been rescued from demons who had done terrible experiments on him. The keepers of their kind, a Special Forces type of unit called the Alpha Council, currently hunted the demons, trying to remove the threat they posed to the vampires.

If the Alpha Council was taking the demon threat

seriously, she better too. Her pulse kicked up a notch and anxiety twisted her stomach.

She spun around and grabbed Harleigh by the arm. "Come on. Let's get inside. Now!"

Harleigh braced, her feet sliding in the sand like a dirt bike skidding around a turn. "Hold on. What's wrong with you?" She gave Natasha an incredulous look. "Just let me get the fish."

Harleigh pulled from Natasha's hold and used the potholder she brought out to grab the handle of the skillet. She began kicking sand on the fire in an attempt to put it out.

"Forget the fire. Let's go," Natasha commanded, turning for her home.

She wrapped her arms about her waist and silently chastised herself for not being more vigilant. Growing up in the shadow of two Alphas, she'd never needed to be on constant guard. Now she wished she'd heeded their advice to have her senses taking in her surroundings at all times.

"Give me a minute. You know it isn't safe to leave the fire going."

Her need to get to safety warred with her desire to help her friend. Obviously, Harleigh wouldn't go inside until the fire was extinguished. Deciding it would be faster if she helped, Natasha scooped up handfuls of sand to throw on the fire. One scoop, two. She lost count, flinging the sand as quickly as possible, all the while sensing the void moved closer.

With the fire finally extinguished, she led Harleigh back up into the house and locked them inside. Natasha peeked out the window, searching for anything usual. The seagrass swayed in the breeze. Waves gently crested against the sand. All seemed quiet, still. Too still.

She jumped at the sound of the iron skillet when it clanged loudly in the sink. Faster than the blink of an eye, she turned to face Harleigh who carried dishes to the table. Her friend set the kitchen table, seemingly unaware of the danger lurking outside.

A mournful howl carried on the air.

“Did you hear that?” Natasha demanded, a tight expression on her face. “You must have heard *that*.”

“Probably just another dingo. No big deal.” Harleigh meandered to the refrigerator and removed two covered bowls. After placing them on the table next to the fish, she spared her friend a glance. “Come on, Tasha. Come eat. I know you are hungry. You’re always hungry.”

Her disarming smile eased some of the tension from Natasha’s body. Harleigh might be right. Maybe she was making too big a deal of the howl. There might be a logical explanation for the void she sensed as well.

She must admit, Harleigh was definitely right about one thing—she was hungry.

The little one growing inside her possessed an accelerated metabolism. The term eating-for-two seemed more like eating-for-six in her case. She needed to feed often, both regular food and blood.

It had not been easy to keep her supply of blood stocked without causing suspicion. The local blood bank and hospitals could only supply so much before they too would run low. She needed to materialize all around the world to supply her increased need, making sure to rarely visit the same site twice.

Her friend’s pulse called to her now with the beat

of its steady rhythm beneath the skin. She fed upon rising for the evening, but no matter how often she took extra blood it never quite satisfied her.

Her feet moved of their own volition in Harleigh's direction. Her gaze bore into the neck which pulsed with each beat of the heart. Tasha's fangs lengthened from her gums. She swallowed. She could almost taste the blood. It would be delicious, warm as it flowed down her throat.

"You okay?"

Harleigh's voice drew Natasha out of the stupor. She blinked several times, coming back to herself. Her steps staggered slightly under the weight of the knowledge she'd almost attacked her friend.

Was she okay? She didn't know anymore. She'd thought everything was fine. Now she wasn't so sure.

She missed Vlad until she believed her heart might break. She was pregnant and faced raising her son alone. Her brother and cousin were in constant danger now that they were after the demons. She had thought Australia safe, away from any possible danger, but she sensed that blank spot. Okay? She wasn't sure if she'd ever be okay again.

Natasha pulled a chair out from the table and sat down next to Harleigh, then plastered a fake smile on her face. "Yeah," she lied, not meeting her friend's eyes. "I'm okay."

Chapter 2

Vladimir gazed out across the frozen land. As the tiger stalked across the new-fallen snow, its white coat blended seamlessly with the barren forest of larch trees. The cat stopped midstride, frozen by the command in its mind.

No, my friend. She is not for you. Turn back to your pride.

Their eyes met, his human black, the animal's light amber. The cat tried to take another step toward the unsuspecting deer.

No! Not today. Vlad pushed deeper into the cat's mind, forcing his will upon the large beast. *She has a family that needs her. I know you are hunting for your cubs, but not this deer.*

He may not have been able to save his own family, but he could save the life of this deer so she might have a few more days or months with hers. Vlad sent his senses flowing out over the land, looking for an alternative source of food. They glided over the icy ground, through the trees. A smile came to his rugged face as he found a lone animal wondering several yards away.

He pushed back into the tiger's mind, sending the image of the wild boar along with the direction the cat should go to find its meal. *There is your meal, waiting for you. Go. Feed your family.*

The tiger's answer formed in his mind. She would heed the command. As the striped beast turned, Vlad brought the engine of his snowmobile to life. Gunning the motor to whip the machine around, he headed through the forest. His eyes roamed constantly over the area, noting each animal, every detail down to which trees were recently marked by his pride.

He noted the long claw marks in the bark, recognizing instantly which of his cats made them. Mishka, the alpha male of the pride, had made the majority, though his females did their share as well.

Vlad inhaled deeply, taking the fresh mix of newly fallen snow and musky forest into his lungs. His hand tightened on the throttle as he leaned over the tank and increased speed. The machine's engine purred beneath his body, the vibration from which melded into a delicious combination with the sensation of the cold air flowing around his body.

The wind whipped through the trees, bending their long boughs. It nipped at his shaven head, his black stubble offering no protection from the freezing temperature. Ice began to form on his goatee, a result of the warm breath blowing between his lips, lips opened by the wide smile of pleasure across his face.

He felt free, unencumbered by the guilt that was his usual companion. Guilt blown away by the wind on his face and the thoughts of the cats he loved.

His cats did not judge or condemn him. With his pride, he experienced complete acceptance. No blame. No censure. Just freedom to be himself. He could be wild, carefree.

The sight of his home on the horizon brought a mixture of joy and sorrow. The dwelling, a stark reminder of his past, looked so much like the house he had kept with his wife and children. At times the place transported him back to centuries long ago. On quiet nights, he almost heard the echo of his children's laughter in the rafters.

It was a simple, A-frame house, made of wood he'd chopped from the surrounding trees. To insulate the dwelling, he packed the seams with a mud mixture created from the ground. He had added a simple porch to the front where he watched his pack play.

But today the pride hunted a mile away. And this would not be a night for relaxing on the porch. Chores needed completing.

He drove behind his home to a tiny shack. With his mind, Vlad threw the doors to the shed open and slowly slid inside. After cutting the engine, he glanced around and easily found what he needed among his meticulously organized tools. A key hung in its usual place. Vlad grabbed it, then marched to the generator in two long strides. A thrust of his hand and a crank of the key awakened the machine. With the slight humming sound playing in his ears, he pushed the red button on the side. The generator purred to life.

After checking to be sure the machine contained a sufficient amount of diesel, he closed the wide doors to the shed and strolled into his home. Pushing through the only door, the smell of his meal accosted his nose. He tossed his coat carelessly over the back of a chair and wrinkled his nose. Vlad quickly crossed the tiny space to the kitchen to clean the mess he'd left. One of the few benefits of living alone, you could be as messy as you wanted with no one to care.

No one to love.

That sums up my life nicely, he thought, scraping the gunk from a plate.

It was his decision. After what happened, how could he not live alone? His sire had seen to it he had no choice. And that was okay.

He didn't need anyone, having been alone for over five hundred years. It had become his way of life.

Sure, he had friends. His fellow Alphas were as close as brothers. He didn't need anyone else. Especially a woman. Definitely not a woman like Natasha.

His shoulders stiffened.

Vlad's hand gripped the plate he held as her scent instantly flooded his memory.

He'd fallen asleep surrounded by the combination of her delicious gardenia scent and their lovemaking. His mind still recalled the intoxicating aroma. It haunted him. His body hardened, his fingers tightening on the plate at the memory until the stupid thing cracked like a suspect under interrogation.

Fates, how that woman affected him. Every waking moment since the night with her had been an experience in pain, real physical pain. Natasha crept into his mind stalking him, threatening to consume him until he ruthlessly pushed the thoughts of her aside.

It had been a mistake, a terrible mistake to be with her. One night of weakness nearly cost him everything.

Thank the Fates she'd decided to be discreet. She obviously had not mentioned anything to her brother. If she had, he would not be standing here now. The warrior felt sure of one thing in this world; should Nicholai find out he'd bedded his sister, Vlad would be the first person to hear about it. He had no doubt he would get the beating he deserved for committing such an offense.

Damned female.

Vlad realized he could not, *should* not care for Natasha. She was better off without him and he her.

****

Yummmmmmm. Natasha slowly chewed a bite of the *Germknödel*, savoring the sugary sweet. She dragged the next forkful through the vanilla cream sauce before bringing it to her mouth. The dough dumpling slid down her throat. The poppy seeded goodness made her tummy quite happy. Only one thing better than that—blood. But the two flavors were not a good mix, so she'd finish this first, then grab a bag of the good stuff.

Barely audible over the song blaring on her radio, a knock sounded softly on her door. Putting the last bite in her mouth, she deposited the dirty dish in the sink next to her glass from earlier. As she ambled to the front of her cottage, she punched the remote, turning down the music.

"Hi," Natasha greeted, pulling open the door. "Nice hair."

She gave Harleigh the once-over with her eyes.

"Like it?" Harleigh ran her hand through the multicolored strands. "I'm in a wild mood this morning."

"I can tell." Natasha stepped aside as her friend entered the room. "I especially like the neon pink and green stripes. They really accent the yellow hair poking out from underneath. Even *I* don't go that wild."

Harleigh gently tugged on one of Tasha's pigtails. "Still have in the purple and blue from yesterday I see."

Natasha sat on her couch and patted the cushion next to her. “Not all of us change our color every day. Doesn’t that ruin your hair?”

Harleigh sat heavily beside her, kicked off her shoes, and tucked her feet underneath her. “Nah. I’ve got a special secret. No damage done.”

“You’ll have to share that one day.”

“Maybe I will, and maybe I won’t,” Harleigh replied cryptically, piquing Natasha’s interest.

Before she could press her friend, Harleigh jumped up and crossed the room to grab her purse. “I wanted to give you this.”

She handed Natasha a flyer before she resumed her seat on the couch.

“Summer Smash?”

Harleigh nodded her head exuberantly, sending the colorful hair dancing. “It’s a carnival. The best one around. I wait all year for it.”

“I don’t do carnivals.”

“You scared of carnies?” Harleigh quipped, earning a smirky smile from Natasha.

“No, smart aleck. I’m just not a big fan of the rides.”

“There’s a lot of stuff other than the rides. There are funnel cakes, ring toss games. Bands. The city does it up right.”

“I don’t know.” Natasha chewed her thumbnail.

“Don’t knock it ’til you try it. You might like it.”

“Maybe.”

“Come on.” Harleigh’s lip stuck out in a mock pout. “You’ll have fun, I promise. It’s the city’s way of welcoming summer, so they really go all out.”

“I can’t believe summer is coming. It’s almost

November."

"Welcome to living in Australia. You want winter in November, you gotta go north."

Bet Vlad's cold in Siberia.

Whoa! Where had that come from? Perhaps a carnival would take her mind off Vladimir, finally allowing her a few hours without thinking of him. He kept creeping into her mind at the strangest times—like a conversation which had absolutely nothing to do with him.

"Maybe a carnival is just what I need," Natasha muttered.

Harleigh flashed a brilliant smile. "So, you'll come?"

"Fine," Tasha capitulated on a throaty sigh. "When is it?"

"Tonight."

Natasha raised one eyebrow in query. "Waited until the last minute, did you?"

"Didn't want to give you time to back out."

"And what made you so sure I'd go?"

"I knew you wouldn't let me down. I'd have begged if you made me."

Harleigh was right; Natasha didn't want to let her down. Since the first day she arrived at the cottage, Harleigh had been there for her. She held Natasha's hair as she vomited, wiped her tears when she cried, and cheered her up when she was down. She'd only known Harleigh a short time, but she considered the woman a close friend. Not close enough to confess she was a vampire, but nonetheless a good friend.

"Let me get my purse." Tasha headed for her bedroom.

Harleigh clapped her hands and slid her feet into her shoes. “This is going to be fun.”

Chapter 3

Jara sat in the vehicle, absently twirling her golden strands. Irritation knotted her shoulders.

"What's wrong?" asked her companion, Finn, from the driver's seat.

She gave his manly physique a slow perusal. It allowed not only for her to take in the sexy demon's physical attributes but gave him a chance to demonstrate just how loyal he was. Being the sister of the Demon King had its advantages and having patient sycophants was one. He'd wait for her reply, and he'd do so willingly. For if not, he would know the wrath of a demon princess, not exactly something anyone wanted to experience.

Jara graced her subject with a smile. "We are so close to finding Sergei, I can't stand the waiting."

Finn shifted toward her. "It shouldn't be much longer. When you scried, the stone warmed over this spot on the map."

The demon princess nodded. "True. I just hope the information Leo found is accurate, and he was sired by the first vampire. If he was, I can use him to destroy he Source."

"What is the source?"

"Not what, *who*." Jara leaned closer to the guard. "The Source is the first vampire. The one from which all others have come. I believe if The Source is killed then all other vampires might die as well. I plan to test that theory."

Excitement bubbled in her blood.

A soft whistle pushed between Finn's teeth. "And this Sergei will kill this Source?"

Jara shook her head, sending her wavy hair swirling around her shoulders. "Sergei could never kill his sire. He *would* never kill his sire. Vampires seem to have a strange sort of love for their makers."

"So, how will he help?"

"I need his blood."

"Huh?" Confusion drew Finn's brown brows down over his red eyes.

Sweet Finn. She really did have to remember not everyone was as wise as she, for only the royal family had access to the Room of Tomes in the royal compound.

"Recently, I found a tome. It contained a wonderful tale that gave me hope when our plan to kill the vampires in Savannah failed. You see, long ago, many centuries now, the demons discovered the original vampire, The Source. Our ancestors tried to kill him, but alas they were not strong enough."

"A demon not able to kill a vampire? That's absurd." Finn crossed his arms over his chest.

"We are talking centuries ago, Finn. There were no bombs, no guns. And this was no ordinary vampire. He was smart, cunning, immensely strong, and if the tales are to be believed, capable of shifting form."

Incredulity widened the guard's eyes. "This vampire could shift?"

"So the story goes. He was quite powerful, invincible. To the point that even his own kind began to hunt him."

Finn scrubbed a meaty hand down his face. "Where is he now? Why have I never heard of him before?"

"Ah, see that is the ten-million-dollar question." Jara glanced out the window of the car to be sure no one lurked within earshot. "Once the demons realized The Source could not be killed, they found a way to put him under a spell. A stasis spell put him in a death-like sleep. They put him deep within the earth where no one would find him, sentencing him to the remainder of his days in a coma-like condition, where he would be aware of his predicament but unable to see or move."

"A horrific end for a horrific being." Finn rested one elbow on the console and the other on the armrest of the door, then steepled his fingers.

Jara nodded. "I would think so. Imagine the hunger he must be feeling, having not fed for centuries."

"But I thought Lane's experiments proved a vampire could be killed by starvation."

The mention of the demon scientist twisted Jara's stomach. She'd recently killed Lane by accident when she was trying to punish an impertinent guard named Cyrus. The princess ruthlessly pushed aside the regret and quickly affected an unconcerned demeanor. She didn't have time for lamenting. She had new plans that needed attention.

"Ahhh, see, Finn, that was my earlier point. Were you not listening? The Source is no ordinary vampire. He is different from all others. If the tomes are to be believed, he has abilities none since him have acquired, such as the ability to shift and go without food."

"How do you know he is not dead?"

"When The Source was put to ground, the king of

the demons decreed one demon would be charged with monitoring The Source. She put a spell on him, an alerting spell. If so much as an eyelash on his body moves, she would have known it. Of course, that demon is now sadly gone, died from dysentery, but before she died, she passed the spell onto her descendants, each one, in turn, inheriting the responsibility when the previous generation dies."

"So, what do you intend to do with this Source?"

"My plan is to find him and kill him, and for that we will need Sergei." Jara spied a tall, muscular male gliding toward an unsuspecting human. "And I believe we just found step one of my plan."

Jara's heart raced as she and Finn exited the car in unison. When their eyes met over the car, she mouthed, "Let's get him."

****

The bone-jarring crash made Natasha's teeth rattle. She bounced on the torn Naugahyde seat, the canvas lap belt digging into her thighs. A hearty laugh forced its way through her lips as she turned the steering wheel of the bumper car and punched down on the pedal heading for her next victim.

"I'm coming for you, Harleigh," Natasha called out around a laugh.

Her friend shot a quick look over her shoulder. "You have to catch me first."

Harleigh took off as fast as the ride would allow. With a quick flick of her wrist, she turned the car and plowed into one of their fellow riders with a loud clunk of metal. Natasha was there in an instant and sandwiched her car in the V the crash created. The trio laughed, each hitting the reverse pedal to escape the pile.

Harleigh glanced down, eyes wide. Her hand reached out in a flash, grabbing at her pants. She drew the material away from her skin, the denim bunched tightly in her closed fist. Her foot pushed down hard on the pedal, sending her car back into the side of the rink.

Noting the panic on her friend's face, Natasha called out, "What's wrong?"

Harleigh did not answer. Instead, in a flurry of movement, her body twisted and turned in the confines of the tiny car. Her friend thrashed wildly as she zigzagged across the rink.

"Bug!" Harleigh screamed while trying desperately to keep a hold on the bunched material in her hand as she pulled at her pants.

"What?"

"There's something in my pants!"

"What's in there?"

"A BUG!"

Natasha laughed, she couldn't help it. Harleigh had a bug phobia. The look of panic, the spastic movements, the fact her friend was stripping right here in the middle of bumper the car arena…it was too much humor to contain.

"Did it bite you?"

"Not yet. Something tickled me. Then the tickle headed north."

Another wiggle and Harleigh's pants were down around her ankles. She kicked off her shoes and swept the jeans from her body, leaving her sitting in her white panties and shirt. She viciously shook the pants.

Natasha's laugh exploded around the hand covering her mouth. Knowing her friend had not been bitten allowed her to appreciate the humor in the situation to its fullest. Her belly shook, shoulders quivered as her laughter rolled through her. She couldn't stop. Her stomach muscles began to ache from overuse. Her eyes teared, blurring her sight.

The green grasshopper fell out of Harleigh's pants, landing with a thud on the cement below. Natasha's watery eyes widened as the thing did a kamikaze move and leapt straight for an oncoming bumper car. It landed on the man's face.

The man hit reverse in his car, taking the bug with him. His eyes crossed when he looked at it on his nose. His decidedly girly scream echoed as he fled away from them, the bug along for the ride.

"O-M-G, I can't believe that happened." Natasha laughed. "You okay?"

Harleigh's face blushed a deep red. "Yeah. I hate bugs."

A shudder ran through her body as she turned the pants inside out to check for more critters.

"Obviously, or you would not have done the striptease."

Harleigh shoved her legs back into her pants just as the other cars came to a stop from the electricity being turned off. "I'm so embarrassed."

Tasha exited her car and waited for Harleigh to do the same before she replied, "Don't be. I don't think too many people noticed."

The women peeked around, noting just how many people had large smiles on their faces. Some of the men were leering, some of the women were quietly laughing behind their hands.

"Look at it this way, Harleigh. You made everyone

happy. Gave them a laugh."

"I can think of better ways to make people laugh."

Natasha threw an arm around her friend's shoulders. "I must admit, you put on a helluva show."

Harleigh laughed. "I guess I did."

"I'm hungry." Natasha's stomach growled its agreement.

"You're always hungry. What do you want?"

Blood. "Cotton candy."

"It's over there." Harleigh pointed straight ahead.

The women made their way over the dusty ground to the yellow concession stand and ordered two large piles of the fluffy pink concoction. Taking a bite, Natasha closed her eyes and savored the taste of the sugary confection as it melted on her tongue. Not blood, but definitely yummy, and it would ease her hunger a little until she got home to her crimson stash.

"Where do you want to go next?"

Natasha shrugged her shoulders. "I don't know. Home?"

"What! We've only been here a few hours."

"We've done all the rides."

"All but one. We haven't been on the Ferris wheel yet."

"I don't do Ferris wheels."

Harleigh's lower lip pouted out. "Ah, come on. *Pleeeeease.* For me?"

"No. They aren't safe." Natasha took a bite of her cotton candy.

"Yes, they are. Come on. It will be fun. Nothing bad will happen, I promise."

Harleigh looped her arm through Natasha's, and they wove through the crowd toward the large wheel.

While they waited in line, it made its revolutions slowly turning to the instrumental music playing through the staticky speakers below. The lights from the ride flashed over the crowd, bathing them in a sickly yellow glow.

"You look like you have jaundice."

Harleigh gave her a smirk. "We're still getting on this ride."

"I'd rather not."

"What are you afraid of? Don't tell me you are afraid of heights."

Afraid of heights? Hardly. Of course, her friend couldn't know heights were no problem for Natasha since she could always materialize somewhere safe if need be.

No, it wasn't the heights that concerned her, but the knowledge if something went wrong, she would be stuck on the ride. With all the surrounding people, she would not be able to dematerialize off the ride.

She needed to get home to feed sooner rather than later. Even after the cotton candy, Tasha had stomach pangs only one thing would satisfy. She figured she had about an hour before the serious pain would hit.

"I'm not afraid of heights."

"Then smile. One quick ride and it will all be over."

Natasha's mood brightened, bringing a smile to her face. "You're ready to go home?"

"Why? Do you want to?"

"Yeah." They moved steadily forward as one by one the seats of the Ferris wheel were emptied and new people were shuffled on.

"All right. After this ride we'll go," capitulated

Harleigh, climbing into an empty seat.

After securing the safety bar, the carnival worker handed Natasha into the next seat. He leaned over to grab the bar to the seat. The movement brought her precariously close to his neck. His pulse beat below his flesh. Teeth lengthened from her gums in response to the delicious sight combined with the steady beating heart. She sharply inhaled the scent of musky male. Natasha turned her head forcefully away from the temptation, willing the fangs back into her gums as the unsuspecting human clicked the safety bar into place.

Her hand went to her belly, covering the small mound. *Soon, little one. Just a little while longer, then Mommy will get what you need.*

She could almost taste the sweet coppery flavor of the blood in her mouth. It would be delicious sliding down her throat, coating her stomach to feed her starving cells. Her tongue moistened her lips.

With every seat full, the Ferris wheel began its slow steady circle, lifting Natasha high over the crowd before bringing her down to the earth once more. She took in a deep breath of fresh air, glad for the reprieve of carnival treats and ride exhaust, and scanned the people below.

In line, a couple cuddled together, nuzzling each other's neck. She longed for someone to hold her hand, to love her. She wished she had someone to ride with her, wrap his arm around her as they rode around and around together.

If only she had a heartmate. If only Vladimir was her heartmate. There sitting with only her thoughts for company, she longed for Vlad—as she had so often over the centuries. The male owned a place in her heart.

They may not be heartmates, but she must admit she had it bad for the guy. For decades, she sought him out. And when she had finally gotten exactly what she wanted—gotten him—she messed it all up.

Apprehension prickled along her skin, pulling her from her thoughts. The tiny hairs on her arms rose toward the night sky. Natasha sensed eyes on her, a penetrating stare that roamed over her body, making her glance down. Her eyes scanned the crowd as the wheel made its rotation. She saw couples kissing, a child crying. She observed a teenager run through the crowd, knocking into a man in his haste.

Her eyes locked with those of the man. When the boy ran into him, his body remained still as a concrete beam, oblivious to the hit from the adolescent. His stare bore into her, tracking her when the wheel ascended.

For the first time that night, she knew a moment's relief at being on the ride as it took her farther from the man below. They broke eye contact when her seat reached the apex. The ride came to a halt, sending her rocking. She reached for the safety bar with both hands. Her eyes darted in front of her to her friend.

Harleigh turned around in her seat. "What happened?" She peered over the back of her swinging seat.

"We are experiencing technical difficulties," a disembodied voice called from below. "Please remain seated. The ride will resume shortly."

"Son of a..." An eerie howl floated in the air, disrupting Natasha's sentence. She scooted in the seat and peered over the side. The man had disappeared as if he had never been. She slid to the other side of the swinging seat.

Gazing below, her eyes roamed the crowd. Her preternatural vision allowed her to see every detail from the color of the striped shirt one woman wore to the patch of black fur that disappeared behind one of the tents.

Black fur?

Her skin tingled. The hairs on the back of her neck pushed away from the skin.

Natasha's gaze locked with Harleigh's. "Did you see that?"

"See what?"

"That!" She pointed in the direction of the tent.

"The tent?"

"No." Tasha blew out an exasperated breath. "There was a wolf. It moved behind the tent over there."

"There are no wolves around here. You probably saw a dog."

"I know a wolf when I see one. I grew up in Russia, for God's sake. I've seen lots of wolves, and I'm telling you it was a wolf."

"Nah. It was probably just another dingo. Like the other night."

"Harleigh, I'm telling you. It was a wolf." She glanced down over her seat, her eyes searching for any sign of the animal. Finding nothing, she slid to the opposite end of the seat and glanced over the side. Nothing seemed amiss. The crowd started to thin, everyone going about their activities. Obviously, no one noticed anything strange.

Maybe she imagined it. A demon that changed into a wolf had attacked her brother. Perhaps she just imagined a wolf because of the other night when she sensed a blank spot. Was she just being paranoid?

"Harleigh, I want to go home as soon as we get down from here."

Her friend turned back around in her seat. "Okay. We'll leave."

By the grace of all that was holy, the wheel started to move. Slowly, seat by seat, the worker unloaded the passengers until at last both Harleigh and Natasha were safely back on the ground and heading for Natasha's car.

The ride back to her home was a quick one. She made sure of it. She wanted to be as far away from the carnival as possible.

Once back in Natasha's driveway, Harleigh jumped on her motorcycle and started the loud engine. "Thanks for coming to Summer Smash with me," she called over the motor.

Natasha wanted to say "any time," but she would not lie. She had no intention of ever returning to the area—even once the carnival left. Something had not felt right all evening. And regardless of what Harleigh said about there not being any wolves in Australia, she knew what she saw.

Things were starting to add up to trouble, and she didn't like it. Worried, her hand protectively covered over her stomach. "Be safe going home."

"I'll try not to let the big bad wolf get me," Harleigh quipped with a wink before gunning the engine to her bike and taking off down the drive.

As Natasha stepped through the front door of the home, the sound of the phone ringing made her jump. She grabbed the thing up with more force than necessary. "Hello."

"Hi Natasha, it's Julie."

"Hi, sis-in-law." Natasha struggled to keep her voice even, knowing her brother was probably on an extension. "How's the honeymoon? You guys back yet?"

"Not yet. We decided to extend it another month."

"Having too much fun to stop?"

"More like too much loving to get any sightseeing done," a deep voice informed her.

"Way too much info there, Nicholai."

Her brother chuckled. "Hello, sister mine. How are you?"

"I'm fine." She hoped her voice sounded steadier than she felt.

A brief pause told her it didn't.

"What's wrong, Natasha?"

That was her brother. She never could sneak anything by him. "Nothing. Everything's fine."

"Tasha." The growl in his deep voice was the only warning before he pushed into her mind.

Afraid he might discover the pregnancy, she pushed the information about the wolf to the front of her thoughts.

"I see the wolf in your mind, sister dear. Tell us what is happening there."

She relayed the events of what happened on the beach and at the carnival as succinctly as possible. "And that's all I know."

Julie cleared her throat. "If you think there is a wolf stalking you, you have to leave. I saw what one did to your brother. Believe me, you don't want to mess with it."

Natasha's hand covered her belly as she erected a

mental barrier to keep her brother from accidentally discovering her secret. "Perhaps I'm just seeing things."

"Tasha, I want you to send your senses out. What are they telling you?"

She did as Nicholai asked. Her awareness pushed out of the home and over the surrounding beach. She discovered a large void. "There is another blank spot. I'm going to see what it is."

She moved to her kitchen window and pulled open the curtains. She blinked once, twice, then squeezed her eyes tightly shut, trying to clear her vision. She could not have possibly seen what she thought.

When she opened her eyes, it was still there. A large, black wolf with a white stripe between its eyes walked down the beach. Riding on its back sat a koala.

She rubbed her eyes. "I don't believe it," she murmured into the forgotten phone.

"What don't you believe?" Julie and Nicholai asked in unison.

"There's a koala riding a wolf. They are strolling down the beach."

A heavy silence met her statement. It was her brother who spoke next. "Say that again."

"There is a koala riding a wolf."

"What are your senses telling you?"

"Nothing. They are just a blank spot moving down the beach."

"Get the hell out of there *now*!" The volume of Nicholai's command made Natasha hold the phone away from her ear.

A shiver raced down her spine at the tone of his voice. Her brother was suddenly all business, all Alpha. Gone was the soft loving tone he normally used with her.

"I'll pack tonight and leave for home immediately."

"I do not want you going to an empty house. The demons have a way of tracking us. They found us in Savannah. They have found you in Australia. I want you to stay with an Alpha for protection."

"Fine," she conceded. "I'll meet you at your place."

"Juliette is still human. We will need to fly home, and we are halfway around the world. It will take a few nights to get home since we will have to take commercial airlines and avoid the sun."

"Why not take Stephan's plane?"

"He is using it. He is with Demetri and Tatiana on a mission."

"I'll go stay with Marcus and Christina until you get home."

"Good. They are with Katrina at Stephan's home in Germany. You can dematerialize there. You know where it is, right?"

"No, so I can't materialize there."

"You know where Vladimir's home is. Go there."

"No," she said a little too quickly. "Um, I don't want to put him out. What about Alex or Desmond?"

"I don't know Desmond well enough to trust him with my sister's life."

She blew out an exasperated sigh. "Fine. What about Alex?"

"I'm not sure where he is. Tasha, I want you go to Vlad. He is much older than Alexander, so he is stronger. He is one of our best fighters. If there is anyone I trust with your safety, it is him."

"But—"

"No arguing. Staying with Vladimir makes the most sense. You know where he lives so you can materialize there. The nights are long this time of year in Siberia. If you leave quickly, it will be dark when you arrive. You will go to Vlad tonight."

Her shoulders slumped in defeat. Her brother's logic was impeccable as usual. If the demons had targeted her, she needed protection. She was not a fighter. She left that role for her brother.

"Fine. You win, Nicholai. I'll…" The remainder of her sentence was cut off by the lump of fear in her throat when she glanced back out the window.

The black wolf stalked up the path that led from the beach to her back door. The koala was nowhere in sight. Her eyes locked with the wolf's. The intelligence in its stare sent a chill through her.

"Natasha? Talk to me," Nicholai commanded.

She let the curtain drop back into place. "The wolf," she whispered into the phone. "It's coming."

"Get out of there." The panic in her brother's voice spurred her into action like nothing else could. "Get out of the house *now*, Natasha!"

She hung up the phone. With fear coursing through her body, her form coalesced until only a wisp of black smoke remained for the wolf to find.

A moment later she reformed in her Russian home, her quick strides taking her to the closet by the front door. She grabbed a heavy coat, knowing she would need it in Siberia. After donning the long toggle coat with the faux-shearling lining, she ran with blurring speed to her bedroom. Withdrawing a suitcase from the closet, Natasha packed a few changes of clothes and some underwear. She didn't need much, just enough to get by a couple of days until Nicholai got home.

Suitcase full, she ran to the kitchen and grabbed a bag of blood from the fridge. She tore open the bag, then drank it down fast.

Grabbing a second bag, she hopped up onto the kitchen counter. She took her time with the second bag, allowing her brain to process the situation. The adrenaline fled her body. Her nerves settled while she drank.

Maybe this wasn't such a bad turn of events. Perhaps this was fate's way of telling her she needed to inform Vlad about the baby. She wanted to keep the child from him so he could find his mate, but what if *she* was that mate?

Stranger things had happened. They had not tasted each other's blood, so she could not be sure they *weren't* heartmates. Maybe, just maybe, a greater power had intervened, determined to bring them together no matter how much she tried to keep them apart.

Or maybe she wanted to convince herself of that so she could run to Vlad for protection and comfort. Perhaps she was being selfish again.

Should I just remain here? she wondered.

Surely, the demons did not know where she lived.

There is no need to go to Vladimir's. Nicholai is being overly paranoid.

As she started to slip out of the coat, something crunching on the frozen ground outside brought her up quick. She pulled the coat tightly around her body. Fear flooded her system once again. Had they found her? She didn't plan to find out.

Tasha grabbed the handle to her suitcase before her

form coalesced. *Ready or not, Vlad, here we come.*

Chapter 4

The oily odor of the diesel accosted his nose as Vladimir pulled the petrol can from the back of his 4x4. His feet crunched in the snow with each confident stride he took. Placing the cans just inside the door of the shed, he turned his attention to the generator. As the machine roared to life, his mind strayed from the task.

It wandered to a familiar place. Away from the harsh Arctic climate to a place of warmth and softness. A place that felt like home in a way his house never had.

His eyelids slid shut as memories of her flooded his mind. Vlad's heart sped up, and his blood warmed when he remembered holding her tight, her soft curves pressed against the hard plains of his body.

Only the knowledge she was better off without him gave him the courage to keep from contacting her. He missed the way her hips swayed when she walked, the twinkle in her laugh, but she deserved much better than him. No doubt, Natasha would be safer the farther she remained from him. Nicholai mentioned she wintered in Australia, but that might not even be far enough to keep her safe.

Natasha.

Just the sound of her name whispered in his mind made his body tighten. The memory of the taste of her skin flooded his mouth. His tongue darted out of its own volition to lick his lips. Being with her only made him want her more. He hungered for her in a way like no other. The flavor of her kiss—addicting. The softness of her skin—exquisite. The thrum of her blood rushing through her veins called to him—tempting. He had barely resisted the impulse to indulge in her life essence, knowing it would have made their act even more intimate.

No doubt her blood would have tasted like she smelled, like sweet gardenias; he just knew it. Even now, the scent surrounded him, taking away the chemical stench of the diesel.

Amazing what the mind can do, he thought.

Vlad tried to push her from his thoughts. It did no good to lament about Natasha, but like a specter from his past, she kept haunting him. If only her scent would leave him in peace. He took a deep steadying breath before opening his eyes.

His dark brows furrowed in confusion. Instead of cleansing her from his mind, the long breath drew her deeper into his lungs. He tasted her on his tongue.

"Vlad."

He spun around at the sound of her voice. By all that was holy, she stood before him. He blinked once to be sure his mind did not play tricks.

His eyes drank her in like a man dying of thirst, traveling slowly down her beautiful face and over the soft curves of her breasts. Even in a winter coat, the flare of her hips held his gaze for a moment before his eyes began their return trip to her face.

She wore fire engine red lipstick which stood out in stark contrast to the black choker about her neck. Hairbands that had plastic pink skulls anchored her harlequin-colored pigtails. A delicate piercing through her nose glittered, accenting the curve of her highly defined cheek. Heavy lines of black eyeliner enhanced her amber eyes such that they leapt from her face. She was a vision of beauty, a dark goddess.

Vlad shut down his senses quickly, blocking out her enticing scent, the beat of her heart. Now if he gouged out his eyes, he'd be all set. She was a temptation he sorely did not need. He had no idea what brought her to his home, but she could not remain.

Vlad stomped angrily toward her, his muscular strides eating up the hard ground. She backed away from his approach, eyes wide as if the sight of him terrified her.

Smart woman.

Natasha wrapped her arms around her waist protectively, no doubt in reaction to Vlad's angry demeanor. She was right to be afraid.

"What are you doing here?" he growled.

He stopped a mere inch from her, so close the warmth of her body surrounded him.

Natasha held a breath. Waiting. Watching him with those big eyes.

"Not going to answer me?" he barked.

"I…" She worried her lower lip between her teeth, his eyes tracked the movement. "I…Nicholai…" She swallowed the next word.

Vlad's eyes traveled down her neck, following the movement of her throat. They came to a rest over her pulse. It sped up under his intense gaze.

Her voice sounded weak. Her pulse beat erratically under her flesh. Flesh that paled before his eyes.

"What about Nicholai? Have the demons found

him? Are they after his mate again?" Vlad shifted his stance, widening his feet and crossing his arms over his chest.

Natasha's eyes rolled back in her head. Without conscious thought, his hands reached out to grasp her upper arms and pulled her toward his body the moment her legs gave way. Vladimir scooped Nicholai's sister into his arms. Her head lolled against his chest. She'd fainted dead away. All he had done was tried to get her to talk, and she fainted. He still did not know why she'd come.

Damn this woman.

Yet here she lay in his arms. Each step he took made his body move against hers, bringing hyperawareness. Thank the heavens he'd blocked his senses, or it would have driven him over the edge as he held her close.

Approaching his home, he noticed the small suitcase sitting by the door. Deciding it was of no consequence now, he opened the door with his mind and proceeded across the threshold without altering his strides. With a thought, he closed and locked the door behind them, sealing himself in with her.

He sat down on the only chair in the small home. Shifting her slight weight so he held her with one arm, he ran his hand down her cheek.

"Natasha." He gazed down at her peaceful face. "Natasha, wake up."

He gently patted her cheek. "Wake up, *milenky.*"

Her full lashes fluttered slightly.

A good sign, he thought, brushing the black bangs from her forehead.

"Natasha," he called again, his eyes meeting hers

when they opened.

She blinked once. Twice. Then her eyes widened and she moved, trying to rise as if his touch repulsed her.

"I…W-what…" she stammered, looking around as she pushed from his lap.

She rose on shaky legs, and his hand flew out to steady her when he too rose from the chair.

"You fainted," he explained and dropped his hand.

She perused his home with a sweeping glance, taking in the sparse décor. For the first time, his home seemed inadequate, lacking in the refinements to which she was accustomed.

He knew her history. She and Nicholai had grown up in luxury. Nicholai still lived in a gilded mansion, and no doubt she did as well.

Natasha probably found his modest home shabby and barren, which would account for the horrified expression on her face. Vlad scowled at the thought.

Well, if the woman felt that way, she was free to leave anytime.

Chapter 5

Tasha slowly struggled back through the murky darkness toward full consciousness. Her first thought went to the menacing male with her. Unable to meet his stare, Natasha glanced around the room. She hadn't expected him to be thrilled to see her, but she at least hoped he would be civil. He must have sensed the baby by now.

She'd wanted to tell him about their child to see the expression on his face when she revealed the secret. Instead, she fainted before she confessed. What could she say now? What *should* she say?

Silence hung heavily between them in the air like a thick fog. Vlad's hand remained on her arm, burning her skin like a brand through her winter coat. The scowl on his rugged face made her pull from the grip, realizing he must be upset about the child. She saw it on his face, in the way he glared at her with disdain.

"I'm sorry," Natasha blurted out.

"For what? Fainting?"

"No. I'm sorry I didn't tell you sooner." She wrapped her arms around her waist in a bracing hug.

"Tell me what?" Vlad braced his feet wide, crossing his arms over his chest. He looked like the fierce Alpha he was, like he could kill just as easily as talk.

Tasha swallowed nervously. "You know."

"Know what?" Vlad scrubbed a hand over his stubbled head. "You are making no sense. Do you need to sit down?"

He offered his chair with a magnanimous gesture of his arm.

"I'd rather stand."

"I should have guessed as much," Vlad murmured.

The Alpha began to pace the room like a caged tiger, agitation clearly visible in his bunched hands and furrowed brows.

"Look, about the baby…"

Vlad stopped the pacing long enough to grab a pack of cigarettes from the drawer by the kitchen sink.

"What baby?" he asked, pounding the pack against his palm.

Natasha swallowed her next words, instead playing his over in her mind. *What baby?*

Had she heard him correctly? Did he not realize she was pregnant?

She met his expectant stare as he opened the cigarette pack and withdrew a cancer stick.

He put the cigarette between his pursed lips, then dug a lighter from his jeans. He gave it a flick as he brought it toward the cigarette.

"Stop!" Tasha waved a hand in his direction.

Vlad froze, the flickering light of the Bic dancing over the plains and hard slopes of his face. He quirked one eyebrow at her command. "What?"

"I didn't know you smoked."

"Only when I'm stressed."

"You're stressed? About what?" *I'm the one whose world tilted on its axis, sending me for a ride that ended with me fainting and you bringing me inside.*

Her stomach knotted at the memory.

Vlad shrugged then lowered the lighter as he took the cigarette from his lips. He leaned against the sink, nonchalant. “You.”

“Me?”

“Right now, you are making me stress.”

“Well, go have a cigarette then. Outside.”

Vlad pushed from the sink, mumbling about not being able to smoke in his own house before he left her alone with her thoughts.

Natasha gazed out the window while he brought the cigarette to his lips and lit up. His chest expanded with a deep inhale before he blew out the smoke in a series of rings. She must admit there was something erotic about the way he cradled the stick between his lips. Something she found masculine, virile.

Everything about him turned her on. His manly scent, which she now realized was a distinct smoky, woodsy fragrance, drove her wild. She loved the way his muscles worked under his skin. His six-foot-six frame was leanly muscled, but the roped sinew and defined musculature were a sensuous combination that gave a one-two punch to her libido. She could watch that male all day.

Natasha sighed.

****

Vlad had left the house *without* touching her. But he wanted to. He pushed the hand not fingering the cigarette down into the pocket of his jeans to keep it from fisting as his gaze roamed the area.

Nestled on a remote, five-hundred-acre plot of virginal forest that had seen more musk ox and wolves than humans in the past couple of centuries, the property was nothing if not private. Not a good thing when your greatest temptation showed up at your door. Or more appropriately at your shed.

She'd stayed away for six months. Why come back now?

Holding the cigarette between his thumb and middle finger, he took a drag.

He didn't need this in his life. He didn't need anyone. Didn't need any complications—and Natasha was most definitely a complication.

He must get rid of her. Send her packing. Get her away from him to keep her safe from his desire.

His phone rang, the heavy metal ringtone blaring in the quiet of the night.

"*Dah*," he barked, after registering the name on the caller identification.

"Vlad, it is Nicholai."

"Want to tell me why your sister is at my place?" Vlad asked, continuing their conversation in their native language.

"Good, she has arrived." Nicholai's relief sounded over the line. "Did not she tell you?"

His eyes landed on the small suitcase standing sentry by his door. "*Nyet*." Though he had a pretty good idea she intended to stay.

"I need her to stay with you for a few days, just until Juliette and I can return home."

"Why?"

"A wolf and koala were stalking her."

"Excuse me?" His eyes narrowed in confusion. "I don't think I heard you correctly, comrade."

"A wolf and a koala. I believe they are demons."

A string of curses left Vlad's lips. *Demons!*

Stalking my Natasha!

She was in grave danger.

"You know this for sure?"

"Not one hundred percent. Natasha said she sensed a blank spot, then she witnessed a koala riding a wolf."

It would have been comical if he had not recently seen firsthand the kind of damage a demon disguised as a wolf could do.

"I do not need to remind you," Nicholai continued, "what the one did to me."

"I recall all too well." Vlad blew out another series of curses on his breath that frosted around his face.

It had been almost a year ago when he received the call from Nicholai's phone. On the other end of the line, Nicholai's heartmate desperately sought help. When he arrived at Nicholai's home, he found Julie hunched over Nicholai's brutalized body. His intestines spilled from his gut, and his blood soaked the snowy ground. Vlad had barely been able to save his fellow Alpha from the damage inflicted during a fight with a demon who shifted into a wolf. The thought of finding Natasha in the same state made his dinner threaten to make a second appearance.

"Before you asked," Nicholai continued in Russian. "Demetri and Tatiana are on a mission with Stephan. And Marcus is off somewhere in Europe with Christina and Katrina. So, you are the best man for the job. Will you protect my sister?"

Vlad took a long inhale of the cigarette before speaking, regardless of knowing instantly what his answer would be.

"Of course. How long before you will be home?" *And she can leave*.

"Since we do not have use of Stephan's plane, it will take us a few days of traveling at night to get back what with having to cross several time zones."

Of course, it will. Vlad took a long drag to calm his nerves. "Call me when you arrive."

"Immediately. And Vlad…" Nicholai's small pause kicked his heart into overdrive. "Keep my sister safe. She is most precious to me."

As if he didn't know just how precious she was. "Of course, Nicholai," Vladimir vowed. "I'll protect her as if she was my own."

"Thank you, my old friend. I knew I could count on you."

"Safe travels to you and your mate, Nicholai."

Vlad cut off the phone and stuffed it back into his pocket before shifting the end of his cigarette back and forth between his finger and thumb to strip the tobacco out of the paper. He stomped down on the burning cherry with his booted foot, then palmed the field-stripped cigarette to take it in the house to throw it away.

So, this was why she arrived unannounced at his home. She needed his protection. And he would give it. What choice did he have? Send her to Alex or Desmond to watch over her. Not a chance in Hell! He didn't want those unmated males anywhere near his…

What *was* she exactly? His female? His mate?

Thoughts like that would get her killed.

It would be pure hell being confined with her for the next few days. He would have to be vigilant, never letting his guard down. He would need to constantly block her from his mind, from his senses. It would be all too easy to let her consume him, then where would they be?

Right back in bed, which was not where he needed this to go—again.

He'd need to set some ground rules, establish some boundaries to survive this. Determination settled over his face as Vlad started toward his home.

Chapter 6

Natasha meandered across the small room to the sink. She ran some cold water over her hands, then splashed her face with a flick of her fingers. As she patted her face dry with a paper towel, the craving hit like an eighteen-wheeler.

Her arm wrapped around her stomach. It growled in protest, demanding satisfaction. Natasha glanced across the barren interior, searching for anything that might contain some blood.

She spied a tiny refrigerator sitting next to the sink. It beckoned her. She answered the call with hope in her heart as she squatted in front of the small fridge and peered inside.

Eureka! Looks like we're in luck, little one.

She patted her belly before her hand wrapped around a bag of blood within.

"Can I help you?" the voice behind her growled in her ear.

Natasha jumped, her backside contacting with the body behind her, knocking her off balance. To keep her balance, she dropped the bag of blood and grabbed hold of the door to the fridge. The bag fell to the floor with a thud as she turned to stare at Vlad.

Normally, he probably would have loved the sensation of her bottom against his groin—heaven knows he seemed to revel in the feel of it on the night they made love—but this was no ordinary experience. His face twisted in distress. Her suitcase dropped to the floor when Vlad's hand cupped his manhood, and he stumbled back. Nothing made a man stagger like having his frank and beans squished up against his body. It was a testicular homicide in the second degree—not premeditated, but none the less brutal.

"What…the hell…d'you do that…for?" The sound of his low moan stopped him from speaking further.

"Sweet baby Jesus." Natasha covered her mouth with her hand to hide the smile that crept onto her face. "You scared the crap out of me, Vlad. I'm sorry. I didn't mean to."

She lifted one arm in his direction. He raised a hand to still her movement. "Don't…touch me."

Well, damned if that didn't smart. He didn't want her to touch him, even to offer him a little comfort. My, how things changed. He certainly hadn't minded her touch the night of her brother's wedding.

Fine. If he doesn't want me touching him, so be it.

Natasha turned around, sending her harlequin-colored pigtails twirling about her face and retrieved the bag of blood from the floor. Without looking in his direction, she stalked through the room and sat in the only padded chair. She punctured the bag with her fangs and drank, glaring at him over the top of the bag.

The blood seeped into her cells, nourishing both her and the baby. The baby moved as she continued to down the bag quickly. Her hunger pangs eased a little with each gulp of the life-sustaining liquid.

Vlad slowly straightened to his full height. The expression on his face, a cross between disdain and pain, softened her eyes. With an awkward gait, he gingerly moved in her direction.

"We need to talk," he barked, his voice still rough with pain.

She just bet they did. No doubt, Vlad would tell her to leave. It was there on his face. He obviously didn't want her in his home, and she didn't blame him.

She had run out after they made love, avoided him for months, and now she had injured his manhood. If the tables were reversed, she probably wouldn't want him around either.

Tasha crumpled the emptied bag in her hand and gazed up at him with her amber eyes. "About what?"

"About you staying here."

Here it comes. Where would she go? Maybe to Alex. He would be able to protect her if she could find him.

"You will sleep in the loft."

Hold on. She must have misunderstood him.

"What did you say?" she asked incredulously.

"You will sleep in my bed," Vlad's whiskey voice slid sinuously over her skin as the image of the two of them sharing his bed popped into her mind. "In the loft."

She glanced up to the loft above the sink before tracking Vlad while he walked over and pulled down a folding ladder from the ceiling. He turned back to face her.

"Day is coming soon. We only have a few more minutes of night. Come," he instructed ascending the wooden ladder, her suitcase in hand. It creaked slightly under his muscular weight.

His point was valid. What else could she do but obey? Tasha rose from the chair, tossed the empty bag in the trash, and silently ascended the ladder behind Vladimir.

"I assume you brought a nightgown to wear?" Vlad held out her suitcase.

Taking it, she replied sheepishly, "Actually, in my rush, I forgot to pack one. But it's all right. I can sleep in my clothes.

The Alpha went to the steamer trunk sitting against one sloped wall. She could not have been more surprised when he turned around.

Vlad stood, feet braced shoulder-width apart, holding a flannel shirt out from his body. "You obviously cannot sleep in your coat all day, so you can borrow this."

He tossed the shirt at her. "I'm sure you will find it warm enough."

She caught the garment easily. "It will be fine. Thank you."

He huffed a welcome.

How was she going to change without him seeing the small bundle in her belly? The shirt would be large enough to hide her tummy, but if he caught a glimpse of her naked, her secret would be revealed.

"Turn around," Natasha commanded, "so I can get changed for bed."

His eyes flared slightly at the demand, the only indication he took any umbrage. "I'll do better than that."

He jumped off the loft, landing as graceful as a cat down below. "Go ahead and change," he called over his shoulder. "I'm going to bed."

Tasha peered over the railing. "Bed? I thought you were sleeping up here with me."

A hard laugh escaped his lips. "Hardly. I'm taking the couch."

Wow! He really doesn't want to be anywhere near me.

This was his house. He'd offered her protection. He should have the bed. "But it's your bed. I'll take the couch."

Vlad stopped, his shoulders tensed. He turned slowly, the hard look on his face made her cringe. "You insult me, Natasha. I would never allow a female to take the couch."

"I didn't mean to—" Her apology died on her lips as Vlad crossed his arms over his chest.

His dark brows furrowed over narrowing eyes. "Go. To. Bed."

"B-but," she sputtered. Natasha couldn't complete the sentence. She wanted to invite him to sleep with her. She needed the comfort of his arms. Wanted to tell him about their baby and see a joyful expression on his face as she did so. But that would not be how this evening would end. Day quickly approached. The pull of the sun would send them both to sleep soon.

"Fine," she capitulated, before turning from the rail. Her eyes rolled in their sockets, taking in the peaked ceiling, sloping walls, and wooden floor. It was a small space. Only large enough for a single bed and the steamer chest.

As she changed into the soft flannel shirt, she heard him move below. She listened while he first moved to the potbelly stove to stoke the fire within, then put a covering over the one window of the house to block out the sun's deadly rays. A soft rustle of clothing informed her he stripped out of his jacket and shirt. Natasha's traitorous mind tormented her by creating a picture of Vlad in only his jeans.

She crawled into the bed. Instantly, his masculine, woodsy scent enveloped her. Natasha buried her face in the pillows and inhaled deeply.

The baby moved again, almost as if he responded to the scent too. Of course, he couldn't be, but it was nice to think the baby already recognized his daddy.

She snuggled down between the flannel sheets. As sleep pulled her under, her last conscious thoughts were of the large male downstairs.

****

Harleigh walked leisurely down the beach, a phone to her head. The soft sound of the rolling waves played over her as she strolled, waiting to hear the telltale beep. It sounded loudly in her ear just as a wave came up to lap at her bare feet.

"Hi, Tasha, it's Harleigh. Just wanted to see how you are doing. I stopped by your house today, but you weren't there. Call me."

She hung up the phone and slipped it back into the pocket of her shorts just as she noticed a black form up ahead. The beast stalked her, the white strip between its eyes the only mark on its obsidian coat. It approached cautiously, its gaze roaming from side to side as if looking for something. Someone.

She reached for its soft fur. It felt silky, not like a usual wolf's coarse coat, but baby soft. Its tongue licked her hand, and a wolfy smile appeared on his long muzzle.

His intense eyes sized her up with their intelligence before its fur began to disappear. Bones contorted, and muscles became covered with flesh. Cracking and popping reached her ears as sinew molded into human form until a man with flowing blond hair and red eyes stood before her.

Harleigh gave him a wide smile. “Hi, Cyrus.”

He graced her with a mischievous grin. “Hi. I was thinking tonight might be a good night for a run. You could shift into a koala and jump on my back again like you did last night.”

Harleigh shook off the offer with a wave of her hand. “No, thanks. I’m not in the mood to goof around tonight.”

He glanced down at his naked body. “Well then, shall we go to your place before I get arrested for public indecency?”

“Even with clothes on you could do that,” Harleigh teased, then handed him the beach towel that had been carelessly slung over her shoulder. “Here. Wrap this around you.”

Cyrus wrapped the fairy princess towel around his narrow waist. “You couldn’t have brought a manlier towel for me to wear?”

“I wasn’t expecting to need to give you a towel at all. I thought you were going back to Mason’s Bluff to see the king.”

Cyrus drew her under his arm while they walked. “Varrick is busy with his mate. He requested I wait a few more days before I go home. He is quite upset with his sister. I think he wants a few days to calm down.”

“I can see why Varrick would be upset. I can’t believe Jara lost the vampire she kept prisoner.”

“Don’t forget about her killing Lane, the one demonic scientist who was our best hope for finding out the secret to vampiric immunity. I’m not looking forward to sharing that bit of news."

"She killed Lane?"

Cyrus nodded.

Harleigh's pink hair flowed about her shoulders when she shook her head. "I'm surprised Varrick doesn't already know. It's been six months."

"Jara is good at keeping secrets. I think I'm the only person who knows what happened."

"How did you find out?"

Cyrus stared ahead, his eyes glazed as if memories were bearing down on him. "I was there. She became upset because her plans to retrieve the vampire were not working out. You know how she gets when she is angry."

Harleigh nodded silently as they strolled.

"Her power built until she could not contain it. She fired the energy at me but missed and hit Lane instead. It killed him, nothing but a pile of ash left where he'd been standing."

"What did you do?" Harleigh looked up at him, concern widening her eyes.

"I got the hell out of there. Dematerialized to a safe place I know." He smiled at her and winked.

"My place," Harleigh supplied.

"Yeah." He gave her shoulders a squeeze. "Thanks for letting me stay with you, by the way."

"What are friends for?"

He stopped and pulled her into his arms. "I'd like to be more than friends, Harleigh."

His eyes searched hers. He began to close the slight distance between them.

Dogs barking out a ringtone to the tune of Beethoven's "Für Elise" stilled the movement. She pulled out of the embrace and yanked the phone from her pocket.

Whew! Dodged that one.

Noting the number on the phone's display, she answered. "Hi, cousin. What's up?"

"Hello, Harleigh. Nothing is up, dear. I'm just calling to find out how you are doing. You and Varrick are the only family I have left, you know."

"I'm sure Varrick and Elizabeth will have children soon. They will make sure the family grows."

Cyrus shifted his weight between feet. "Who is—" Harleigh raised her finger to her lips to silence his question.

"Who do I hear in the background? The voice sounds familiar."

"Just someone on the beach. You wouldn't know him."

One of Cyrus' brow rose questioningly.

"You are on the beach? With other people? With all those germs? Shouldn't you be somewhere safe like the Demon Compound in Wyoming?"

"I'm fine, cousin. You know I've always made my own way through life, living life while throwing caution to the wind."

"I remember. You never did care what others thought or what dangers might be lurking."

"That's right." Harleigh smiled. "Besides, I'm sure you have more important things to worry about than me."

"Why? What have you heard?"

Harleigh noted the suspicion in her cousin's voice. "Nothing. I just figured being a demon princess you had lots of official duties keeping you busy."

"Oh, well. Yes. I suppose I—"

The deep, rich timbre of a male voice murmured across the phone, but she could not make out what it said.

"Who is with you?" Harleigh asked curiously.

"That is no one, dear."

The sound of her cousin covering the phone receiver kept Harleigh from saying anything further. Waiting for her cousin to resume their conversation, she listened quietly to the mumbling of voices, one female, one male in the background.

"Harleigh, darling. I wanted to ask a favor of you, but I'm afraid I have to go. There seems to be a…situation requiring my attention."

"You know I'd do anything for you, cousin, but I understand if you need to go, Jara." Harleigh's relief lightened the features of her face as Cyrus' face paled with the recognition of her cousin's name.

"All right then. Ta, ta, Harleigh, dear."

"Later, cous'."

Harleigh turned off the phone and verified the connection was severed before turning to Cyrus. He stared at her with wide eyes.

"I didn't know Jara was your cousin," he accused with a small voice.

Harleigh resumed walking in the direction of her home. "I don't advertise that fact. It's not like it's a point of pride."

Cyrus jogged to catch up. "So, you are part of the royal family. You're the king's cousin."

"Yeah, but don't sound so astonished."

"But you…I…" Cyrus pushed a hand through his blond strands.

"Yeah. I get that a lot. Which is why I keep my lineage a secret. Look, it's no big deal, okay? I'm not any different because I'm related to the king of the demons."

Cyrus stopped her on the porch to her home by grabbing her arm. He turned her to face him before he spoke. "Do you have a royal title?"

"Mmm-hmm." Harleigh pulled her arm from his grasp.

"What should I call you?"

She pushed through the back door to her home. "Harleigh."

Chapter 7

Natasha ran the pads of her fingers down Vlad's body. An electric current of pleasure coursed through him. The digits trailed slowly, too slowly. She toyed with him, pushing him to his limit. Testing him.

Well, this test he could pass.

He stood still, using all of his carefully honed skills of self-control. He fisted his hands at his sides to keep from touching her. His eyes closed while her fingers traversed his body, trailing over his shoulders and down over his pecs. She took his nipples between her fingers, giving them a slight twist that sent pleasurable pain shooting to his groin. His manhood jumped approvingly in response.

Her sensuous fingers continued their path down, tracing each defining line of his abdomen before dragging through the indentations over his hips. Down, down her fingers roamed, heading for the place he longed to be touched most.

Natasha's sweet gardenia scent surrounded him, drove his desire higher. Vlad took a long, deep breath, drawing the addictive fragrance into his lungs. It filled him inside and out. The powerful perfume wrapped around his brain, sinking in until he knew he would never forget it. It was like her—lovable, innocent.

Innocent. Innocent. *The thought pushed through the erotic haze like nothing else.*

She was *innocent. Not in the virginal sense, but she was naive. Naive to the dangers the world presented, the dangers* he *presented.*

This was wrong.

Her scent made him want her with an uncontrollable ferocity. He needed to stop this now before they went too far…again!

Vladimir's eyes flew open, and he stared at the ceiling above. The thing rested too far away. He popped a questioning brow.

Oh yes, I'm not in the loft.

He rolled over on the couch and scrubbed a hand up his face. It made a raspy sound over his goatee. Still hazy from the intense dream, he struggled to remember. He'd slept downstairs because of…

A soft mewing sound brought full awareness to his mind. Natasha rolled over in his bed. A bed that would now smell like gardenias. Unconsciously, he took a deep breath.

His body hardened instantly, demanding he go to her. Take her. His inner desire awoke, wanting to mate.

Vlad ruthlessly stomped down the impulse and took control by closing his senses to her, her scent, her heartbeat. He permitted nothing of her to soak in. His hold over his baser instinct seemed tenuous at best. He needed space. Needed room.

Vlad pushed from the couch, sore muscles protesting the movement. The small couch was never designed for sleeping, especially for someone as large as he. He had been forced to sleep on his side with his feet hanging off the end all day. Luckily, the days were short. Another two hours on the couch and he doubted he would have been able to move.

Vlad stretched, leaning to one side, then the other, then bent at the waist, stretching the backs of his legs. It felt good, but not enough. His body, tight with lust and tension, made him realize he needed to work off the strain, and since the woman sleeping in his loft was off limits, he would have to make do with the next best thing—a workout or maybe…

The craving flowed through his body, taking hold. Damn, he wanted a smoke something fierce. Nothing like a little nicotine to ease the body and mind.

He pulled at the drawstring to cinch the waist on the sweats he'd worn to bed. After securing them tight, he went to the kitchen and grabbed a cig. Thinking better of it, he put the thing back in the drawer. Perhaps after his workout. Even though his body easily took care of the carcinogens in the cigarettes, it was still a bitch to work up a sweat with smoke-filled lungs.

On silent feet, he left the home and made his way around back. A few more weeks and the temperature would be too cold even for him, but this evening it seemed perfect. The chilly air nipped at the exposed flesh on his bare chest, giving his mind something to concentrate on other than the female in his home. Vlad took in a deep breath of clean air.

He crossed by the shed, noting the hum of the generator inside. *Good. When Natasha wakes, she will have electricity and running water.*

Vlad stopped in front of a black punching bag suspended from a large larch tree. Exactly what he needed—to go a few rounds with his faithful friend. He gave the trunk of the tree a push that sent a blanket of snow falling to the ground. After all, he would rather be coated once than to be covered with the stuff each time he landed a punch.

He brushed the snow from his head and shoulders.

Better than a cold shower, he thought, squaring his body to the bag.

Vlad's first punch sent the thing into the trunk of the tree. It rocked from the force of the blow, sending a final light dusting of snow to the ground. As the black bag made its return, he reared back with his other fist, easily connecting with the thing to send it flying once more.

He threw a series of hard punches. Right. Left. Right. Left. Alternating his fists until he noticed bloody knuckle prints on the vinyl.

Vladimir switched his stance and gave the bag a roundhouse kick. The sting of his bare foot contacting with the padding became a welcome addition to the pain in his fists. It kept his mind clear of everything but the movement of his body.

His breath came in hard bursts. A sweat broke out over his body. Steam rose from the exposed flesh as he assaulted the bag with alternating kicks.

Time disappeared. Gone, like the light of day. The darkness of the moonless night cradled him, welcomed him. There was only him. The ache in his body. The blissful pain that took away the hurting, took the longing for things he could not have.

He did not like when his Alpha duties did not consume his time. With nothing to occupy himself, his thoughts of Natasha became too loud for his skull to contain.

A sharp inhale stopped his kick midarc. He pivoted on his grounded leg, his arms held next to his chest, hands fisted. He slowly lowered his leg to the ground.

"How long have you been there?" He raked Natasha with his hard stare.

She stood beside the shed wrapped in her long coat, the top of his flannel shirt peeking out from the collar. Her legs were exposed between the coat and her boots. The woman had only his shirt on under the coat and didn't that make his libido pop up to say hi.

Her hair appeared mussed. Tasha's fire engine lipstick long gone like the choker worn the previous night. She wore no makeup, nothing to add to her beauty, and yet she was the most beautiful sight he'd ever seen. Her soft, amber eyes perfectly accented her patrician features. Her full, pink lips were parted slightly. Breath, barely clouding in front of her face, added an ethereal feature to her glow.

So much for the workout getting his mind off her. In one second, all the effort with the bag had been negated. His body tightened, coiled as if to spring upon her. Vlad fought his rising lust when all he wanted to do was strip the coat from her body, so she stood before him wearing only his shirt.

"I've been here long enough," came Natasha's reply.

"Can I help you with something or are you just going to stand there gawking at me?" He knew he sounded clipped, but Vlad wasn't sure how much longer he could refrain from touching her, especially when desire sparkled in her eyes as they roamed his body, scorching him with their heated stare. She needed to leave, soon—before his control snapped.

"I was just wondering—" Her voice dropped away when her eyes found the erection tenting his pants.

Damned woman.

Didn't she see the effect she had on him? Oh wait, she did.

He adjusted himself as if it would help to hide the evidence of his arousal. His desire exposed, his inner beast clawed to get out. It was a losing battle. Eventually, he would succumb to its lustful yearnings.

Unless…

If he just held out a little longer. Nicholai mentioned he would be home in a few days. All Vladimir needed to do was hold out against the pull Natasha had on him a short time longer, then he might be able to not only keep his dignity but keep her safe. And her safety was everything.

He crossed his arms over his sweaty chest, trying to hide the glistening that seemed to draw her gaze.

"You were wondering," he prompted, his eyes narrowing.

She cleared her throat. "I was wondering if I should start breakfast."

"I'm afraid there isn't much in the house. I wasn't expecting company."

"I could go out and get something," Natasha offered.

Not going to happen. He'd sooner tie her down then let her out of his sight. "No. You won't. There are some canned goods in the shed for an emergency. We can survive on those until your brother arrives home, and you can go stay with him."

Her eyes dropped to the ground as if in defeat, and her lower lip pushed out in a sexy pout. If he didn't know better, he would think she didn't want to leave. But he knew better.

After all, she was the one who snuck out of his

room after they made love. She probably couldn't wait to get away from him again.

An old-fashioned telephone ring came from the pocket of her coat. Her hand withdrew a cell phone. She glanced down.

"Who's calling?" Vlad strolled to where she stood.

"No one. I have a voicemail." She pushed a button on the phone.

He easily heard the message when it played. A woman named Harleigh asked if Natasha was all right and wanted her to return the call.

"Do not call her back," Vlad commanded.

"Why not?"

"It is not safe. We do not yet know how the demons track us. Do not use your phone until we know you are safe."

"That is ridiculous. I don't even know for sure demons are after me."

"I will not let you take the risk, Natasha. Your brother has charged me with your safety. I forbid you to use your phone. It could be tracked."

When Tasha placed the phone back in the pocket of her coat, a satisfied smirk took Vlad's face. At least Nicholai's sister could be reasonable…at times.

"Fine," she capitulated. "You win for now. But don't—"

Horror crossed her face. Her mouth gaped open as she backed away from him.

Vlad knew he wore an intense expression, but not a savage one. He held no malice toward her, she had conceded to his will after all. Why did he scare her?

"What's wrong?" he asked.

"Don't move," she whispered, stilling her steps.

"Behind you."

Slowly, he turned his head. A large Siberian tiger locked eyes with the Alpha. It loped toward them, placing one paw in front of the other like a tightrope walker on a rope. It stopped in front of Vladimir and butted its large head against his legs.

"Mishka," he greeted, reaching down to rub between its ears. "I see your winter coat is coming in nicely, my friend."

"You named this beast?"

"Yes." A genuine smile graced the features of his face, softening his black eyes. "Allow me to introduce you. Natasha, this is Mishka. He is the male of his pride."

Vlad squatted down, taking the white tiger's head between his hands to give it a shake.

Where is your family? He sent the question into the tiger's mind. The answer came to him as he stayed within the mind of the beast.

"His pride is in the woods. He is leery of you. Come and meet him formally."

"Will he bite?" Natasha asked.

"Not once he accepts you. Come here. I will not allow him to hurt you."

As Natasha approached, he took her wrist in a gentle grip and led her hand to the tiger's nose. "Let him smell you. Give him a minute to absorb your scent."

The tiger tensed. *Natasha is okay. You can trust her. She will not hurt you or your family.*

Vlad sent a feeling of comfort and serenity to the tiger, willing him to accept Natasha. Mishka nuzzled her outstretched hand with his nose, causing a nervous giggle to escape Natasha's lips.

"He likes you," Vlad assured her, keeping possession of her wrist. "Pet him. Show him you like him too."

Vlad guided her hand along the back of the tiger. A purr vibrated under the ministrations. Her body relaxed, and wonderment replaced the horror on her face. He let go of her wrist, pleased when she continued to stroke the large cat without any encouragement from him.

The animal made a soft throaty sound, and his pride stalked from the forest. A female and her three adolescents emerged from between the trees.

Natasha drew in a sharp breath. "I didn't even know they were there."

Vlad smiled, then knelt on the cold ground in greeting. "They are well camouflaged."

The adolescents crawled over his legs, stumbling in their haste. Their mother nuzzled his face, giving it a lick with her rough tongue. It stung, but he allowed it, realizing it as a sign of acceptance and love. One by one, the cubs took turns greeting Natasha. She gave each a playful rub before turning to find their mother eyeing her warily.

Vlad quickly pushed into the tigress' mind. *She is with me. Natasha will do your babies no harm. Go greet her. Let her know you accept her. She is a friend.*

Cautiously, the tigress stalked to Natasha, approaching her with a steady stride. She sank her fingers into the thick fur. The pride surrounded her, pushing up against her to roughhouse a little. Tasha's nervous laugh had him on his feet to intervene. Vlad pushed the male's large head. Mishka replied with a show of teeth and stepped away from Natasha. Sensing the tiger's laughing intent, Vlad allowed the display.

While the male nuzzled his mate, Vlad's fingers stroked through the thick fur. Watching the two cats together, his mind could not help but turn to the woman beside him. Natasha playing with his pride made him want her more, made him want to be stroking his fingers over her smooth skin instead of through Mishka's pelt. She'd been brave, pushing through fear to reach out to them. She accepted them, and they, in turn, quickly accepted her. A smile engulfed his face when she bent down to play with the adolescents.

A genuine laugh pushed through her lips. Natasha's laughter had a way of stealing his heart. Centuries ago, the magic of her smile wove its spell around his soul, soothing a part of him long ago buried. It was one of the things he'd first noticed about her. Of course, the rest of her wasn't bad either.

Tasha's round little bottom bounced as she spun to keep the cubs in sight. Her coat gaped open at the neck when she bent, giving him a delectable view of her bosom. His body tightened painfully. He forgot the male tiger under his hand as her tongue darted out to moisten her lips.

She appeared sexy as hell, folded over to stroke the cat's fur. He imagined the sensation of her fingers stroking him. Holding him.

"Natasha." His voice sounded husky with desire. He did not bother to hide it from her. "I think we should go inside."

She straightened, her gaze flying to his. She knew. He could tell by the way she looked at him with sultry eyes. She wanted him as desperately as he wanted her.

Natasha's beauty made him let down his guard, and

he breathed the scent in the air. The aroma of tigers mixed with the surrounding forest and snow. But an additional perfume also tickled his nose. Hers. It was saccharine, dark, pure female seductiveness.

Vlad's control snapped. He advanced on her, impressed when she held her ground. He cupped Natasha's face in his large hands. His mouth descended on hers, taking her lips in a punishing kiss.

Tasha melted against him, grasping his shoulders for support. Her nails dug into his flesh as if to anchor herself, driving his passion higher.

Vlad's tongue swept into her opened mouth. She tasted as sweet as he remembered. He must find every delicious corner. His tongue left no spot untasted. Natasha moaned into his mouth, the sound vibrating against his tongue.

The warrior broke the kiss to look into her eyes. He needed to make sure she understood where this headed.

"Tasha." The Alpha waited until she gazed up at him from under her thick, dark lashes. "If this continues, I will not be able to stop. We will finish this in my bed."

She closed the small space between them, pressing her lips to his. Natasha deepened the kiss this time, leaving no doubt as to her understanding of the warning. Too soon, she pulled back, and their eyes locked.

"Take me inside." Natasha smiled at him.

That was one command he didn't mind obeying.

Chapter 8

Natasha gazed into Vladimir's obsidian eyes. Eyes that darkened with passion at her command. The muscles beneath the flesh on his shoulders danced under her fingertips when he lifted her into his arms. His hand on her back branded her, burning into her skin. Making her his.

Being back in his arms seemed right. The play of his muscles and sinew against her side as he marched them back toward the home brought a carnal awareness of the male. With the tigers watching them go, Vlad opened the door with his mind when they approached, the hinges squealing slightly in protest.

She forgot the sound when his lips found hers. The rough rasp of his goatee brushed around her mouth, heating her blood. Vlad's lips pressed against hers in a demanding kiss. She instinctively opened for him, needing the taste of his kiss.

His tongue danced with hers, thrusting in time to his steps across the cabin. Without breaking their kiss, his powerful legs bunched beneath her. With a mighty leap, they landed softly on the loft.

When he placed Tasha on the bed, she gazed up at him expectantly. He crossed his arms over his chest and braced his feet wide.

That is the Vlad I know. Commanding, always in control.

How Natasha would love to shatter that control. Keep him off balance, like she felt around him.

"Take off your clothes." His whiskey voice slid up her spine as he reached for the drawstring on his pants.

Natasha's tongue flicked out to lick her suddenly dry lips. His eyes tracked the movement. She did not miss the slight jerk of his manhood under the sweats.

It stood thick, long. He filled her body and soul when they made love. She reached a hand out as if to take hold of the object of her desire.

Her hands stilled when he moved his hips away. "Take off your clothes, Natasha." Vlad's voice brooked no argument. "Before I rip them from your body."

She swallowed the lump in her throat. The raw desire and lust on his face made her heart race. His brutal words made a hundred butterflies flutter in her stomach. Her core clenched at the raw sexuality he exuded.

"Natasha," Vlad growled a low warning.

She rose to her knees. Her hands molded the coat to her body as they made their way slowly up to the top toggle button. She popped it loose, then the next. Haltingly her hands traveled down the jacket, undoing each button with care. She shrugged from the garment, tossing it carelessly to the floor before looking up at him expectantly.

"My shirt," he commanded. "Take it off."

She pushed him. He trembled slightly from the effort it took not to descend on her. Loving the satisfaction of knowing she toyed with his control, Natasha's hands slid up her thighs, catching the hem of the flannel. She moved the shirt north, holding onto the material until it just reached the junction of her thighs.

His eyes widened, riveted on the movement of her fingers.

Vlad wanted her, his need evident on his face, but she wasn't done playing. Natasha let the fabric fall, denying him a glimpse of her most feminine part. His nostrils flared. She realized he scented her arousal and wondered just how far she dared to tease him.

Tasha's fingers found the top button of his shirt. Repeating the same deliberate pace, she took with the coat, she popped each button from its hole, one by one. She opened the shirt, peeled it away from her body, while arching her back to give her lover a generous view of her swollen breasts. A low rumble sounded from deep within his chest. Her eyes flew to his.

"Lie down," Vlad growled between clenched teeth.

She complied, while his muscles ripple beneath his skin as he took off his pants. Her breath quickened. Her heart raced. A magnificent specimen of masculinity, Vlad's handsome face and corded neck sat on broad shoulders. His perfectly sculpted chest led to chiseled abdominals. His manhood stood erect, jutting out from his body thick and long over thighs which bunched as her gaze swept over them. They flexed as if he were about to pounce.

For the first time since he placed her on the bed, he moved. Vlad took one of her legs in his strong hand, cupping the back of her knee. His other hand ran down her calf, over the boot she still wore. He removed the shoe with ease and reached for her other leg.

After removing the other boot, he retained possession of the leg. Vlad's lips lowered to her calf. The Alpha laid a trail of tiny kisses up her leg. Natasha moaned as he headed north. His lips were soft, a stark contrast to his goatee. The combination sent a burning wave of heat through her body.

He set her on fire. Made her forget about anything but him. Vlad surrounded her, consumed her. And Natasha reveled in the sensation.

It had been like that when they first made love. It was one of the reasons she ran. She hadn't been ready to lose herself in him. But she was ready now. Being here with him, being loved by him felt right.

Felt perfect.

She needed this. Needed him. And she willingly gave into the desire.

His lips found her inner thigh. A slight nip made her jump, but his strong hands on her thighs held her in place.

Vlad blanketed her body, settling between her opened legs. The soft curves of her body welcomed him. His lips molded over one of her breasts while his hand cupped the other. He drew her puckered nipple between his teeth, and his tongue laved over the sensitive flesh. Vlad's hand kneaded the other globe, working the supple, creamy flesh, driving her higher.

Her body coiled under the attention. Natasha's back arched. Her breasts pushed into his touch. She climbed toward the precipice. Her body wanted, demanded release.

Natasha moved her hips against his, grinding his hard length against her most sensitive spot. *He got the hint*, she noted with satisfaction as he began to thrust against her. He wasn't even inside her yet, and she was about to find her release.

Suckling at her breast, his hand trailed down her body, over her rounded stomach to find the junction of her thighs. Vlad's fingers pushed through the tight curls to find the tiny nub. His thumb circled the delicate spot as his fingers slipped into her. They pumped in time to the draws of his mouth, sending Natasha over the edge of ecstasy.

Like the fireworks grand finale that boomed in the background the first time they made love, Tasha's orgasm hit her with such force it sent a flurry of light dancing before her closed eyes. Her hard breath pushed from her lungs, cheeks reddening from the afterglow. Her hand fisted in the sheets when he tried to pull from her breast.

Natasha eased her grip when she realized his tempting mouth headed south. Her body trembled with the aftershocks of the climax, sending delicious shivers through her body. This male possessed amazing talents, and she would gladly be the beneficiary of his skills all night.

Natasha's hands found his stubbled head, resting there while he feathered kisses down her stomach. His tongue circled her bellybutton. Once. Twice.

He went stone still beneath her hands.

Vlad's hand came to her belly, and he laid his head down on the small mound.

A worried expression consumed her face. "What is—"

A harsh shushing sound from Vlad's mouth sent his warm breath over her stomach. Goose pimples pebbled her flesh. This was it.

He knows.

Natasha worried her lips between her teeth as his head slowly rose from her stomach. Vlad's dark eyes pinned hers, his mouth gaping open. His black eyebrows narrowed.

"You are with child." Vlad moved into a seated position.

"I wanted to tell you."

Tasha tried to read the play of emotions on Vlad's face. He seemed surprised at first, but it quickly turned into anger. She feared he wouldn't want her or the baby. She'd been afraid he would be upset about the baby, and apparently, she'd been right.

"Don't worry," she continued hastily. "You don't have to do anything. I will raise the baby. You don't even have to be in our lives. It isn't a trap. I am able to take care of us. You won't have to do a thing."

"Stop, Natasha. Breathe." The features of his face tightened. Through clenched teeth, he uttered, "How far along are you?"

"S-six months, almost seven." She stared up at him with large doe eyes.

The expression on his face became thoughtful as he calculated the amount of time. "Are you saying the baby is mine?"

"Of course. Who else would be the father?" Anger heated her face. Did he really think she would come to him with another male's child growing in her belly?

He stood and paced the small space. "We are going to have a baby?"

"Yes." Tasha tracked him as she pushed into a seated position.

"I thought you were bearing another's child," he murmured.

Vlad turned sharply and pinned her with an intense stare while his power flowed over her. "I was ready to kill the bastard for daring to touch you, for leaving you to raise a child on your own. You are telling me *I* am the bastard?"

She nodded, unable to find her voice. He was petrifying when he became enraged. What angered him so? Did he really hate the idea of them having a child together so much?

"Fates above, Natasha!" His ire prickled over her skin. "How could you keep this from me?"

"I-I did not want you to feel trapped. I wanted you free to be able to find your heartmate one day." She inhaled sharply at the harsh look on his face.

"And therefore, you decided you would keep my child from me."

"So you could find your mate, Vlad," she explained hastily. "I just wanted you to be happy. I love you too much to let you sacrifice your happiness for me."

His face softened, and the tingling sensation left her skin. Vlad sat down next to her on the bed, placing one large hand over her rounded belly. "Natasha, do you not think you should have allowed me to decide what would make me happy?"

"But your heartmate is out there, waiting for you. You deserve to find her. I don't want you saddled with me and a baby."

His hand rubbed back and forth across her stomach. "Who's to say you aren't my mate?" His black eyes jumped from her belly to her face. "We have not exchanged blood. How can you be sure we are not heartmates? I certainly have been drawn to you since the first time we met."

Shock lifted her brown brows. "You have?"

"Of course." Vlad gave an easy shrug of one

shoulder.

"Then why has it seemed like you have been purposely avoiding me every time we were in the same room?"

"Because I was."

Okay, now she was really confused. "If you were drawn to me, why did you avoid me?"

"You were Nicholai's sister *and* Demetri's cousin. They are very protective of you, Tasha. I did not wish to complicate our friendships by getting involved with you. But now, everything has changed."

She shook her head, sending her multicolored locks swirling about her shoulders. "No. It hasn't. You can go about your life. I can provide for the baby. I will not tell anyone the child is yours. Nikko and Demetri will never know you are the father."

Vlad took her chin between his finger and thumb and forced her to gaze into his dark stare. "Natasha, you insult me. I would never allow you to raise our child by yourself. I will be a part of the baby's life…regardless of the consequences."

"But you'll never be free to find your mate."

"Enough!" His voice echoed in the rafters of the cabin, making her jump. In the blink of her eye, his fangs sank into her delicate skin. She experienced a moment's pain, like a pinprick, then pleasure washed over her. Offering her neck to him, she cradled his head in her hand while he drank.

All too soon, the sucking stopped, and his tongue glided against the flesh to seal the wounds.

When he raised his head, the look in his eyes told her all she needed to know.

"You are mine." Possession darkened the tone of

his voice. "I suspected as much, but now I have no doubt."

Hope lightened the tension in her shoulders. "Are you sure, Vlad?"

"Take from me so your fears will be eased."

His hand cupped the nape of her neck, then he pulled her forward, leaning his head back to expose his neck to her. The sight drew the fangs from her gums.

Tasha's heart raced. This was it. Vampires could tell by the taste of their mate's blood they were heartmates. Her brother, Nicholai, had tried to explain the sensation to her. Would she be able to tell Vlad was her mate? Only one way to find out.

Her fangs sank into the flesh. Blood flowed onto her tongue.

Mine!

Her body tightened as the blood raced through her veins. The sinuous feel of his blood nourishing her cells, flowing through her body, filled her with passion. She needed him. Wanted him.

Only him.

The instant his blood touched her tongue, she realized she belonged to him. Knew it down in her soul. They were mates.

Heartmates.

Happiness unlike she'd ever experienced before filled her, making her chest swell. She licked the wounds on his neck closed needing to tell him, needing to say it aloud.

"We're heartmates."

He chuckled. "It would seem so." Vlad pulled her into an embrace. "And we are going to have a child."

"Are you pleased?" She wrapped her arms about

his waist.

His fingers smoothed the strands of her hair. “I have never been happier in all my centuries of life.”

A smile took her face. “Me too.”

And she was. For the first time since discovering she was pregnant, she felt truly hopeful. She’d found her heartmate—a miracle. They were having a child—another miracle. She must have done something right to have the Fates reward her so.

Some couples waited hundreds of years to have a child. She and Vlad were fortunate enough to have one right away. A true miracle. Her very own personal miracle. She felt truly blessed.

“Do you need anything? Does the child need anything?” Vlad asked.

“I’m fine for now. Just hold me.” A contented sigh left her lips when his strong arms wrapped around her. “But knowing our son, I’ll need a bag of blood before too much longer.”

“Son?” Vladimir pulled back slightly, looking down at her with awe in his eyes. “We are having a boy?”

Tasha nodded, the smile on her face reaching her eyes. “Yes. And I hope he looks just like his father.”

****

The vampire’s eyes snapped open, staring sightlessly across the crowded room. The regal home was aflutter with activity, but his attention remained somewhere far away.

It started building hours ago. A prickling in his mind along a mental channel not used in many centuries.

One of the vampires he’d sired was dropping his

guard. It took the ancient only seconds to recognize the source of the mental disturbance. Emotions poured over the mindlink forged on the night he'd converted the young lad.

They came in waves. Surprise. Anger. Elation, unlike he had ever experienced, made him narrow his eyes in focus as he tried to follow the link deeper into the mind of Vladimir.

Centuries ago, the vampire learned to keep him from entering his mind by erecting thick mental barriers. It must be at least four hundred years since he'd been able to sense Vladimir.

But tonight, those barriers were down, and Sergei sensed Vlad's excitement building. Finally, Sergei felt the young one again. Although now, he supposed, Vlad was no longer young. He would be about five centuries old.

"What is it, darling?" the female demon asked from the chair in which she sat.

When he did not reply, she persisted—the determined wench—splitting his attention from his connection to the younger vampire.

"Sergei!" Her shrill tone drew his gaze. "I asked you a question."

He hushed her, dismissing her with a wave of his hand. "Shut up. I need to concentrate."

Jara pushed from her chair, moving to stand in front of him, her eyes glowing blood-red. Long blonde hair stood out from her head as power swirled around her, fueled by her outrage. He had never seen anything look so wild and untamed.

So sexy.

Her stare burned into him; fingers flexed sending

tiny blue sparks of electricity to arc wildly from the tips. They trailed down the sides of her body to the floor, charring the carpet where they landed.

His stomach twisted. This demon was as deadly as she was beautiful. It had been a long time since anyone piqued his interest this way. Playing with her was akin to playing with a scorpion. And he loved to play with danger. It had been the reason he'd agreed to come with her the night she and a guard approached him out of the blue with a promise of reuniting him with his sire.

"Relax, my love," he soothed. "I meant no disrespect." He watched her hands closely as they relaxed, the blue sparks disappearing.

The vampire pulled her onto his lap, ignoring the stares the action earned from the others in the room. He ran his fingers through Jara's hair, so the silky strands slid over her shoulders. "What did you ask me?"

She relaxed against his chest. "I asked you what is wrong."

"Nothing is wrong. Nothing at all. In fact, everything is once again right."

"What do you mean?"

"I just found something lost centuries ago," he informed her.

Jara pushed away from his body to look into his eyes. "How? You were sitting right here next to me. What could you have found?"

"I found my lost child."

Puzzlement crossed her pretty face. "You are making no sense, Sergei. What child? You lost a child?"

He gathered her back against his chest, resting his chin on the top of her head. "Let me tell you a story.

"Long ago, many centuries from this time, I sired a vampire. He was magnificent. Strong, confident. A true warrior on the battlefield." Her fingers slid up and down his arm as he continued. "This male was everything I ever wanted. He was one who could stand by my side for eternity. I knew I would never tire of him. I would adore him forever."

"What happened?" the woman in his arms asked, seeming genuinely interested.

"Her. While I fell in love with him, he was in love with his wife—the woman who gave him four whelps."

"You loved this man?" Jara pushed against his chest as if to rise. "Should I be jealous?"

He gave her a squeeze, keeping her against him.

"Perhaps," he answered as honestly as he could. "I admittedly still pine over him to this day. His loss has weighed heavily on me over the years."

"But you and I…we…" He waited for her to continue. "You swing both ways."

It was more of a statement than an accusation, and for that, he was grateful.

"I am attracted to beauty wherever I find it. It makes no difference to me if it is male or female."

Jara sifted her weight in his lap, bringing her bottom to rest over his groin. "Finish your story," she commanded.

He chuckled at her arrogance. She acted like a spoiled child, always demanding, never asking politely. He had yet to decide if he would keep her, but for now, she was a delightful plaything for his amusement. Deciding to indulge her, he continued. "I knew as long as his family lived, he would never be free to love me in the way I needed. Being the first vampire I sired, there was a special bond between us. Something I would never find with another. I wanted him and refused to allow anything to stand in our way."

"So you killed them."

His demon was smart. He would give her that.

"Yes. It was easy really. I simply hired someone to kill them while he was in his day sleep."

"I take it, he had not converted them."

"No. They were still quite human. Easy pickings."

"And when he awoke?"

"He found them, of course. I gave him some time before I arrived at the home and announced I had freed him of his responsibilities."

"What did he do after you told him *that*?" asked a male demon, named Finn, who looked remarkably like a particular unkempt, long-haired, kilt-wearing, Scotsman from the thirteenth century.

Sergei met his red stare over the head of his current lover. "What any respectable male would do. I should have expected it really, but in my lustful desire, I did not anticipate his reaction. Like a fool, I thought he would be grateful to finally be with me once he no longer had the burden of a family. However, sadly that was not the case."

The demon in his arms, stirred, running her fingers over his short honey-colored hair. "He was not grateful, was he?"

"No, Jara. He flew into a rage, the likes of which I have never seen to this day. I nearly lost my head that night."

Jara straightened away from his body, tracing the faint line around his neck with her finger. "Is that how you got this scar?"

"Yes," he admitted reluctantly, not liking to divulge any weakness, especially in front of this group of demons. They would turn on him. He did not have their loyalty. Only Sergei's desire to find his master kept him here.

Finn's brows raised questioningly. "I thought vampires didn't scar."

"They do if the knife is made from titanium," Jara supplied, turning toward the male demon who was running his fingers through his long, coarse hair.

Sergei put the sultry demon away from him as he rose to his full height. He needed to be alone to concentrate on the mindlink between him and Vladimir, so he might discover the information potent enough to cause Vladimir to drop his mental barrier. He planned to use their link to discover as much current information as possible about the vampire he'd sired. Perhaps he could locate the male, take things up where they left off. He had a score to settle, and he'd waited long enough to do it.

Chapter 9

Vladimir pushed from the bed and paced the small loft.

"A boy," he murmured. "I'm going to be a father."

Tasha nodded exuberantly. "Yes! Yes, you are."

Her intense gaze tracked his movements. His eyes glazed over. Lost in thought, his lips worked silently as he marched back and forth. Was he sending a prayer up to the heavens? Was he cursing the predicament he found himself in?

If only they'd formed a mindlink, she would have no trouble discerning his rumination. Unfortunately, Natasha could only watch and wonder…and vow to remedy the situation soon.

Wanting to be in the mind of a mate was as natural to vampires as sleeping during the day. Creating a mindlink allowed the pair to monitor each other's safety, communicate no matter how many miles separated them, and gave them access to memories. It was the most intimate thing two people could share. Tasha couldn't wait to find out what lay in the crevasses of her heartmate's mind.

"Tell me what you are thinking," she prompted, propping herself on her elbows as she lay on his bed.

His eyes, black as midnight and fringed with even darker lashes, pinned her with their steely stare when he stopped the restless pacing. Burning over her flesh, his gaze raked her body, reminding her of their nakedness. He'd just given her one amazing climax, and she was ready to return the favor.

On fire was the best way to describe how she felt. Her body flushed, her feminine core achy. It clenched in anticipation—in invitation. Her body wanted the male standing at the end of the bed.

With its deep hollows and uncompromising angles, his was a warrior's body, battle-hardened from years of fighting and training. One which might have been sculpted by the gods themselves—designed to swing a sword in lethal arcs as he led men and barked orders.

His skin smelled of smoke and earth. Facial features nearly perfect in their beauty contained lines softened by the dark goatee circling his full lips.

Vlad stood stone still, save the muscle which flexed along the line of his strong jaw. "You don't want to know what I'm thinking."

His eyes darkened, impossibly so, holding within their obsidian depths the promise of sinfully delicious acts. Bending her left leg at the knee, she coyly placed her thighs together, taking her most feminine part from his view. The muscle of his jaw ticked again when she licked her suddenly dry lips.

"Tell me what you want, Vladimir."

She toyed with a predator, one coiled and ready to pounce. The knowledge of which sent a fresh wave of desire straight to her core. The scent of her arousal perfumed the air, making his nostrils flare when he breathed deep.

His mouth slashed a straight line across his face, lips pulled taut. He forced his eyes away from her body and scrubbed a hand back and forth over his stubbled head. Resuming the pacing he murmured, “What I really want more than anything in this world is for you and our child to be safe.”

Surprise widened her eyes. Where had that come from?

“We are safe. We are here with you.”

“I wish that was true.”

“It is, Vlad. You are an Alpha. We couldn’t be any safer.”

His steps paused, and Vladimir turned to face her. “Oh, *lapushka*, if only that was all it took for me to keep you safe.”

Tasha smiled. “You called me sweetheart.”

A smile that mirrored her own took his face, softening the features but not quite reaching his eyes. “You are so much more to me than just a sweetheart. I have watched you become an independent woman, strong and brave. You thoughtfully work through every problem, letting your intelligence process the information before making any decisions. You are not only smart, but you are beyond beautiful. Every man who lays eyes on you wants you, and I am no exception.”

“Then come over here and do something about it.”

Vlad shook his head. “I can’t.”

Brows furrowing in confusion, she purposely glanced down at his erection. “Seems to me like you can.”

“It will hurt the baby.”

Laughter burst through her lips. “No, it won’t.”

He crossed his arms over his chest and braced his feet apart, affixing an I’m-large-and-in-charge stance. “It most certainly will. When my wife became pregnant, the midwife cautioned us against intercourse, saying it could harm the child growing within her belly."

A pang of jealousy washed over Natasha. Nicholai had mentioned Vladimir had been married when he was converted. She also knew his wife and his children were no longer in this world. No one knew what happened to them. Natasha assumed they died of old age centuries ago which made her jealousy morph into sympathy.

"That advice was from what, about four hundred years ago?"

"Closer to five," he corrected.

"Well, doctors have learned a thing or two since then. Like for instance, you can have sex and not hurt the baby in the least."

One dark brow lifted in disbelief over his eye. "You are sure about that?"

Tasha rolled her eyes. "I'm sure, silly. Don't you know anyone in this century who has been pregnant?"

Emotions played over his face, but Natasha couldn't quite identify them.

"I've been rather isolated."

The news did not surprise her, unlike the look of sorrow on his face. She'd always assumed his seclusion and remoteness were by choice. Could she have been wrong all these years? Had this amazing man been living a life of self-imposed isolation? The loneliness he would have experienced must be crushing, day after day in this wilderness with only the tigers to keep him company. The thought of him suffering alone tore at her heart.

Reaching both arms out, she sat up. Vlad took the invitation and perched next to her on the bed. His arms wrapped around her, holding her as if afraid she might dissolve from his grasp. His hand lovingly stroked her hair, making her eyes close, before he guided the two of them down onto the flannel sheets.

Her side tingled everywhere their bodies touched. Natasha opened her eyes and discovered Vlad propped on one elbow, gazing down at her. Hunger burned brightly in his eyes, making them sparkle. His heart raced in his chest. Heavy breaths sawed from his lungs. She affected him as much as he did her, and she reveled in the power of it.

He restrained himself around her, she sensed it. She had yet to see the powerful animal beneath his façade, but she desired that animal most. She needed him to make her his in the most primal of ways. He was so close to giving her what she wanted. A little extra push and she'd have him right where she wanted him.

When she chewed her bottom lip between her teeth, his shaft jumped against her thigh in response. Was he waiting for her to make a move? Fine.

Their eyes met.

"I dare you to kiss me," she challenged.

His lips descended on hers. The quickness of the movement caused her to gasp. Vlad wasted no time deepening the kiss. It appeared she'd awakened the sleeping tiger, and he'd come out ready to play hard.

This was no slow, languorous kiss. Their tongues dueled in her mouth. His lips pushed against hers with bruising force. Fangs collided, the scrape of their razor tips an erotic sensation. He tasted the way he smelled, smoky and spicy.

His fingers slid into the thick weight of her hair, fisting in the strands to hold her head at the angle he desired. Vlad's lips left hers to trail over her cheek, then down the line of her jaw to her throat. The scrape of his fangs against her flesh sent a shiver up her spine. They played over her delicate skin, teasing, taunting. His tongue flicked out to taste her. It swirled over the spot where her shoulder met her neck, the place her pulse beat strong.

Her heartbeat quickened behind her ribs, muscles tightened in anticipation. A fresh gush of moisture pushed between her thighs in ready for him. Her fingers splayed over his back before they curled around his shoulders. Vladimir's muscles bunched under the smooth skin. Her nails dug into his flesh when his fangs slid home.

The world tunneled to only him, the feel of him, the scent of him. He surrounded her, taking her over, and she went willingly. A soft mewling sound escaped her throat as he suckled at her neck. So good, so right, her mate at her neck. Each draw sent her body ratcheting higher. Her passion climbed toward the precipice. She needed him inside her. Now!

Her hands shifted to his chest, and she gave him a push, following when he rolled on his back. A quick flick of his tongue over the wounds in her neck to seal them and he pulled away. Vlad stared up at her expectantly, and she was happy to oblige.

No feathery trail of kisses, no preamble. Tasha struck hard and fast, taking his vein. His blood poured from the twin lesions, tasting rich and hearty. It flowed over her tongue, thick like honey, sliding down her throat to nourish her body. Her cells cried out in relief when the powerful blood filled them.

Her body came alive. Tasha's muscles became

more toned, her skin tingled. Her strength increased with each draw. She'd never get enough, not in all the lifetimes they would share. The taste of him was instantly addictive. And then it happened.

It slid into her mind, snapping into place like the last puzzle piece, locking their minds together. Vlad was there, touching her mind as she now touched his. They'd exchanged enough blood to form a mindlink. She couldn't wait to try it out.

As her tongue laved his skin to close the tiny wounds on his neck she thought, *Damn, you taste amazing.*

I happen to feel the same way about you, lapushka, he sent back through the link.

She couldn't exactly explain it, but the mindlink felt different from the one she shared with her brother. Their link seemed sensual and intimate where the one with Nicholai seemed perfunctory and reserved.

I have to agree with your assessment, Natasha. Using this link with you is incredibly intimate.

Used to guarding her thoughts from Nicholai, the link with Vlad almost seemed intrusive. She pulled back.

His arms tightened around her back as she raised her head to look at him. Her multicolored hair fell around her face while he spoke.

"You know I would never purposely intrude on your thoughts, *lapushka.* They were there on the surface to easily read. I would not betray your trust by taking that which you wish to guard. However, I hope you will trust me enough to allow me complete access to your mind. I want to know everything about you."

"I know that is the way between heartmates. They

share everything. I want to know everything in your mind as well."

His eyes widen slightly. "There are some things best left buried. You don't want to see my memories. There is no benefit to visiting my past." His eyes softened as a wicked smile took his face. "And there is so much to be gained by staying in the present."

Lust and desire flooded her mind. His lust and desire for her poured into the link, feeding her passion. Hunger for him flowed through her veins like liquid fire, settling in her core. Perhaps this mindlink had its uses after all.

She met his heated gaze and became immediately lost in the depths of his eyes. Everything else forgotten, her soul focused on her mate. She kissed his thick chest, carefully attending to each pectoral before heading south. Her tongue traced the hollow of every abdominal muscle before it circled his belly button.

Lower, he commanded, earning a devilish giggle from her lips.

Tasha planted her hands on either side of his body to support her weight and pressed a kiss to his stomach before inching lower. His hands covered hers, their fingers lacing.

"Use only your mouth," he stipulated in a rough voice.

She smiled against his shaft and looked up to find him staring down at her with such intensity it took her breath from her lungs. Obeying was the only option, and she happily did so.

Her tongue darted out to lick the length of him from base to tip. It circled the wide tip before she welcomed it into her mouth. Vlad sent the sensation of her ministration through the link.

The warmth of her mouth surrounded him. Her strong lips cradled his flesh as she worked them up and down. Fates above, no wonder men loved this so much. The sensation felt incredible.

His hips got into the action, sending him farther into her mouth. When he hit the back of her throat, she moaned, and the sensation sent over their mindlink curled her toes.

Never had sex been like this. Feeling your partner's pleasure as acutely as your own doubled the experience. She sensed his release building and tried to cup the sensitive globes below.

His fingers tightened, keeping her hand still. *No, you don't. Only your mouth. If you touch me, I'll explode.*

I thought that was the purpose behind this.

Oh no. The purpose behind this is to show you how amazing making love will be with your mate. Now release me and straddle me. I must be inside you, immediately!

Needing no second invitation, she did as instructed but at her own pace. Natasha unhurriedly moved her mouth up his long shaft, taking a moment to give it one last long suck before relinquishing it. Her tongue trailed up his torso in a lazy glide, swirling and playing over the muscles.

Their lips met in a deep kiss. Her tongue thoroughly explored the cavern of his mouth, sliding around each fang. He moaned into her mouth, and she swallowed the throaty sound.

When she straddled him, he released her hands to take hold of his member. Positioning it at her entrance, he slid home in a long, deliberate thrust. The combination of his sensations coming over the mindlink coupled with the sensation of him filling her pushed her to her limit. She didn't fight the fiery passion he stoked within her. Natasha let go as he took her to the height of sensation. She tumbled over the edge, muscles clamping down on him, gripping him like a velvet glove. Tasha felt herself locking down on him like a vise, her scalding heat burning him.

His hands grabbed her bottom, fingers dug into her flesh. He pushed her down when his hips rose. The unexpected thrust forced a small sound of surprise from her lips. Surprise gave way to ecstasy as he wrapped an arm around her back, pulled her to his chest, and took her.

Setting a furious pace, their bodies came together in a heated rush. Flesh against flesh, they became one. One body. One mind. She no longer knew where he stopped, and she started. It didn't matter.

The slide of her body against his created a sinuous draw against her little bud. Tasha's passion rose in a quick climb. In minutes, her body fragmented. She came apart in an explosion which sent waves rippling throughout her body.

Her hair veiled them from the world when her lips found his. She screamed into his mouth as her pure, hot rapture crossed their link and dragged him into the furious undercurrent, pulling him under with her waves of pleasure. His legs pushed them off the mattress, thrusting him deeper within her core when he climaxed. He filled her completely, branding her, making her his.

As if you were ever anyone else's.

She smiled against his lips. *I could never be*

anyone else's.

****

Sergei opened his eyes and smiled wickedly. His prodigy had found himself a mate. Sergei had retrieved glimpses of the woman from Vladimir's mind. She looked pretty enough, he supposed. But that hair! She really needed to do something with those multicolored locks. What was she, some sort of jester?

Mostly what he had been able to sense were feelings. Vlad's passion and desire warred with his concern for her safety, and he had good reason to be concerned. If the past few hours were any indication, Sergei would eventually find Vladimir using their mindlink. It appeared the longer he was with his heartmate, the easier it was for Sergei to push through the mental barrier he'd erected.

"Oh, this is just too good," Sergei muttered aloud.

"What is too good?"

His gaze darted to the demon standing in the now open doorway to his room. Jara. A nice diversion and a means to an end—that summed her up nicely. If only he didn't have to play nice. But she possessed information he needed, the whereabouts of his sire. So, it seemed, at least for a little while, he would have to indulge her. Of course, indulging her didn't mean telling her the truth.

"My being here with you, Jara, is too good to be true." He gave her what he hoped would be perceived as a genuine smile. "What has brought you to my room, my darling?"

"I came to retrieve you for dinner." Her gaze roamed over his body. "But I see you are not dressed."

Indulge her. Just a little longer. "I do not understand why we must be so formal. Surely, my trousers and sweater are sufficient clothing to eat."

"Not if you wish to eat with a princess. I expect some formality. It is my right. My brother and I are royalty after all."

So spoiled. If he ever met this indulgent brother she kept referring to, he might just have to give him a lesson in how to deal with a petulant sibling. Fates knew that he'd taught more than one such lesson over the centuries. He was a rather good teacher if he did say so himself.

A genuine smile reached his eyes as the memories of past lessons played in his mind's eye. Oh, the lessons he'd love to teach her…after she helped him achieve what he wanted most. "My apologies. Allow me to change, and I will meet you downstairs in a few minutes."

"Don't keep me waiting long," Jara warned. Her thick mane flowed in golden waves as she turned on her heels and paraded from his room.

That self-indulgent, spoiled, sadistic bitch! His internal rant raised his ire as he crossed the room. Sergei barely refrained from slamming the door to the room when he closed it. He'd dress for dinner. He'd play the attentive, understanding love interest. But only because it suited him to do so. Once he got what he wanted, he'd teach the demon a lesson she'd never forget. Sergei's hands rubbed together in anticipation.

Chapter 10

Quick strides took Harleigh across her living room to snatch the mobile phone from its resting place on the coffee table. She punched in the number to Natasha's cell. While she listened to the blasted thing ring, she changed the color of her hair with a thought, expelling less effort than it took to change into animal form. She loved changing her hair, it gave her a new start each day, gave her hope that today might be a good day.

Ring. Ring. Click. Optimism blossomed in her chest. Would today be the day Natasha finally answered the phone?

The sound of Tasha's recorded voice dashed the possibility of speaking to her friend. *Dammit!*

"Natasha, this is Harleigh again. You're startin' to worry me, girl. You haven't been home. You won't return my calls. Call me, so I'll know you're okay. 'Kay?"

She rang off and turned to find Cyrus staring at her from where he lay on the couch. His shaggy hair looked tousled, eyes leaden from sleep. The blanket he'd used the previous evening rode low on his body, exposing his muscular chest and arms. Damn, the blond could look sexy.

"Good day." He gave her a flirtatious grin. "Like what you see? If so, I could show you a lot more."

His hand fisted in the blanket and drew it slowly

down his body. Harleigh glanced away quickly, even though it wouldn't have been the first time she'd seen his manly bits. When demons shifted between their animal and human forms, they often saw each other with no clothes. A long time ago she got over the shyness and embarrassment at seeing others in a state of undress. But that didn't mean she felt comfortable around a male who had expressed an interest in her that went beyond friendship and who happened to be lying naked on her couch, looking at her with a leer that suggested he'd loved for her to join him under the blanket.

"G'day, Cyrus. I take it you slept well." Harleigh ambled to the kitchen to pour them juice. A soft rustling behind made her concentrate hard on her task. She poured slowly, giving him time to finish dressing before she turned her attention back to him.

"Trying to call your friend again, princess?" he asked.

The sound of his zipper rising indicated safety. She turned to face him, holding out one of the juices she'd poured. "Yeah. Still no answer. I'm starting to get really worried."

When he reached for the glass she held firm, refusing to relinquish control until his eyes met hers. "Don't call me princess."

"But you're related to King Varrick and Princess Jara. That makes you part of the royal family. If not princess, then what is your official title."

"I do not go by a title."

"But you have one." Cyrus made his way to the kitchen table.

Harleigh sighed as she gathered her juice and bowl

of fruit from the counter. He just wasn't going to leave this alone, like a dog with a bone…or more appropriately a wolf with a fresh kill. "Yes."

"Tell me what it is."

"No." Harleigh let out a deep sigh as she settled next to Cyrus.

"Then let me guess."

"No. Leave it, Cyrus."

"I can't."

"Obviously." Taking an apple from the bowl, she blew out another exasperated breath. "Can we change the subject, please? Let's talk about something else."

"Like what?" The male demon grabbed a grape from the bowl, flicked it into the air, and caught it easily in his mouth.

"Like my friend, Natasha. She's missing."

"Maybe she went for a walkabout."

Not when she's pregnant. It's too dangerous.

She'd just keep that bit of information to herself. Cyrus didn't need to know about her friend's condition. "I seriously doubt it."

"Then perhaps she went back to her winter home."

"To Russia? I don't think so. She loved it here."

"You sure? Maybe the weather is getting too hot for her."

"So, she just left without saying goodbye?"

Cyrus shrugged. "Maybe."

"Maybe not. I don't think she would do that."

"Have you been back to her house?"

Harleigh shook her head. "No."

"Why don't we start there? Let's go to her house after breakfast and check the place. Perhaps we'll find out something useful."

Perhaps they'd find her lying on the floor unconscious. The thought twisted fear down around her spine. A shiver shot through her body. She hadn't considered Natasha might be hurt until now. Holy crap on a cracker! Why hadn't she gone over to the house to check on Natasha when she couldn't reach her?

Harleigh stood so abruptly her chair skidded in her haste. "Let's go," she ordered, heading for her purse.

"Where?" Cyrus grabbed an apple and stood.

He was shirtless, but at least he had on jeans, and Harleigh decided that was dressed enough for a rescue mission. She pulled the strap of her purse over her shoulder and fished out the keys to her car. "We're going to Natasha's house. She's not a morning person, so if she's there she'll probably still be in bed."

Ten minutes and a few broken speed limits later, they stood on the front door of Tasha's beach home. Harleigh knocked on the door. No answer. Cyrus banged on the entryway while Harleigh peered through the window beside the door.

Everything appeared normal. The furniture sat in place, nothing askew. The fresh flowers sat on the kitchen table, wilted but otherwise fine.

Cyrus joined her, cupping his hand around his eyes before leaning against the glass to peer in.

"Looks perfectly fine to me," he announced straightening beside her.

"I'd feel better if we could see the rest of the house."

"Got a credit card in your purse?"

"Yeah. Why?"

"Let me see it." Cyrus held out an expectant hand.

Harleigh removed her wallet and gave Cyrus the

card. In seconds, he jimmied the lock and the door open. "After you, princess."

"I told you not to call me that. My title isn't princess, by the way."

Harleigh crossed the threshold with Cyrus on her heels. "Then tell me your official title."

"No. We've been through this, Cyrus. I don't want you using my official title."

Her sense of smell, acuter than a human's, informed her something was off. A sour odor accosted her nose. Her gaze swept the living room then she took in the kitchen. The counters appeared clean, the chairs pushed in neatly around the table. Two towels hung from the handle on the oven. Nothing seemed unusual.

Dirty dishes sat in the sink…*Wait!*

Harleigh strolled to the sink as Cyrus continued to push about her title.

Damn, that demon.

Ignoring his imploration, she noted the food stuck on the plates. Poppy seeds stuck to what appeared to be vanilla cream sauce. Plum jam peeked out from beneath a bit of dough. A glass of curdled milk—well, that explained the smell.

"I recognize this food. It's remnants from what Tasha ate the night we went to the carnival. She'd never leave dirty dishes sitting in her sink for so long. Something's wrong," Harleigh announced, moving through the room.

"What is it?" Cyrus followed her down the hall.

"Those dirty dishes have been there for days." Harleigh checked one room after another as the pair made their way to the master bedroom. The guest bath…clean. The guest room…straight. The office…orderly. At the end of the hall, she reached out to open the door to Natasha's bedroom.

Cyrus' hand reached the knob first. "You'd better let me go in first."

"Why?"

"What if there is something in there you shouldn't see?"

Harleigh took a deep inhale. "There's not a dead body if that's what you were getting at."

"I knew that. I'm not olfactorily impaired, you know. But something stinks. In fact, it smells like vampire."

"Just open the door, Cyrus." Her tone sounded aristocratic even to her. She didn't like ordering others around, but she also didn't want to acknowledge her friendship with a vampire just yet because she knew he'd freak out, so Harleigh decided better to insult than incite.

"Yes, your royal highness," Cyrus replied, then opened the door wide with a grand sweep of his arm.

"Stop it with the royalty stuff. I mean it, Cyrus."

Harleigh glanced around the room. The ocean-blue bedspread lay pristine on the bed, not so much as a throw pillow moved out of place. On the vanity rested a hairbrush and comb, along with several bottles of perfume sitting in a row. Cyrus strolled to the closet and opened the bifold doors. Tasha's clothes hung neatly within. All seemed in order, nothing out of place…other than the fact Natasha had vanished without a trace.

"It's like she's been abducted by aliens," Harleigh observed. "Poof, gone."

Cyrus closed the door and crossed his arms over

his chest. "Why don't you scry for her?"

Of course! Why hadn't she thought of that earlier? Most demons used a scrying stone and a map to locate someone. They did so by holding the special stone over the map until it warmed over a particular place, indicating where the person they were looking for could be found. But Cyrus' suggestion had one problem.

"I don't have a stone," Harleigh informed her friend as they wandered back through the home.

"Not a problem. I have one."

Hope bloomed in her chest. "Good onya, mate! Let's go get it. Is it back at my place?"

Harleigh headed for the hall at a brisk pace, anxious to find her friend.

"No, it's at *my* place."

Harleigh stopped, turning to meet the steady stare of her companion. "You mean it's at Varrick's compound?"

Cyrus nodded. "Yep. Looks like we'll be seeing King Varrick a little sooner than he expected."

****

Natasha rolled onto her side and drew the fur blanket up under her chin as she snuggled against the chest of her lover. She inhaled his woodsy scent deep into her lungs, reveling in the instant passion coursing through her body. They had made love throughout the night. She felt deliciously sore but not quite replete. She'd never get enough of this male.

An old-fashioned telephone ringing garnered her attention.

Don't answer that, Vlad commanded over their mindlink while his arms tightened around her back.

She stuck her tongue out at her mate. *I wasn't*

going to.

You considered it. I read your intention in your mind.

Stupid mindlink. It would take her a while to get used to someone else being in her mind.

But it is a benefit as well, lapushka. *For example, I happen to know just how much you love this.*

Vladimir gently pushed her onto her back and wandered down her body, feathering a path of tiny kisses over her flesh. The lower he traveled the tighter her body coiled, core clenching in need.

His smugness flowed through their link. *See, I speak the truth.*

She couldn't argue. She did love when he did this. His touch ignited a passion, sending her up in a ball of flame. She just wished she didn't feel quite so sticky from the previous evening. They'd been too tired after making love to clean up before falling asleep.

Vlad stilled, his lips poised over her navel. His large hand rubbed her rounded tummy. She sensed his awe and wonderment at their child.

I hear his tiny heart beating within your womb. It beats so fast, yet strong.

That's because he's healthy. A strong, strapping boy just like his father.

Vlad crawled up her body. The pride in his eyes melted her heart. A wide smile that showed her fangs brightened her face.

"I hope he has your eyes," Vlad whispered, brushing a wisp of hair from her forehead.

"And his father's handsome face."

He scoffed. "I hope he doesn't get saddled with my features."

Tasha cupped his face in her hands. "I happen to love your features."

She leaned forward for a kiss, shocked when Vlad pulled away.

"No kissing," he barked.

Confusion furrowed her brows down over her eyes. "What?"

"No kissing." He rose from the bed. "Kissing you always leads to other things, and there is somewhere I want to take you. Get dressed."

"Where are we going?"

"Outside, so be sure to dress warmly and put on a coat."

Vlad grabbed a set of clothes from the steamer truck and descended the ladder, leaving Natasha alone in the loft.

What does he have planned? she wondered, gathering clothes from her suitcase.

You'll see. And don't bother trying to read my mind to find out. I've blocked that particular bit of information.

That's not fair, Vlad.

It's one of the benefits of being older. Now get that beautiful body of yours dressed so we can get going.

Happiness unlike she'd ever experienced made her giddy, and she chuckled.

Ten minutes later, she sat behind Vlad on his snowmobile. Natasha wrapped her arms around the waist of Vlad's leather jacket as they sped through the surrounding forest.

The air, cold and dry, came at them in gusts. Natasha rested her cheek against his back, while the scenery sped by. Snow-covered boughs hung heavily from the trees. The world around them gleamed so white; even though it was night, it appeared light. Shrubbery encased in snowy blankets lay between the trees. Large rocks on the ground were barely visible from under the snow. A few flakes began to fall from the clouds.

Movement caught her eyes. She squinted the image into focus. In the distance, she glimpsed an animal's silver-white pelt, glistening with flakes of snow. *Mishka.*

His growl filled the night air as his pride emerged through the trees. The cats raced alongside the snowmobile.

Vlad yelled a greeting and cranked down on the throttle. The chase was on. Exhilarating and wild, the ride through the snow brought joy to her heart, especially when Vladimir's deep laugh shook her arms. His elation came through their link. He loved the tigers almost as much as he loved her. This night, playing with his cats while being with her, made this the best night of his long life.

Having fun, Tasha?

You know I am! Natasha's laughter rang out as she urged him on when the cats started inching ahead of them. The tigers plowed through the underbrush, careless of the snow. Each wore a dusting of the powdery stuff. It glimmered on their coats. They were the most beautiful sight she'd ever seen.

Wait until you see where I'm taking you, then tell me if you still feel that way.

How much longer, Vlad? The anticipation is killing me.

His answering chuckle rumbled in his chest. *We're*

almost there, lapushka. *Just over this ridge.*

Natasha straightened, looking over his shoulder as they crested the hill. Below them stretched a whitewater river, the current flowed over the rapids, making beautiful white caps. In the few places where downed trees lay in the icy water, snow gathered in thick blankets on their trunks. A few trees sloped out from the bank. Their snow-laden limbs hung over the river. The landscape lay undisturbed, no tracks to mar its perfection.

Vlad brought the snowmobile to a halt and looked at the large tigers who gathered around the vehicle. “Go now, my friends. We are done playing for tonight.”

Mishka gave a muted cuff as if to thank them for the run—or perhaps to protest the end of their game, Natasha wasn’t sure which. The pride melded into the white, shadowy forest.

“You were right, Vlad. This is beautiful.”

“You haven’t seen anything yet,” he informed her.

A twist of the throttle sent them careening down the hill and next to the partially frozen river. They stopped in front of a large mound of snow, and Vlad dismounted the vehicle.

Helping her off the machine, he asked, “Shall we?”

Tasha put her hand in his, enjoying the way his strong fingers wrapped around hers. Vlad made her feel protected and cherished, like he would do anything in the world for her.

Of course, I would. You are my mate.

He led the way around the mound, wearing a dusting of snow that glimmered in his black buzz cut and on the shoulders of his leather coat. Shortening his strides so she could keep up, he led her to a breach in the snow. Long icicles hung from the top, decorating the dark opening.

"What's that?"

"A cave."

"Where does it lead?"

A sexy grin took his handsome face. "That's what I want to show you."

He pulled her into the cave, making sure to take both her hands until her eyes adjusted. The opening, only large enough for one person to fit, made Natasha follow behind Vlad. While he walked slightly hunched over, she could stand. The walls of the rock were relatively smooth as if they'd been worn down.

By water erosion, Vlad supplied.

I figured as much.

In no time, they pushed through the corridor and emerged into the most beautiful place she'd ever seen.

I told you, you would feel that way.

Natasha stopped and took in the amazing sight. Before her lay a grotto. A hot steamy shower of water fell from the cave's roof forming a pool below. Multicolored stalactites hung from the ceiling above, their rocky surfaces shiny from the spray of the falling water. Small, smooth rocks surrounded the pool to create a ledge.

Vlad brought her hand to his lips, kissing each knuckle. "Do you want to go for a dip? The water is a perfect temperature for bathing. I thought you might prefer this to taking a sponge bath in my home."

"I noticed you didn't have a shower." She also noticed the snow had melted on their heads and shoulders from the warmth in the grotto.

"I have no need of one. I can materialize here any

time I want, and now you can too."

What a wonderful thought.

Vladimir smiled, then released her hand and began to undress. Natasha quickly followed suit, dropping her coat and clothes to the rock floor in reckless abandonment in haste to reach the water.

Steam rose in grand plumes from the surface of the pool, creating a warm haze that played over the surface of their exposed skin. Vlad leapt as high as the space would allow and dove headfirst into the pool, disappearing beneath the rippling surface. By the time his head broke the surface, she'd made her way to the ledge, surprised to find the rocky surface warm under her feet. She felt his eyes on her as she dipped her toe into the water.

"Come in," he purred, running his arms enticingly just under the surface of the water. "The temperature is perfect."

Tasha kept her gaze locked with his, needing his reaction. She sauntered down the natural incline, the water caressing her flesh. It slid over her skin, wet and silky, gliding higher with each step. Deliberately provocative, she slowed her steps, coming to him through the steam and rippling water.

He allowed his hunger to flow into her mind, feeding her own until she ached with need. He stalked toward her through the water. The expression on his face made her womb clench, the baby stirred as a fierce hunger pang knotted her stomach. He stopped his advance.

"You're starving. Why did you not tell me?"

"I didn't realize."

"I should have insisted you feed before we left.

Here, take from me." Vlad moved in her direction once more.

"I shouldn't. I took so much from you last night."

His arms wrapped around the small of her back. "I insist." He bared his neck. "Take from me."

She pushed against his chest though it did no good. He didn't allow her retreat. "No, Vlad. You gave me too much last night."

"But our child…"

"Will be fine if I drink from the bag. Pop back to the house and get us both a bag. It'll only take a minute." She ran her nails down his stomach, wrapping one hand around his thick shaft. "And when you get back, we'll put this to good use after we feed."

He growled when she stroked her hand up and down the length of him. "You are a master in the art of persuasion, Tasha."

She flashed him a demure smile. "And you are a master in the art of making love. Now go, get us something to eat so you can remind me how masterful you are."

A wicked gleam leapt into his black eyes. A nod of his head was the only warning he gave before he disappeared. Natasha swam across the pool and crossed her arms on the rock ledge to support herself. She'd just laid her head on the arms when her phone went off. Using her vampiric speed, she rushed from the water to answer it.

"Hello?"

"Hello, sister-in-law. How are you?"

"Oh, hi, Julie."

"You sound disappointed to hear from me."

"No, not at all." *I thought you might be Harleigh.*

"I'm just surprised you aren't Nicholai."

"He's off getting…a little refreshment."

"So, he's feeding?"

"Uh-huh. Went to…the restroom. He'd better get back soon, I think the last passenger has boarded."

Tasha knew her brother most likely locked himself in the bathroom of the airplane, then dematerialized to a stash of blood with the intention of getting back to his seat before takeoff. He'd talked about having to do that from time to time. "I'm sure he'll get back in time."

"Actually, I'm glad he's…indisposed. I am calling to let you know Nicholai and I are at least another day away, thanks to one of our flights being canceled on account of snow."

"Oh, that's okay." *I'd like the extra time alone with Vlad, anyway.*

"However, Demetri and Tatiana have finished doing whatever they were doing for Stephan and will be arriving at Vladimir's house soon. Nicholai said we didn't need to call you to let you know, but I thought you should be aware."

"But—"

"Oh-oh. We are about to take off, and I'm getting a dirty look from the flight attendant. I better shut off the phone. We'll see you soon. Oh, and Nicholai said to tell Vlad he better be taking good care of you or he'll answer to him. Bye."

With a click, Julie rang off. Thank goodness she called. The last thing Tasha needed was Demetri to walk in on her and Vlad. She'd have to make sure to warn Vlad when he returned.

A heavy sigh left her lips as her hand cradled her growing tummy. "When did life get so complicated, little one? I just want happily-ever-after with your daddy. Instead, I may have demons after me. I have an overprotective cousin on the way. I have an even more overly protective brother on the same. Your daddy won't be any happier than I am about those last two bits of news."

Why can't life be simple? Natasha didn't need more drama. If only she had someone to talk to ease her fears and make her laugh. But the only person who could do that was a continent away.

She missed Harleigh's humor, the way she made it seem like everything would work out fine. Her friend was always so upbeat and happy. Unlike the serious males in her life.

Tasha looked down at the phone resting in her hand. Surely one little phone call couldn't hurt. Vlad was just overreacting—being overprotective of her like Nicholai and Demetri. And with them on the way, she really needed a friend to talk to.

She smiled and pressed Harleigh's number.

Chapter 11

Jara smoothed the nonexistent wrinkles from her silk blouse and brushed the invisible lint from her navy pencil skirt, trying to look her best. Sergei would arise at any moment. It was inconvenient really, this thing vampires had about sleeping during the day and being awake all night. Wouldn't be needed if they could tolerate the sun, she supposed.

They really were vile, disgusting creatures. Too bad they possessed a natural immunity to all human illnesses which helped to keep them alive for centuries. Were it not for the fact she required one's assistance, she would not lower herself to take one as her lover.

"But it simply cannot be helped," she murmured.

"What cannot be helped," Leo asked.

His face boasted angular, harsh lines that were both exotic and handsome. At seven feet, most beings gave him a wide berth.

While Jara appreciated his size, she most valued his intelligence. Recently, he helped her create a bomb based solely on information he garnered from the internet. They used it to take down a known vampire hangout in Savannah, Georgia.

Jara smiled. *Yes, Leo comes in handy from time to time.*

The princess turned to find her loyal subject gazing at her with interest. "It cannot be helped that we harbor a vampire."

"Not to question you, but do you mind if I ask why he is here?" Leo settled back into the recliner and crossed his leg, resting his ankle on his opposite knee. The demon's posture bespoke of relaxation, but Jara knew better.

Leo was a bear of a demon, thickly built with a large muscular body, who moved like the predator he was. Slow, easy movement belied the fact that at all times, he sat coiled and ready to strike. Fiercely loyal to her, he'd proven himself time and time again, and she saw no reason not to reward that.

"The bloodsucker is here to serve my will."

The guard inclined his head. "Naturally, princess."

"He is but a means to an end. Once he has served his usefulness, I will require your services to dispose of him."

Leo cracked his knuckles ominously, one corner of his mouth curved up in a crooked smile. "It will be my pleasure. Do you mind letting me know when my services might be needed?"

Jara crossed the media room to alight in the seat next to his. She lowered her voice when next she spoke. "He is the first offspring of The Source. After I use him to resurrect The Source, I want you to kill him, *but* not until *after* we find The Source."

Leo's brows shot up in interest. "How will you do that?"

"All I need to achieve my plan is a special locating spell and Sergei's blood. Once I have located The Source, we'll find him, blow him up, and be rid of all vampires forever!" She licked her lips at the delicious taste saying her plans aloud left in her mouth.

"You have Sergei. Why not drain him now and be done with this? I can make another bomb in no time."

She leaned forward and patted his knee. "I know you can. In fact, I'm counting on your new skill to help my plan come to fruition, but it is not that easy, I'm afraid." She glanced at the door once again to find it still closed. "I don't know the locating spell. No ordinary spell will do. The demons who trapped him made it all but impossible to locate the monster for fear someone would awaken him."

"So, Sergei must live until you can find the location spell."

"Exactly. I need to get into the Room of Tomes to collect the book that not only contains the location spell, but also the original spell which put him into stasis."

Concern widened Leo's eyes. "But it is located in Varrick's compound in Mason's Bluff, and you cannot go back there for fear he will discover you killed Lane."

"I know that," Jara snapped. Her hair rose from her scalp as her energy built in direct correlation to her ire. "Don't you think I've been trying to come up with a way to get the Tome that contains the spell?"

Leo bowed his head, and his eyes fell to the floor in supplication. "Forgive me, princess. I meant no disrespect."

No disrespect? Having the audacity to point out the one short-coming in her plan wasn't exactly what she'd call being respectful. She should teach this male a lesson in respecting one's better. Just as the blue energy arced from her fingertips, a knock sounded on the door.

"Jara, are you in there my sweet?"

Sergei! Damn that vampire and his timing. She

took several deep breaths, willing her pique to quell for it would not benefit her for her supposed lover to know how powerful she was. Once she was again in control of her power, she called, “Come in, my dear.”

****

Harleigh and Cyrus materialized inside the compound at Mason’s Bluff, Wyoming. Her cousin, Varrick, would know immediately they were there. Being the king of the demons, he could easily sense their kind. He’d know two more demons had joined him inside the mountain.

Cyrus led her down the hallway, heading for his room. Carved from the mountain, the granite rock that made up the floor, curved into walls and ceiling. Harleigh slid her hand along the rough wall while they walked, the habit formed when she ran through these halls as a child. Iron sconces hung every two feet on both sides, holding the candles lighting their way. Ahead wooden doors lined both sides of the hall. Apartments for the demons in residence lay behind them. It was one such apartment they were now heading toward so Cyrus could retrieve the scrying stone she needed to find Natasha.

“Which apartment is yours?” Harleigh asked.

“It’s just down one more hall.” Cyrus quickened his stride. “We’ll grab the stone, then see if King Varrick will receive us.”

As they rounded the next hallway, they came to an abrupt halt. Before them stood Varrick’s second in command, Caden. His thick form struck an imposing stance, with feet wide and hands fisted on his hips. Dark hair, cut so short an opponent could not get a handful during a battle, covered his scalp. The guard’s handsome face, with its wide cheekbones, straight nose, and red eyes, possessed a harsh look to it this day. His tall, battle-hardened body towered over Harleigh's petite frame, but he did not intimidate her—much.

She flashed her best smile.

"G'day Caden," she greeted informally, noticing Cyrus flinch beside her. "How ya been?"

The guard leveled his intense stare between the two of them. "To what do we owe the pleasure of your company, little countess?"

"You're a countess?" Cyrus bumped her with his elbow.

Harleigh rolled her eyes. Great! Now Cyrus would be going around calling her by the royal title all the time. She decided to ignore his question. If she were incredibly lucky maybe he'd forget—probably not.

"We came to get something from Cyrus' room and, of course, to see my cousin."

"The king happens to be in the receiving room. I'll escort you there to see him."

"That isn't necessary." Harleigh glanced at Cyrus who resembled a child caught with his hand in the cookie jar. "Varrick isn't expecting us. We'd hate to bother him. We'll talk to him later."

"He sent me here to retrieve you." Caden gave her a pointed stare. "Follow me."

He turned and retreated down the hall without checking to see if they followed. Obviously, he did not doubt for a minute she and Cyrus would comply with his order…which, of course, they did. When the King of the Demons summoned you, you went.

"What's wrong?" Harleigh leaned against Cyrus and whispered.

"Do you think King Varrick will be upset I came here even though he told me it was not a convenient time for me to speak with him?"

"Is *that* what's wrong with you? You're worried about Varrick freaking out because you went ahead and came to the compound?" She never understood quite why everyone seemed so scared of her cousin. He'd always been rather sweet to her, at least the few times she'd gotten to see him when she was growing up. "Don't worry about Varrick. He's a big pussycat."

"Actually, he's a lion, and he will probably bite my head off, literally." Cyrus swallowed nervously.

Caden pushed the massive mahogany doors to the receiving room open, simultaneously announcing them as they entered. "Your Highnesses, I present Countess Maria Harleigh Grace and her escort Guard Cyrus."

Really! Could he have made their entrance any more dramatic? Harleigh didn't think so.

Her eyes swept the room. The granite walls curved from floor to ceiling, which in turn, curved down to form regularly spaced columns. In the middle of the room, a three-tiered fountain flowed, identical to the one in the Room of Tomes. Fire poured over the tiers to pool in the large basin, sending yellow and orange light flickering around the room, which illuminated the polished walls.

At the end of the cavernous room, two thrones sat on a rock dais. Though the demons sitting upon the wooden chairs hid the velvety padding, Harleigh knew from experience the thrones were plush and comfortable. She'd played on them as a child, pretending to be queen. As an adult, however, she had no desire to be a ruler.

The king sat before them in all his regal glory. Even she had to admit he looked rather handsome, if not intimidating. Thick blond hair framed his face. High cheekbones, a perpetual five o'clock shadow, and red eyes combined to form a savage face. He had a lion's cast to his face, but it didn't detract from his looks.

His mate sat next to him, a slip of a girl with golden eyes and long blonde hair. Adorned in sandals which matched the white dress that wrapped around one shoulder and fit snugly against her small frame, she appeared like she should be going to a toga party. Harleigh couldn't help but notice the vine of ivy tattooed around her right ankle. It snaked down her foot and hid underneath. Because they were newly joined, this was the first time she'd met her cousin's mate, but the woman gave off a good vibe. Harleigh instantly liked her.

"Harleigh, my dear, come closer and meet Elizabeth," Varrick's deep voice echoed in the massive room.

She moved forward, taking Varrick's outstretched hand. He gave it a friendly squeeze and beamed at his mate. "Elizabeth, this is my cousin, Harleigh. Harleigh, Elizabeth, my mate."

His hand dropped hers and immediately touched Elizabeth's as if he could not bear for them not to be touching. Varrick turned his attention back to Harleigh, expectantly.

"It is a pleasure to meet you, your royal highness." The countess curtsied.

"Oh, my gosh," Elizabeth exclaimed. "Don't you dare call me anything but Elizabeth. We're family after all. I have to put up with that royal stuff from the other demons—at least that's what Varrick says—but I won't have it from you."

Yep, I knew I'd liked this woman. They would be fast friends. Between comparing tattoos and making fun of being royalty, they'd have much in common.

Harleigh smiled. "Elizabeth, then."

"Varrick told me you live in Australia as if I wouldn't know from your accent."

"I do."

"I'd love to go there. Everything I've seen about it on TV looks amazing," the queen gushed.

"You are welcome at my house anytime. Just come on down…under," Harleigh quipped earning a chuckle from Elizabeth.

"And what about me?" Varrick asked with a twinkle in his eye that Haleigh had never seen before. He brought Elizabeth's hand to his mouth and nipped the back of the hand tenderly.

"You know I'd never go without you," she assured her mate.

"Oh, I know. I make sure you don't ever want to be too far away from me." The king leered at his queen, making her cheeks flush a deep red.

Harleigh cleared her throat. It suddenly seemed rather hot in here. "We don't want to keep you. Cyrus and I will go."

Without taking his eyes from his mate, Varrick replied, "Don't leave. Not yet. First, I wish to speak with Cyrus."

Cyrus approached on quick feet and took a knee in front of the dais. His forearm rested on his leg as he bent his head. "I am at your service, my king."

"Stand," Varrick commanded, tearing his gaze

away from Elizabeth. It hardened when it landed on Cyrus. "You called me regarding a situation with my sister, Jara. And although I requested you wait until later to discuss the matter, you came here."

"We came to get something from his apartment," Harleigh interjected.

Varrick went on as if she hadn't spoken. He had a habit of doing that to people, and it ticked Harleigh off when he directed the habit at her.

"Since you disobeyed me and came here before I summoned you, I can only assume what you have to tell me is of the utmost importance."

"It is." Cyrus shifted as if the king's stare burned into this flesh.

"Then rise and tell me what is so damned important."

Cyrus obeyed immediately. "Everything was going well in the Canadian compound. Lane was experimenting on the vampire and making headway, but then vampires somehow found the place and raided it. They made off with the vampire we captured. When Jara scried for him, it turned out he was in Savannah, so Jara and Lane dragged all of us guards there. I discovered the bloodsucker who escaped frequented a restaurant in the city that catered to vampires. We were going to catch him there, but the place blew up. I don't know if they caught the vamp."

Varrick's eyes widened. "Tell me Jara didn't blow it up. We don't need a police investigation."

Cyrus shrugged. "I'm not sure because by then I was on the run."

The king's eyes narrowed. "Why?"

Cyrus shifted uneasily on his feet. "Well, I kind of

pissed Jara off, and instead of using her energy to zap me, she missed and disintegrated Lane. Needless to say, I got out of there and never returned."

Red crept into Varrick's face. "Are you telling me Jara lost the vampire, blew up a restaurant, *and* killed our best hope for finding a way to keep us immune to human disease? And all of this she did without telling me!"

That last sentence pushed out through clenched teeth with such venom Harleigh fought the impulse to take a step back. *Looks like cousin Jara has some 'splaining to do.*

Varrick's power rolled over them as the corona of blue light glowed around his throne. His eyes darkened to a blood-red before his facial feature shifted to become slightly more beast-like than man. A prickling heat danced over Harleigh's skin. Both she and Cyrus took a step back. She now understood why so many feared her cousin.

Damn, he was a scary sight, and if even half the stories about his fighting ability were true…well, let's just say she didn't want any of his ire directed at her.

Their hands still clasped together, Elizabeth gave his a squeeze. "You are scaring our guests," she admonished in a low tone.

"It is not them who should be scared. It is Jara. How could she betray me like this? She knew I did not want any more vampires hurt. She knew how important it was to me that Lane discover a way to keep demons immune from illness. And yet, she disobeyed me, my edicts. She will answer for her insolence. I must find her immediately!"

His breath sawed from his lungs in hard, short

bursts. Varrick's face reddened before their eyes.

Caden stepped up next to Harleigh. "I think it is time to take your leave, countess."

Truer words had never been spoken, she decided as a tremor went down her spine. Varrick's power increased to a near suffocating level. She was surprised the mountain remained standing. She suspected the only thing keeping him in check was the touch of his mate.

Cyrus took her arm and led her from the room with Caden on their heels. When he closed the massive door behind them leaving him inside with Varrick and Elizabeth, Harleigh's phone vibrated.

She pulled the phone from her pocket, looking down to note the caller. Natasha's number. Finally!

Her fingers shook, her nerves rattled from Varrick's display of power. By the time she punched the button to answer, the dogs barking out a ringtone in the tune of Beethoven's *Fur Elise* stopped.

"Crap missed her." Harleigh turned to Cyrus.

His ghostly parlor indicated he'd been equally as affected by Varrick's power. "What do you think he'll do to her?"

"To who? Natasha?"

"To Jara. What do you think Varrick will do to his sister?"

"I don't know. What does a king usually do about treason?"

They moved down the hallway toward Cyrus' room in silence, each contemplating just what the answer to that question might be. Harleigh checked her phone and discovered a voicemail. Hoping it might be Natasha, she went to punch in the code to check it just as the sound of dogs barking alerted her to another call.

She checked the caller ID.

“Speak of the devil,” she muttered, giving Cyrus a pointed look as she pushed the button to answer. “Hello, Jara.”

Chapter 12

Vlad materialized in front of his small refrigerator. Wrenching open the door with a quick jerk, the blast of cold air that hit his dripping body sent goosebumps to pepper his naked flesh. He instantly thought of the warm grotto and the sexy female waiting for him within. A sad smile spread across his face as he reached for two bags of blood. Only one bag left, but that chore could wait.

A beautiful woman waited for him in steamy water. If he lived another thousand years, he'd never forget the way she looked, gliding down into the rippling water, the misty spray from the falls glistening on her skin. His shaft jumped, eager to be put to good use. He didn't know what in his life he'd done to deserve her—in fact, he didn't deserve her. She was a goddess and so far above him in many ways.

She was royalty; he had been a farmer. She grew up with gilded ceilings and chandeliers; he had one light and a tiny shack. She was as light as the sun and as good as the gold that surrounded her; he had a dark past that still cast its gloomy shadow on his life.

Natasha deserved better than him. Yet for some unfathomable reason, she'd chosen him. Or perhaps the Fates had chosen for them, but it made no difference now. They were heartmates, and that made him powerless to deny the attraction between them. If only being with her didn't come with a price.

His sire would never permit him loving another. He'd proven it centuries ago. In fact, Vlad recently experienced his sire's oily presence in his mind. He hoped the male had not discovered Natasha before Vlad realized he was there and slammed the mental barrier back into place.

Vlad sent his senses out through the home and over the surrounding land. Contentment settled in when he found nothing out of the ordinary.

With a thought, his form coalesced into itself and rematerialized in the grotto. Through the steam he saw her, kneeling next to where their clothes lay. Tiny droplets cascaded down her body to the rocky floor. Her wet hair clung to her body, the purple and blue streaks barely noticeable in the black strands darkened by the water. She wore no makeup, didn't need any as far as he was concerned for her natural beauty needed no enhancement.

Natasha's amber eyes met his through the haze, and she graced him with a dazzling grin. Lust knotted his stomach. He dove into her mind, couldn't help himself. Vlad needed to know what brought the look to her face. She was admiring him just as he was her. An answering smile took his face, and he stalked toward her.

"Here," Vlad whispered, handing her one of the bags. "Drink, you'll be needing your strength."

"Why, whatever do you mean?" Natasha responded coyly, before taking the bag and tearing open the top.

The warrior sat beside his love and gave her his best you-know-what-I-mean look, earning a sexy giggle from her that wound up his spine. "So, what were you doing while I was gone?"

Concern flashed across her face. Had he not been staring so intently he might have missed the emotion. "What is it, Natasha?"

His awareness flowed out through the cave, over the river, and into the surrounding forest, detecting nothing but his pride and a few other creatures. He pushed deeper into her mind, easily discerning what caused the expression.

"You called Harleigh after I explicitly told you not to?"

She at least had the decency to look properly contrite. How could she do that? Did she not realize just how much danger she was in?

The blood boiled in his veins. At any time, their situation could go tits up. Nicholai believed demons might be after her. If Vlad let his mental guard down for a second, his sire would be after her. Being with him put her in more danger, but at the same time, he needed to be with her, to love her, protect her. The dichotomy might drive a lesser man mad.

"It was just a quick call. And she didn't answer."

"But you left a message," he growled, making her flinch.

Tasha nodded her head and drank the entire bag before speaking. "I just wanted her to know I am fine. She'll worry."

"Better she worries than you end up dead because someone uses her to track you down. How could you put yourself, our child in danger, Natasha?" His voice echoed mightily off the rock walls.

Tears pushed into her eyes. "I didn't…" A sob choked her words as the tears broke their dam. Her hand protectively covered their unborn son.

Vladimir's heart melted at the sight. He gathered her into his lap, cradling her in his strong embrace. "Shhhh." He kissed then nuzzled the top of her head. "I know, *lapushka.* I know you did not think calling your friend would bring any harm to our child. I can see your intentions in your mind. You thought only to ease her concern."

Tears wet his chest in warm rivers. Her sorrow pushed at him. Confusion as to why he'd reacted so strongly to what she'd done filled her mind. She didn't understand, couldn't understand unless she knew his past.

Vlad took a deep breath. Did he dare let her know about his past? Another sob shook her body. His arms tightened lovingly around her, and he realized in that moment he'd do anything to stop the tears he'd caused.

His hand smoothed her hair. "I am sorry if you think I overreacted. There is a very good reason why I'm protective of you."

"Why, Vlad? Help me understand."

He closed his eyes, steeling himself against the memories, then opened his mind to her.

Look into my memories, Natasha. I will show you what happened. Why I am the way I am. I only ask you forgive me once you see my past.

Her hand tightened on his bicep as he opened his mind's eye looking back on the worst time of his life.

He'd been dying, an accident. When his horse spooked and threw him, he'd hit his head on a rock and lay bleeding in a ditch on the side of the road until a man came along.

In the darkness of the night, Vlad had been sure no

one would find him, but this man did. How lucky. The man asked if he wanted to live. Of course, he did. Vlad had a wife and family who needed him. The man scored his wrist and put it to Vlad's mouth. When he tried to pull away, the man took control of his body forcing his compliance. Then the man bit into Vlad's wrist.

The conversion burned like fire, but when it ended, he became stronger, faster, more agile. Everything a young man could want. His sire introduced himself as Sergei and informed Vlad he was a vampire.

Natasha shifted in his lap as the images leapt forward in time.

Vlad awoke from his day sleep to the sound of a death rattle. Crawling from the cellar under his home, Vlad discovered the noise emanated from his wife. He ran to her, cradled her in his arms just as she took her last breath. Blood covered her dress, making it cling to her body. The sticky stuff matted her hair.

He peered down and noted the deep cuts slashing across her body. The scent of her blood both repulsed and excited him. He threw back his head and let out a strangled scream.

Vlad's thoughts turned to his children. After gently laying his wife on the kitchen floor, he went in search of his offspring. Vlad's bile rose in his throat when he discovered the assassin had found all four of his children and ended their lives. In one day, while he'd been asleep under the home, someone attacked his family, killing them all.

After all this time, his grief still weighed on him as he relived the memories of that horrible night. That kind of loss never went away. The loss would always own a place in his heart, his soul. A tear fell from his eye.

"Oh, Vlad!" Natasha wrapped her arms around his neck. Her tears for him wet his flesh. "Who did that to your family?"

"I didn't know at first. I had no idea who would want to harm them. They'd done nothing. They were innocent children." Vlad swallowed the lump in his throat. "My sire showed up within minutes of me finding them. Sergei tried to comfort me, hold me. He…his touch was not that of a concerned friend, but more like that of a lover. He told me to let him take the pain from me. He could love me enough to make up for the loss of my family. He'd be enough for me."

Natasha pushed back slightly, looking into his eyes. "Your sire fell in love with you?"

Vlad nodded. "Weeks before the slaughter, he tried to get me to leave with him, but I'd rejected him saying my family needed me. Of course, the real reason I didn't leave was I adored my family. They were everything to me. I'd been blessed because my wife wasn't repulsed by what I'd become. She was fine with me being a vampire as long as I remained with her. Her love for me was total and complete as mine was for her. And our love overcame any fears she had about me."

"Did you ever find out who killed your family? It couldn't have been Sergei because he'd have been sleeping too at the time of their deaths."

"Once I realized what he intended, that he wanted to make me his lover, it dawned on me that he might be responsible for the death of my family, so I confronted him. He admitted to me he'd arranged for a murderer to go to my home and destroy my family, so I would be relieved of my burdens, and we could be together. He was so casual when he said it, like it was no more effort than hitching a horse to a wagon. He didn't have an ounce of remorse."

"What did you do?" Natasha whispered then worried her lip between her teeth.

"I flew into a rage and leapt at Sergei. I wanted to rip him limb from limb with my bare hands for what he'd done." Ire heated his face. "He was in my mind, knew what I intended and seized control of my actions. I stood frozen, anger boiling in my blood, impotent to act against my sire." He paused, needing a moment to remind himself he'd worked hard to never feel that way again. "In that moment I realized, I had no choice but to accept what happened. Sergei could read my thoughts, control my body. I had to capitulate to his will. He reminded me of it every chance he got."

Vlad refused to show her what the following decade had been like. She didn't need to see his abuse and mistreatment at the hands of his sire. There were some things he just couldn't share with anyone, and she didn't need to witness the disgusting details.

"Eventually, I became strong enough to block him from my mind. I planned his execution perfectly. Had the sword in my hand and struck a clean blow. He dodged at the last second and dematerialized before my eyes but not before my sword struck true. I could only hope I'd killed him."

"What happened?"

"Nothing, so I thought I must have struck a death blow. Then I sensed him rifling through my mind several months later. By that time, I'd befriended Demetri, and he'd brought me into the Alpha Council. I used the mindlink with my sire to convey one last threat before shutting him from my mind for good. I told him the Council was after him, and I'd be coming for him. I never heard or felt him again, so I assume he went into hiding."

The look in her eyes, a combination of love and awe, humbled him.

"You're an amazing man, Vlad."

"Not amazing enough to protect my family." And didn't that just bring a whole lot of the never-gonna-let-anything-like-that-ever-happen-agains.

He pressed her against his chest, cradling the back of her head with his palm a moment before he held her slightly away. He gazed deeply into her eyes as he spoke, wanting her to see the truth of his convictions. "I will never allow such a thing to happen again! Not to you, not to our child. The Fates have blessed me with a second chance for a family, though I cannot come up with a reason for them to do so, and I will not fail a second time."

He took her mouth in a deep kiss, pouring all his emotions into the passionate embrace. He'd relived enough sorrow and devastation. Now he wanted to celebrate what he had—a heartmate, another chance to be a father. Vlad wanted to remind himself what it felt like to rejoice in life. He no longer wanted to be lost in desperation and isolation. He wanted to be lost in her.

Natasha's empty blood bag dropped to the floor forgotten. She shifted her body, straddling his lap without breaking their kiss. Her hands rested on his shoulders, and her legs knelt on either side of his thick thighs.

Vlad ran his nose along her jawline, taking a deep inhale when she arched her neck to tempt him.

"Do you have any idea how exquisite your scent is, Tasha?" When his teeth grazed her delicate flesh, she trembled in his arms. "It's enticing, delicious."

His tongue flicked over her skin in tiny circles and made its way south until he found the place where her shoulder met the neck. Her pulse beat under his lips. Temptation incarnate, she made his fangs slide from his gums.

"Take from me," she commanded. Her hand rested on the back of his shorn head, urging him on.

The words flamed his blood, quickened his heart. Her trust in him, her desire for him flooded his mind.

Natasha's needs, her safety came before any desire. He would not take from her, she'd just fed. She needed the nourishment.

He trailed a series of reverent kisses down her chest. "You are so amazing," he murmured around one breast before taking the nipple in his mouth. It puckered against his tongue as he softly suckled.

Tasha's hips moved slowly back and forth. Her moist core rubbed against his shaft, coating him with its warm heat. She was ready for him, wanted him.

He scanned her body. Their eyes met. He kept his gaze locked with hers, needing her reaction. His fingers slipped between their bodies to slide through her dark curls. His palm cupped her mound as his fingers slid inside her tight channel. He rotated his digits, pressing against her sweet spot. She gasped at the sensation.

Fire leapt into her eyes, burning into him to ignite a similar passion within his body. Flames danced along his skin. Her eyes glazed, her body tightened around his fingers. He sensed her reaction to his actions in her mind, reveling in the way her body coiled.

He increased the speed of his fingers tunneling, setting a preternatural pace while his mouth suckled on the creamy flesh of her breast. She pushed tightly against him, her back bowing. Her body spiraled tighter and tighter until it burst from their shared passion.

Natasha convulsed around his fingers with surprising strength and cried out his name like a prayer when she came apart in his arms. The sound drove his inner beast mad with desire. The noise he made was all pure animal.

With blurring speed, he stood and positioned her body between him and the wall next to the waterfall. Water sluiced over their bodies as Vlad turned her to face the wall, pinning her against the smooth surface with his body. As he thrust into her from behind, his fingers curled around hers, pulling her arms over her head and against the wall.

His inner beast roared in triumph as his hips thrust hard into her. The slapping of their flesh drove his passion harder. His possessive nature bounded out, and he thrust deeper.

She spread her legs wider making him bend at the knees slightly to accommodate. His fingers tightened around hers. He pulled her arms higher over her head, stretching her body. She was his. His to possess.

His to love.

"I'll never let you go, Natasha," he roughly murmured against her ear, before he explored the droplets on her neck with his tongue.

Natasha threw her head back against his shoulder and cried out when another orgasm took her. Fisting him like a velvet glove, her body convulsed around his length.

Vlad released her hands as his body swelled behind her, his member long and thick inside. She pushed against the wall and leaned back into him, turning her head so her mouth lay against his neck. The sting of her fangs induced a euphoric state. His mate taking sustenance from him pushed him over the precipice, and he went up like dynamite. The Alpha growled ferociously, pumping wildly into her as he exploded into a thousand tiny pieces.

Spent from the soul-gripping orgasm, his hips slowed their pace, eventually stopping when she licked the tiny holes closed on his neck. His arms wrapped around her waist, holding her to him as one large hand spanned her rounded belly. Movement under his palm brought a smile to his face. The baby stirred.

He gently separated them and fell to his knees when she turned to face him. He laid his cheek against her stomach and again felt his son. The awe and wonder of such a miracle filled his soul.

Her stomach growled.

"You're still hungry?" he asked, not keeping the incredulousness from his voice.

I guess there is something to the saying "eating for two."

She peered at him through thick lashes and smiled sheepishly. "I guess so. Your son has an insatiable appetite just like his father."

"Oh, Tasha," he purred, reaching for her, "you have no idea just how insatiable my appetite is."

****

"Leo, darling." Jara smiled wide. "I have a task for you."

"Yes, princess," her dutiful subject replied.

She did so appreciate the respect and obedience she garnered from this male. If only Sergei would be as compliant, but no matter. She'd soon have what she needed from the bloodsucker, and then he'd be out of her life—for good.

Her smile widened to reach her eyes. "I need you to run an errand for me."

"Another one?"

The smile dropped from her face, and Jara narrowed her eyes on Leo. "Yes, another one. You will do as many errands as I want you to do."

"Of course, princess." His eyes went to the floor.

"Besides, you executed your last errand perfectly."

His eyes flew to hers. "I wouldn't say perfect. Sneaking into Varrick's compound was next to impossible."

"But you got the tome I needed."

"I did," he acquiesced, "but they almost killed me in the process."

"Yes, yes." Jara waved her hand dismissively. "You already shared how guards came bounding into the Room of Tomes and nearly took your head from your shoulders."

Leo rubbed the still healing wounds from the battle. "I barely got out of there alive," he murmured.

"But you did—get out of there alive—and you brought me the ancient text I needed. Thank goodness, Harleigh let it slip that Varrick knew about Lane and was angry with me. Imagine what might have happened if I went to retrieve the tome myself." She made a dramatic pause before continuing. "Now that I have the spell to reverse the stasis, all I need is a little reconnaissance, and I'll be ready to move forward."

"What do you mean by reconnaissance?"

"I did the location spell to find the Source, and believe me, it was not easy."

"Is that what you were doing when you locked yourself in the kitchen earlier?"

"Yes. I discovered he's in a remote part of Siberia. You must go there and check the place out. I don't want to go in blind. Go, see if you can discover where he was laid to ground."

"How will I find him?"

"Here." Jara handed a map to Leo. "I've marked the place the spell indicated. It would seem to be in the middle of nowhere. Go there and see what you can find out. I want to know everything. What's near there? What the terrain is like. Where exactly The Source is buried. Everything! No detail is too small."

"When do you wish me to leave?"

"Now."

"But my wounds." Leo pushed against the bandage around his neck. "I still haven't fully healed. Can't someone else go or at least let me wait a day or so to be back to one hundred percent."

Jara shook her head. "Do you think I would trust Finn to an errand so important? Only you can be trusted to complete this task. And as for waiting, I've waited long enough. I'll have my vengeance on the vampire race now! The sooner we kill The Source the sooner we'll rid the world of vampires."

"But—"

"No more buts, Leo. Go now, right this minute. If you must, you can shift into your animal form to do the reconnaissance. That should take care of your wounds and keep them from bleeding."

"Yes, princess."

A genuine smile curved her lips. "That's what I like to hear."

Chapter 13

Demetri Romanoff materialized into the Siberian forest and instantly sent his senses over the land, looking for any sign of trouble, as his heartmate, Tatiana, materialized next to him. Dressed in her usual leather bodysuit and shit-kicker boots, she appeared every bit the *femme fatale* he knew her to be.

She was all lithe muscle, like a graceful cat. His male libido automatically registered the curves of her body and the length of her strong legs that were hugged lovingly by the leather she wore. But it was her yellow eyes that held his gaze. They appeared almost too bright for her beautiful face.

She walked toward him, her leather duster flaring with each sure step. Her movements more predator than prey, made his body harden with desire. This woman challenged him, mentally and physically like no one else dared, and he'd come to crave the contest.

"You look ravishing, *kotik kisa.*" Demetri reached for her hand and placed a kiss on the back.

When he tried to pull her in for a kiss, Tatiana pulled her hand from his grasp and placed it firmly on his chest to stop his movement. "Not now, big guy. We need to locate Natasha."

She pushed past him and headed for Vlad's home. Demetri followed, trying to tame the lust for his mate.

Tatiana knocked on the door. When no one

answered, Demetri pushed his awareness throughout the home.

"No one is here."

His mate rolled her eyes. "No kidding."

A smile pulled at one corner of his mouth. "Sassy, woman. I would have thought you'd have learned to be more respectful to your elders."

She glanced over her shoulder, giving him a sultry look that warmed his blood. "And I thought you *enjoyed* my smart mouth."

"Only when it's being used in very particular ways." Demetri swatted her heart-shaped bottom.

"Where do you think they are?"

The question forced his thoughts back to the reason for their visit.

"I'm not sure. I don't feel them nearby."

"Me neither." Tatiana peered in the window. "Everything looks normal."

"Let's wait inside."

"Don't you think that's rude?"

"Vladimir will not care. Besides, what would you have us do? Stay out here in the cold?"

With a thought, Demetri unlocked the door to the home and opened it wide. "After you."

Tatiana shook her head. "Anyone ever tell you, you're pushy."

"I believe you remind me every chance you get."

Demetri followed her into the small cabin, his gaze immediately roamed the place, noting every detail from the color of the black appliances to the placement of the couch and chair.

He moved behind his mate and wrapped his arms about her waist. Next to her ear, he whispered, "Having the place to ourselves gives me an idea."

Tatiana leaned into the embrace, resting her head on his shoulder. "And what would that be?"

"It starts with peeling you out of the leather." He pulled her coat aside and kissed the spot where her neck met her shoulder. Her heart beat faster, her breath left her body in tiny huffs. Demetri reveled in the knowledge he affected her as much as she did him. His libido grew behind the zipper of his jeans.

He couldn't keep his hands off her. The more they were together the more he craved her. He was addicted to her in every way; her body, her feistiness, her challenges. She threw down the gauntlet every chance she got, and he gladly picked it up every time.

Demetri's kisses trailed up her neck to her jaw, and she turned in his arms. Her hand snaked up his thick bicep to cup his neck as the other wound around his waist and settled on his back. His hand moved into the silky, blunt-cut strands of her raven hair. Tatiana rose on her toes, her lips a breath away from his when she spoke.

"Romanoff, I hear something."

The rumble of an engine made him send his senses out once more. "They are coming."

Tatiana dropped to her heels and cocked her head to the side, reminding him of a curious cat. "Sounds like a motorcycle."

"In this snow, doubtful. More than likely it's Vlad's snowmobile."

Demetri reluctantly dropped his arms to his side as did his heartmate before they turned in unison to face the door. Funny how often they did things like that. Their instincts were evenly matched, she was as much a warrior as he, but it still didn't keep his protectiveness from flaring. If something threatened his mate, he'd rip it apart.

The couple met Natasha and Vlad at the door to the home. Natasha burst through the door laughing, with Vlad hot on her heels. She came up short when her eyes met Demetri's.

"Hello, you two," she greeted.

Her voice sounded weary, and Demetri wondered why. She looked good. Her face, flushed a vibrant red, seemed to glow and her eyes sparkled.

Demetri held his arms wide. "Come give me a hug."

Tasha hesitated, a concerned expression crossed her face. She'd never withheld affection before. He was not only her cousin but her sire as well. The two of them were close. Demetri was more father than distant relative, and they'd always had a great relationship. Why did she show reluctance now?

A fluttering heartbeat registered to his preternatural hearing. He immediately pushed his senses into his cousin's body and found the infant.

She was with child!

Demetri, what is it? Tatiana sent over their mindlink.

Do you not hear it?

She's pregnant! Tatiana's shock came through the link, mixing with his own in a turbulent concoction that fueled his confusion and growing anger.

His cousin was pregnant. Unmated. Call him old-fashioned, but that just wasn't the way it was done. She'd disgraced not only the family honor but herself. She was too young to have an infant.

She's older than I am, Tatiana gently reminded him.

But you're mated.

Demetri's ire grew. How could she! Who did she lie with to get into this kind of trouble? Demetri's eyes darted from Natasha to Vladimir.

"What the hell did you do to Natasha!" Demetri's question came out as an accusation and flew across the room to smack Vladimir in the face.

Vlad straightened his shoulders, squaring them against Demetri's anger. His legs braced wide as he crossed his arms over his chest. "I suggest you calm yourself, comrade."

Vlad hadn't denied it. He must be the father. Demetri's face flushed with rage. His eyes narrowed on the male across the room. His fists bunched, muscles tightened ready to pounce. One leap and he could be on the bastard. Only his mate's hand on his forearm forestalled the attack.

His gaze leapt from his prey to the long fingers pushing into his flesh. His gray gaze tracked up Tatiana's arm to lock on her cat-like eyes. Love stared back at him.

Demetri, don't you remember what it felt like when you believed I might be pregnant?

That was different, we are heartmates.

Are you sure they are not?

Demetri paused at the question. His eyes reluctantly left his mate to pin his fellow Alpha with his stare. "You have dishonored our family. Have you never heard of a condom? Were you too good to use one? Now Natasha is carrying your child, unmated."

Demetri allowed his power to flow throughout the

room. Tatiana shifted subtly beside him and watched as Vladimir's eyes widened slightly in realization.

Vlad moved, scooping Natasha behind him. His hands drew into tight fists while his body fell into a fighting stance. "She is not unmated. Tasha is mine. *Mine!* And if you threaten her with your power again, I will take your head from your shoulders."

It was a promise, not a threat, and Demetri knew it. He saw it in the lines of the Alpha's face. "I wasn't threatening *her*. I was threatening *you*."

"Now, boys," Natasha cut in. She moved next to Vlad, lacing her fingers in his.

"Natasha, you stay out of this," Demetri warned. "This is between Vladimir and me."

Nicholai, where are you?

I am on a flight with Juliette. Why, cousin? You are upset. Your anger bleeds through our link.

It is your sister.

What is wrong? Has someone hurt Natasha? Nicholai's concern flooded through the link.

She is uninjured. But I think you should get here as soon as possible. We have a situation.

The flight will take three more hours. Tell me what is wrong.

Demetri hesitated, debating exactly how to tell Nicholai his beloved sister was with child.

Demetri, what is it?

Blatant honesty was always best, Demetri decided. *Tasha is pregnant with Vladimir's child.*

What! *Are you sure?*

She's standing before me. I sensed the babe, and neither she nor Vlad denied it.

Nicholai materialized next to Demetri. The growl

that left his throat was the only warning Vladimir got. In a burst of vampiric speed, Nicholai blurred across the small room and grabbed Vlad by the throat. He lifted the warrior off his toes and moved across the room with Vlad dangling from his grip. As Vlad's hands clasp around Nicholai's forearm, he slammed the Alpha to the ground, leaving an indentation around his body when the floorboards flexed under the strength of the blow. Vlad's breath left his lungs in a hiss of air.

"Give me one reason why I should not kill you right now," Nicholai commanded around a mouth full of fangs.

Natasha raced to her brother's side and placed her hand on his shoulder. His free arm scooped her behind him. "Get back, sister mine," he ordered as he gave her a gentle push away.

Vlad dematerialized, leaving only a wisp of black smoke to waft between Nicholai's fingers. He instantly materialized between Natasha and her brother. "Touch her again, Nicholai…" The threat hung unfinished in the air.

Nicholai advanced on the couple. "She's *my* sister."

"She's *my* mate!"

Nicholai's foot stopped mid-stride. "What did you say?"

I told you. Tatiana sent over their mindlink, along with her smugness. *You called Nicholai here, didn't you?*

I did not. I simply informed him of the situation.

Why would you do that?

He needed to know.

But you must have known he would... Vladimir's

deep voice stopped the remainder of her thought.

"I said," Vlad growled slowly. "She. Is. My. Mate."

"How…Why…But…" Nicholai stammered.

"I think we should all sit down and talk this through," suggested Tatiana.

The five of them settled. Nicholai and Demetri sandwiched Tatiana on the couch while Vladimir handed Natasha into the chair. He stood behind her, his hands resting possessively on her shoulders. The expression on his face appeared a mix of anger and daring as if he thought either Demetri or Nicholai might challenge his right to his mate.

But Demetri knew better. He might wish someone softer for Natasha because she was so delicate, but being recently mated, he realized when the Fates picked a mate there was no fighting it.

"Nicholai, what are you doing here?" Natasha asked.

"I thought you and Julie were flying back from your honeymoon." Tatiana turned toward Nicholai. "That's why you asked Demetri and me to come check in on Natasha."

"I was. When Demetri informed me my sister was pregnant, I materialized here immediately." Nicholai sighed. "I'll need to get back on the plane before it lands. No doubt there will be some memories that need erasing."

Natasha shook her head. "You told him I was pregnant, Demetri? Couldn't you let me tell him?"

Demetri's heart clenched in his chest when tears pushed into her eyes. "Don't cry, little one. I meant no harm."

"But *I* should have been the one to tell him. It's my right to tell people when I want them to know." A tear escaped down her cheek.

"Please, do not cry, sister mine. I would have found out the minute I saw you later tonight."

"But…" The rest of Natasha's sentence was cut off by a sob as tears streamed down her face.

Demetri's gut twisted.

"Get out. All of you get the hell out," Vlad hissed. "Now! I want you out of my home. You have upset Natasha, and I want you gone."

"Not going to happen," Nicholai challenged.

"I can make it happen," Vlad shot back, moving out from behind the chair.

"There's too much testosterone in this room." Tatiana rose from the couch. "Vlad settle down. I think you should ask Natasha what she wants before you go making threats against her brother." Tatiana rounded on Nicholai. "And Nicholai, don't you think you owe Natasha an apology for coming in here and attacking her heartmate."

Nicholai had the good sense to look remorseful. "I guess," he muttered.

Tatiana turned toward Demetri. "And don't forget the role you played in creating this situation. You owe Tasha an apology too, Demetri."

He most certainly did not! He had nothing to apologize for. His behavior had been perfectly rational.

Your behavior, his mate informed him, *was perfectly chauvinistic. It's the twenty-first century. You shouldn't have overreacted when you thought she was an unmated mother. You certainly didn't need to immediately contact Nicholai and drag him in to complicate this. Natasha's pregnant. You know how special and rare that is. How can you cause her such stress, knowing a vampire pregnancy is rarely carried to term?*

Guilt weighed heavy on Demetri's shoulders. His anger had pushed all rational thought from his mind. He hadn't stopped to think about the dangers associated with the pregnancy. His eyes left his mates to find Natasha's.

"Natasha, how far along are you?"

"Almost seven months."

"Fates above." Tatiana murmured. "That would mean—"

Demetri did the math in his head. "The two of you—at the wedding?"

Natasha nodded.

"Is everything all right, physically I mean?" asked Nicholai as he leaned forward to rest his forearms on his knees.

"Yes." Natasha smiled and wiped the tears from her cheeks. "The baby's fine."

Vlad looked down on his mate, even Demetri saw the affection in his eyes. "Tasha, are you hungry? Do you need to feed?"

She smiled up at him. "No, Vlad. I'm still full from what you brought to the grotto. But thank you for asking."

"Something's wrong. What is it, Natasha?" Vlad reached out to take her hand.

"It's nothing." She let out a pained moan. Her hand reached for her head. "Stop it. All three of you, get out of my head."

Demetri realized Nicholai and Vladimir must have

believed her no more than he did, for they all three pushed into her mind to glean what was wrong at the same instant. He couldn't help but admire the two males for their actions. After all, as the saying went, great minds think alike.

"Leave the poor woman alone." Tatiana shot Demetri a deadly look.

"Why does your back hurt?" Nicholai inquired. He always could read his sister quickly.

Vlad knelt next to her chair. "Did I hurt you in the grotto? You should have said something."

Nicholai and Demetri tensed at the same instant, rising to their feet.

"What did you do to my sister?"

"He didn't do anything," Tasha assured them. "My back is just a little sore. Probably from Vlad's bed."

Demetri and Nicholai groaned in unison. Neither of them wanted to be reminded of little Natasha in Vladimir's bed. The thought made Demetri want to pound something, preferably Vlad's face.

"It's no big deal. See the pain is already subsiding." Natasha smiled at the group.

"Juliette just informed me the captain of our flight came over the intercom and announced turbulence is coming. I must return to the plane."

"Because the flight attendants will be making sure everyone is in their seats?" Tatiana asked.

"No, because I need to be with my mate to be sure she is safe."

Natasha smiled. "Go, brother. Tell Julie I said hi."

Nicholai pinned Demetri with a cold stare. "I leave my sister in your hands, cousin."

Vlad stood. "The only hands Natasha will be in are

mine."

Demetri glanced outside, noting the sky had lightened to indicate the impending sunrise. An idea came to him. "The sun will be rising soon. Why don't we call it a night? Nicholai go to Juliette, see her home safely. And we'll all meet back here tomorrow evening, so we can discuss this situation further."

Nicholai's eyes narrowed. *You intend to leave Natasha alone with Vladimir?*

She is his heartmate, Nicholai. You can't fight the Fates. Just look at Tatiana and me. She tried to fight our mating for a year and didn't win the battle.

Nicholai's chuckle traveled over their link.

"Until tomorrow evening then," Nicholai said before he dematerialized from the room.

Natasha rose from her chair, her hand on her back. "Demetri, I…"

A thick growl outside interrupted her. Four sets of eyes darted to the window simultaneously. A large bear ran through the forest.

"You don't see that every day," Tatiana observed.

"It is most unusual," Vlad concurred. "I can't recall the last time I saw a brown bear in this forest."

"It looked like a grizzly," Demetri informed them.

"Impossible. There are no grizzly bears in Siberia. It must have been an East Siberian brown bear."

Living in Wyoming for over a century, Demetri knew a grizzly when he saw one. Strange or not, he'd bet his log home that was a grizzly. And didn't that just make him want to stay here and figure out what was going on.

Chapter 14

Sergei scrubbed a hand down his face, pulling the skin taut, and let a heavy sigh push through his lips. He needed to go charm the bitch. If only he didn't need her to find his sire. After running his hands over his black dress shirt and pants to assure they were wrinkle free, he pasted what he hoped would be a charming smile on his face and headed down the stairs.

As he approached the library, Jara's shrill voice stopped him in his tracks. The door stood slightly ajar, so he plastered himself against the wall to eavesdrop.

"This, dear Finn, is the Tome of Necromancy. And you may not touch."

"I would not attempt to do so," Finn assured her. "May I ask where Leo is this evening?"

"I sent him on an errand. I located The Source."

Source of what, Sergei wondered as someone clapped their hands.

"Congratulations, princess."

"Yes, well, was there ever any doubt I would?" Jara's arrogant tone grated on Sergei's nerves.

"I never doubted you," Finn assured her.

"As you shouldn't." Sergei heard what sounded like a book closing. "Finn, I'm feeling like a snack. Do you think we have time to go out and get something to eat before that damned vampire wakes?"

"I'll be glad when we can get rid of him."

"Patience, Finn. I need him. Just for a little longer."

Sergei wondered just what she planned on doing with him after his services were no longer needed. He didn't trust her or the other demons in the house.

The sound of clothing rustling made him dematerialized to the top of the stairs to watch the pair of demons walk out the front door as if they didn't have a care between them. He, on the other hand, felt the weight of the world on his shoulders.

The key to finding his sire lay in this house, somewhere. If only he could discover it. And what better time to search than when the mistress of the house was away.

Sergei materialized in the library. His eyes scanned the room. Everything seemed in place. The desk in the corner stood free of clutter, looking barely used. The throw pillows rested against each other neatly on the settee. Every book stood in neat rows like good little soldiers. Everything seemed perfect, except for one little thing. Had he not been so curious about what the Tome of Necromancy was, he might have missed it, but luck was with him.

There, on the third shelf, a spot of disturbed dust. He moved closer for a better look. It appeared someone recently removed one of the books from the shelf. He read the spine of the book located in front of the spot.

"Tale of the Jilted Lover."

Not a book he would expect either Finn or Leo to read, and he couldn't exactly envision Jara reading it either.

He pulled the book from the shelf. It slid to the end of the ledge and stopped. The click of a lock unclasping sounded beside him. A slot on the opposite bookcase popped out from the side. Sergei smiled while he walked over and pulled the compartment open. It contained an old book which he took from its hiding place.

He laid the book on the desk to give it a good perusal. Bound in aged leather, the edges of the pages were jagged at irregular intervals as if chewed upon by tiny rodents. Sergei flipped the book over and examined the cover. Letters flowed in an arch, hand-written in scrolling golden print. He could not read the print, but it seemed to resemble the tribal tattoos so popular with modern culture.

Hoping the pages within would not contain the same script, Sergei opened the book. A musty stench of soil and rot accosted his nose. The tome smelled of death, and based on the aged parchment paper that made up its pages, he'd guess the thing was older than dirt.

As luck would have it, the language inside happened to be Ancient Sumerian, a language he understood. He carefully turned the decrepit pages, glancing over the words written thereon until two words jumped off a page. The Source.

Might he finally get some answers? Sergei sent his senses throughout the house. When he didn't sense Jara or any of her minions, he started to read.

In the time of darkness and plague, a great being arose. Two great lines split from the one. One to forever walk in darkness, the other in light. As time passed, the being came to favor one side of his line. Being of darkness himself, the being chose the darklings, forsaking his other line.

The light ones dubbed the being, The Source.

Ah, so he finally had a reference for this Source Jara kept talking about.

The light ones realized they could not survive without his favor, so they hid from The Source, afraid he would strike them from the earth. But a few brave souls trailed The Source. He roamed the earth, murdering the innocent, searching out and destroying each light one he found. The light ones endured, documenting many atrocities until at last a great king was born.

This king dubbed the light ones demons and vowed to end their suffering at the hands of The Source. The king scoured the lands, gathering his people to his castle. They lived in peace and harmony for many years until a darkling happened upon their dwelling.

The darkling came in the shadows of the night, bringing death to most of those within the castle walls. Only a few demons escaped with the queen and the prince.

As the prince grew, his mother told him of the great man his father had been, and this inspired the prince. He grew to hate the darkling for killing his father, rightfully hated all darklings, as well as, The Source for creating them.

The prince became a proud, noble demon, and upon his mother's deathbed, he vowed vengeance against The Source. He waited centuries, building his forces until at last, he declared war on The Source. It was said that The Source was all powerful, all knowing, but the light ones still battled. They followed the darklings, finding them with The Source in the land of the people with the almond-shaped eyes.

Could it be referring to the Orient? Sergei

wondered. A nagging feeling of familiarity crept up his spine to wind around his mind. "My sire and I were in Asia. We came under attack. I believed the vampires Michael Garsoe and Gage Lucio were to blame. Could I have been mistaken?"

He read on.

The prince sent his brother to kill The Source, but The Source had surrounded himself with a great fighting force. The darklings were too powerful and could not be fought hand to hand with swords. The demons did the only thing they could, resorted to using their magic.

A memory flashed in Sergei's mind of Michael. He'd been a good friend, seemed to be trustworthy, then suddenly the next night, he acted possessed, changed in a way no one had understood. If this tome referred to their time in Asia, then perhaps the demons had put him under some kind of spell. Ultimately, he and his sire lost Michael somewhere between Alaska and Siberia. Could this story be about Eldrick? He must know more.

The demons found The Source alone one night, wondering in the cold, frozen land. The prince's sister wasted no time. She bespelled The Source, putting him into a deep sleep, and hid him away. To ensure he'd never leave should he awake, she placed a spell over the site so none could dematerialize from the grounds. In so doing, she saved demon kind.

Their band of vampires left Asia and traveled to Alaska then into Siberia. His sire disappeared during that time. They assumed the Alpha Council had something to do with the disappearance, but maybe they'd had it wrong.

Demons be warned, take to the mountains and the islands. Hide from the darklings for they can only bring you harm. They carry in them great illness but show no signs of ailment. Now caution is also sagacious for The Source can be awakened again. The blood of his offspring can return him to the world when given with the specter incantation.

Hope surged through Sergei's blood. If he correctly interpreted this text, it all made sense. Most vampires didn't know about the existence of demons, but somehow demons seemed to know of them. His sire was the most powerful vampire in existence, but he'd disappeared. Sergei believed he wasn't dead, he would have sensed it, and yet he couldn't find him either. If he'd been placed under some kind of stasis spell, it might explain why. And if the text could be believed, his blood could awaken his sire. Was that why Jara sought him out?

"Oh, this is too perfect," he muttered under his breath. "She's been using me while I've been using her."

Once he got his sire back, he'd kill the deceitful bitch. An evil smile came to his lips as he slipped the tome back into its hiding place. He'd just exited the library when the front door opened.

"So, you'll use his blood to awaken The Source and kill him."

Jara stopped short when her eyes met Sergei's, and Finn bumped into her back. Sergei pretended not to have heard Finn's last comment. Now he understood. Jara intended for his blood to awaken his sire so she could do what the other demons couldn't—kill him.

Sergei forced what he hoped would look like a

genuine grin. “Jara, my sweet, so glad you came home.”

She crossed the foyer to place a chaste kiss on his lips. “You’re awake.”

“Aren’t you glad to see me?”

“Of course, my dear.” Her tone sounded sugary sweet. “I’m just surprised to find you up and about. Did you miss me?”

“But of course,” he lied, taking her into his arms.

A genuine smile took his face as a plan formed. He’d play along, let her wake his sire, then together they’d make her rue the day she ever thought to use him.

Chapter 15

Vladimir awoke, muscles bunched tight from the adrenaline coursing through his body. His heart pounded in his throat, mouth opened in a silent scream lost in that place between consciousness and sleep. His arms tightened automatically around the woman beside him when images of Natasha and their son lying dead flooded his mind's eye.

It was just a dream, he assured himself.

"I'll never let anything happen to you," he whispered into her soft, colorful hair.

Tasha stirred in his arms, rolling onto her back, and he allowed the movement, needing to see her. He gazed down on her beautiful face. Her black eyelashes lay on her cheeks in two dark crescents. Her full, sensual lips were pursed in a tiny pout. She appeared a little pale, probably because she needed to feed.

He'd made sure she'd eaten and drunk more blood before going to bed. After the way her brother and Demetri responded to the news of the pregnancy, she'd been upset. He really couldn't blame Nicholai and Demetri for their reactions. Vlad wasn't good enough for her, and they knew it. But the Fates made her his mate, and he could do no other than care for her and their child.

His hand cradled her belly. The fluttering heartbeat reminded him of hummingbird wings. Their son sounded strong.

His fingers pulled the material of her gown up. They crawled over the fabric, bunching it above her navel. When her smooth skin lay exposed to his view, Vlad placed a light kiss over the apex of the small mound that held his child, then rested his cheek on the warm flesh.

He didn't deserve her, didn't deserve a second chance at fatherhood. He'd thought his chance at having a family was gone and buried, but now he'd been given another chance by the Fates, and this time he'd get it right.

This time, he'd make sure Natasha and their child were protected at all costs. He'd be with her, shield her from danger. Be there to watch over them, care for them. Surely, fate wouldn't be so cruel as to take his family again. But if it tried, he'd stop it this time.

Something pushed against his cheek. It happened again. Vlad sat up and placed his hand over Tasha's stomach. It rose to push against his fingers. A smile lifted the corners of his lips.

"I feel you, little one," he whispered.

"He feels you too."

His eyes locked with his heartmate's, and his grin widened when he noticed the love in her eyes. They sparkled with it, turning her amber irises golden.

"I'm sorry I woke you."

She returned his smile, and it made his heart want to shout. "I'm not sorry. I love watching you when you don't think anyone is looking."

"Why?"

"Because, you let that gruff, hardhearted persona down, and I see the real you. The male who cares for me. The male who will be wrapped around our son's tiny finger."

"I don't know about that. I'm a rather tough parent. I expect great things for our son."

"But you won't be a cruel parent. You won't push him beyond his limits. I know you, Vlad. I'm in your mind. I sense the love you have for him. For me."

And there it was. She might have been the one to say it, but he felt it. His heart seemed heavy, full of the love for her and their unborn child. She spoke the truth. He did love them. But he had yet to say those three little words, and Vlad decided to rectify that immediately.

"I love you, Natasha." Saying the words freed him. The weight of his self-loathing and blame for the loss of his family lifted from his shoulders, and for the first time in centuries, he experienced hope again. "And I love this little one."

As if in response to the declaration, the babe pushed against his hand once more. It was the most amazing feeling.

Tasha laughed. "Seems he's wanting to let you know he loves you too. I think he's trying to say hi."

Vlad placed another light kiss on her stomach. "Patience, little one, you'll have an opportunity to tell me hello soon enough."

"Vlad," Tasha waited until their eyes met before continuing. "I love you."

His heart beat hard in his chest. If he lived another century, he'd make sure to never let this woman down. He'd strive to be worthy of her love and faith in him. The burden of providing for a family and seeing to their protection sat heavy on his shoulders, but he'd gladly bear the responsibility. For her and their child he'd bear any weight.

I love you too, milenky. He purposely used their most intimate form of communication to declare his love so she would experience the sincerity behind the sentiment.

"I know you love me, Vlad. And I love it when you call me dear."

She rolled her hips, the movement no doubt a means to increase her comfort, but the gesture brought her core closer to his lips, and her delicate female scent perfumed the air. His body instantly hardened in response. In a thousand centuries, he'd never get enough of her.

"And I'm glad you feel that way because I'll never get enough of you." Tasha sent her desire through their mindlink. It washed over him in waves, making his blood boil with hot passion. His mouth watered at the thought of tasting her.

Vlad settled between her legs, thankful she had not worn panties to bed. His hand wrapped around her thighs before he spread her wide. They held her down, opening her sex to him. Delicate and pink, it glistened with her excitement. His mouth watered as his fangs descended from his gums.

He ran the points along her inner thigh, and Tasha arched as a long moan escaped her lips. The moan turned into a pained cry, and Vlad instantly released her. "What's wrong?"

"It's just my back. When I moved, it hurt. I must have slept wrong."

"Are you sure that's all it is?" Vlad sat on his heels.

"I'm sure. It will probably go away in a few minutes." Tasha gave him a naughty look. "Know what I heard is good for a backache?"

"What?"

"An orgasm."

"Well then," Vlad settled back down on the bed, sliding a large hand under each of her thighs. "I'll have to see what I can do to help your back."

His tongue slid over her folds in a long lick that made her hands fist in the sheets. She tasted salty-sweet, like his favorite snack, a delicious combination of woman and musk. He lapped at her, thrusting his tongue into her folds to taste the honey within. His tongue swirled, brushing over the sensitive nerves until her head thrashed in wide abandonment on his pillow. When lips closed around her tiny nub and his fingers replaced his tongue, thrusting into her, Tasha rewarded his efforts with a soft mewling sound.

He suckled, working her with his mouth, until her hands gripped his head and her nails bit into his scalp. She held him captive between her legs, pushing his mouth firmly against her sex. He understood the silent plea and increased the suction. The addition of one more meaty finger thrusting inside sent her over the edge.

Her feminine channel gripped his fingers as her body jolted with the force of the orgasm. A shudder went through her, pinning her legs to his head. He glanced up her body and noted the red flush to her cheeks, the way her pink lips parted with her heavy exhales. He'd never seen anything sexier in his life.

Her body went boneless, her long legs fell open to rest on the bed. One of her hands left his head to push her fingers through her hair, pulling it away from her face.

“Holy crackers,” she breathed.

“Is your back feeling better?” Vlad didn’t keep the male satisfaction from showing on his face.

“My back, my body. Everything feels better.”

Vlad rose over her, bracing his weight on straight arms. “Ready for round two?”

Tasha nodded enthusiastically and grabbed his ass with both hands. She pulled him against her weeping core. Her moist heat coated him, made him crave to be inside her. In one smooth glide, he slid in, burying himself to the hilt.

Her inner muscles welcomed him into her body with a firm squeeze. Her juices bathed him in their warmth, drawing his balls tight. Fates above, she felt so good.

His inner beast roared in pleasure. His hips pistoned against her, and the sound of their flesh coming together filled the loft.

“You feel incredible,” Vlad ground out around clenched teeth. “Are you sure I’m not hurting your back?”

“What back? Do I have a back?” Tasha shifted her hips, and he sank deeper into her core. “I only feel one thing right now.”

“Only one?” Vlad lowered his head to her full breast. Her pink nipple puckered as his tongue swirled around it. When he sucked the creamy globe into the hot cavern of his mouth, his mate’s hand reached up to grab his broad shoulders.

“More than one.” She kneaded his muscles as they bunched and flexed under her touch. “Definitely, more than only one thing."

He left their mindlink open, feeling their passion pass between them. It made a circuit, increasing their need with each pass as it traveled between their bodies. He lifted his head to meet her steady gaze. Her lids were half-closed. Tasha's cheeks flushed as one hand reached out to cup his face. Hot, delicate fingertips brushed over his goatee before they touched his lips. They traced the curves, her eyes darkening with desire, the scent of her arousal wrapped around them until he wanted to drown in it.

Her ragged cry of joy nearly sent him over the edge. Her eyes locked on his throat. He knew what she wanted, what she needed, and he'd happily oblige. Balancing his weight on one arm, he cradled her neck with his free hand and brought her mouth to his pulse. Tasha's fangs sank into his flesh, hard and fast. She drew at his throat in long pulls which sent a rush of pleasure pouring through his blood.

She took from him what she and the baby needed, ancient blood that would nourish and sustain them. He could do no less than provide. It thrilled him to do so. Vlad swelled within her.

Passion coiled, drove him toward the breaking point, making his body tighten further. The speed of his hips increased, but she matched thrust for thrust until the coil shattered, and together they fell over the precipice into ecstasy. His release pulsed into her body, white-hot sparks of pleasure that curled his toes.

Knocking at the door brought them back to earth just as the last pulse jerked his shaft. Tasha ran her tongue over the puncture wounds in his neck. He lowered her head to the pillow. Her black hair with its purple and blue stripes spread over his pillow. A flush colored her cheeks deep red from the combination of feeding and intercourse. Natasha's tiny pink tongue darted out to lick the crimson from her lips in the most enticing way. She looked utterly seductive, and even though they had just consummated their love, his shaft stirred within her creamy heat.

"I know you two are in there," Demetri called through the door.

Of course, he did. Just as Vlad sensed that Tatiana and Nicholai joined Demetri on the porch to his home.

"I used our link to tell Demetri we'd be just a minute," Natasha informed him.

"Did you also inform him he is interrupting and should leave us in peace for several more hours?"

"As nice as that sounds, the sooner we find out why they are here the sooner they will leave, and we can have the rest of the night together."

Now that theory had merit, Vlad decided. He separated their bodies, albeit reluctantly, and quickly donned a pair of black jeans and a heavy shirt while Natasha pulled on one of his sweaters and her pants.

Vlad materialized by the front door and opened it wide. "Come in."

Nicholai's nostrils flared, taking in the scent of sex that hung heavily in the small space. The expression on Demetri's face indicated he'd noticed the same aroma. Well, the two of them should have given him and his mate a few more hours of peace if they didn't want a reminder of their love.

"Thank you," Tatiana greeted when her two companions remained silent.

The trio made their way into the home, each

choosing to stand rather than sit on the couch as they'd done the previous night. He suspected this was intentional.

Natasha materialized next to him, and he gripped her elbow to gently guide her to the only padded chair in the room. He handed her into the chair under the watchful eye of the group. "Sit. I know you're back has been hurting."

Nicholai's brows furrowed. "You are still in pain?"

Tasha graced the warrior with one of her placating smiles. "I'm fine. It just spasms from time to time."

Vlad could tell Nicholai felt unsure as to whether or not to believe her by the way his body shifted slightly, and his eyes narrowed.

"Are you sure, sister mine? Your body should have healed any injury by now." Nicholai pinned Vlad with a hard stare. "Unless your mate won't give your body respite."

Vladimir's temper flared to life. "Now see here…" Tasha's fingers closing around his wrist halted the rant.

"Nicholai, do not insult my mate." She stood, hands fisted on her hips. "Vlad takes excellent care of me and the baby. If you came here to insult him, then you can leave. He is my heartmate. I love him. I will not allow you to come into our home and toss wild accusations at him."

The corner of Demetri's mouth quirked up in a half-grin. "Seems our little girl has become a woman, Nicholai."

It was endearing that his mate stuck up for him, but Vlad didn't need anyone fighting his battles. He opened his mouth to confer his own warning to Nicholai.

A roaring chuff drew everyone's attention. In

unison, five sets of eyes darted to the door of the home.

"What was that?" Tatiana asked.

"Mishka," Vlad answered. "Something has upset him."

Vlad pushed his awareness out into the night. He found the pride agitated and running quickly through the forest.

Vlad reached the door first and pulled it open in time to witness the pride streak by. He concentrated on the male tiger to glean his thoughts, then stared into the woods.

"What is it?" Demetri asked, stopping next to him.

"The tigers saw a bear. It attacked."

Tatiana joined the two of them. "A bear attacked a pride of tigers? Isn't that unusual given how many tigers just ran by?"

"Very," Vlad replied succinctly.

A large bear with brown fur lumbered by in the tracks left from the cats. Though barely visible through the thick forest, Vlad watched him pick up speed and tear after the tigers, leaving large clumps of debris in his wake.

"That was a grizzly," Demetri said.

"Impossible. It must have been a Siberian brown bear," Vlad argued.

"No, that was a *grizzly*. I've lived in Wyoming long enough to know one when I see one. It must be the same one from last night."

"I'm going to investigate." Vlad stepped out on the porch.

Nicholai's hand on his bicep stopped Vlad's next step. "Do you sense that?"

Vlad sent his instincts out again, this time finding a

blank spot. “A demon?”

Tatiana approached the door. “I feel it.”

“As do I,” Demetri said. “And it’s moving.”

Vlad’s consciousness flowed into the night, seeking connection with the bear. What he found sent an involuntary shiver down his spine. The bear was a demon!

Vlad turned to discover Natasha too had come onto the porch. Concern for her safety made his stomach twist and shoulders bunch.

“Get inside,” he demanded. “It isn’t safe out here.”

“How did the demon find me?”

When Tasha didn’t move, Vlad turned her by the shoulders and guided her into the house. The others closed rank behind him.

Nicholai took his sister’s hand. “Tasha, I just contacted Julie. She thinks you should go to our home.”

“I think that is an excellent idea,” Tatiana agreed.

“But I don’t want to go. I don’t want to leave Vladimir.”

As Nicholai released his hold, Vlad wrapped his arms around Natasha’s waist. “I think you should go to Nicholai’s place. It isn’t safe here with a demon roaming the woods. You go to Nicholai’s, and I’ll contact you when we have disposed of the threat.”

“Julie would love the company,” Nicholai chimed in. “She just said it would give the two of you a chance to know each other better.”

Vlad’s gaze locked with Natasha’s. “You go to Nicholai’s, get to know Juliette a little better. I’ll meet you there in no time.”

“You promise?” Natasha asked. He wanted to kiss the worried look off her face and would have if they did not have an audience.

"I promise I'll do whatever it takes to keep you and the baby safe."

"Natasha, enough of this." Demetri crossed his arms over his chest. "We waste time standing here talking. You will dematerialize now to Nicholai's home. Contact me when you arrive."

Vlad should have been irritated at Demetri's highhandedness, but instead he was grateful to have the backup.

"She'll contact me," Vlad corrected, hoping his concern showed in his eyes while he gazed deeply into hers.

Tasha sighed. "I'll contact both of you."

"All three of us," her brother amended.

His mate's eyes rolled in their sockets. Relief poured through Vlad, taking the strain from his shoulders.

"Fine," she at last conceded. "Go, hunt the demon. I'll be waiting safe and sound with Julie."

She stood on her tiptoes and gave him a long, thorough kiss that earned a collective groan from the group. "I love you," she whispered against his lips before dropping away.

"I love you too," Vlad replied and gave her bottom a pinch. "Now go."

"Fine."

Her body coalesced before their eyes, leaving only a black coil of smoke in the room.

"Let's go find that demon," Tatiana ordered, before heading out the door with blurring speed.

"Damn that woman," Demetri muttered, going after her.

Vlad smiled when he realized he wasn't the only one with a troublesome and stubborn mate. He and Nicholai followed the couple, catching up to them as they trekked through the woods. The tracks were easy to follow. The demon made no attempt to cover them, proving he was either stupid or ignorant of the vampires in the vicinity.

Vlad noticed the way Demetri stayed slightly ahead of his mate. He was still recovering from starvation at the hands of the demon scientists. He'd packed on some impressive muscle since being retrieved from captivity and currently boasted the physique of a heavy-weight fighter. Which, with Demetri's fighting skills, would be more than enough to intercede between his mate and the demon should it be necessary.

I'm here, safe and sound, Natasha sent over their mindlink.

Thank you. How is Juliette?

Well.

And how are you feeling?

Tired and my back has begun to hurt again, but I'll be fine.

Perhaps you need another treatment.

I'll take one of your 'treatments' any time, my love.

Despite the fact they tracked a demon the size of a bear through the wilderness, a smile played over his lips. He'd like nothing better than to spend the night treating her, but first he had a threat to dispose of.

Be safe, Vlad. I don't know what I'd do if something happened to you.

You rest, and I'll be there before you know it.

I love you.

I love you too, milenky.

He bemoaned the loss of her from his mind but knew she must contact Nicholai and Demetri. He pushed his senses out over the frozen land. They brought a plethora of information to him. The woodsy scent of the nature around him mixed with the perspiration from the fleeing animals. The pride no longer ran, but instead settled in its usual place near the grotto. A blank spot moved in their direction. Vlad immediately connected with Mishka. He sent the animal the impression of danger and urged him to move the pride.

The animal's acceptance and trust flowed back to Vlad, then the pride moved in the opposite direction from the blank spot.

Vlad put on a burst of speed and the others followed. As they crested the snow-covered hill, the grizzly pulled itself from the icy river and vanish behind the grotto. Clearly, the demon tried to throw them off his scent by crossing the river. He must not know that vampires figured out how to detect the demon's presence.

The four Alphas materialized on the opposite side of the river, and Vlad led them around the snowy mound which concealed the grotto. Just as they rounded the corner, he caught a glimpse of brown fur disappearing inside the cave entrance.

"The demon must be looking for a place to hide," Tatiana whispered before the group entered the cave.

Vlad pushed ahead as fast as he dared in the darkness. He ran his hands along the wall for guidance until his eyes adjusted to the miniscule amount of light.

When the quartette popped out inside the grotto, the steam from the water clouded their vision. Seeing nothing unusual through the thick haze, Vlad scanned the area. His senses flowed over the water, through the steam to find…

Nothing?

"Do you sense anything?" he asked no one in particular.

"Nuh-uh."

"Nothing."

"Not a thing."

All three replied simultaneously.

"Where did it go?" Tatiana asked. "We were right behind it."

Demetri moved around the water's edge. "I know it came in here."

"We all saw it, sensed it." Nicholai moved around the opposite direction of his cousin. The two met on the other side near the waterfall.

"It's gone," Demetri announced.

"Can they dematerialize?" Tatiana asked.

"I don't know," Demetri replied, walking back to join his heartmate. "I never saw one do it when I was taken prisoner."

Nicholai joined the group. "Well, he obviously isn't here now."

"We need to inform Stephan of this development," Demetri suggested.

****

Thirty minutes later Stephan and Desmond, one of the newer members of the Alpha Council, materialized into Vlad's home wearing the usual Alpha garb of black camo pants and a black turtleneck shirt, no doubt with weapons hidden on their persons. Vlad greeted each in the way of the warrior, by clasping forearms and giving a nod of the head. After he informed them about the apparent demon and his supposition as to why it might be here, Stephan crossed his arms over his thick chest.

"So, Vladimir, you think the demon came here looking for Natasha?"

"It seems reasonable. One tracked her in Australia," Nicholai informed the group.

Stephan gathered his black hair back into a leather strap. "Why would the demons be after Natasha?"

"I don't know," Vlad confessed, and it bothered him to no end.

"Maybe because she's pregnant," Tatiana suggested, then crossed her long legs that were encased in leather.

Son of a bitch, why hadn't he thought of that? Vlad's stomach churned, and bile coated the back of his throat. They already knew demons had kidnapped a pregnant vampire and according to what Demetri shared, had done terrible experiments on her and the child, killing both in the process. If they so much as touched Natasha, he'd kill them. Hell, he'd kill them just for thinking it.

He pushed away from the wall he'd been leaning against.

"Natasha is pregnant? Who's the father?" Stephan didn't keep the incredibility from his voice.

"I am." Vlad braced his feet wide and crossed his arms over his chest.

"Bloody hell." Desmond pushed his fingers through his brown hair and with his aristocratic, English accent commented, "Vlad's going to be changing nappies, is he?"

Vladimir growled. Damned Brit missed the point.

His heartmate and child were in danger, and Desmond talked about changing diapers. He wanted to throttle the newbie. His hands fisted.

Stephan stepped between him and Desmond, obviously reading Vlad's irritation.

"I won't allow them to hurt her. I'll keep her safe whatever it takes," Vlad declared.

Stephan rested a hand on his shoulder. "We all care for Natasha."

Vlad knew she was like family to most of them. Hell, she *was* family to half of them.

Before he could comment, Stephan continued, "We'll see to her safety. We'll find this demon and destroy it."

Nicholai shifted his stance, his hands curling into fists by his sides. "How do you recommend we do that, Stephan?"

One black brow raised over the Alpha leader's blue eyes. "I recommend we go hunting."

The warriors let out a collective war cry.

Chapter 16

"Leo, what did you find out?"

No preamble, no thank-God-you're-okay, just "what did you find out." He should have expected as much having worked with the princess for years. Correction, worked *for* the princess for years.

Leo's wounds had healed when he took his animal form, but the itchy pain remained. He scratched his neck as he crossed the library to pour himself a stiff drink. His hand skimmed over the vodka the bloodsucker had laid claim to and grabbed the whiskey.

"Leo…" Jara's voice broadcasted her irritation for all to hear. Her Majesty wanted his report, and he knew better than to keep her waiting.

"I found him." He poured himself a full glass and slammed the fiery liquid down in one long gulp before pouring a second round.

Jara clapped her hands in excitement. An evil grin played over her face, twisting it in a way Leo found rather disturbing. He downed the next glass, barely tasting the fire water as it rushed to his belly to warm him from the inside out.

"Annnd…" Jara gave a dramatic pause. When he didn't respond she continued. "So, tell me exactly what you found."

"There is a cave. He's in there, behind a waterfall."

"You actually saw where he lies?"

Leo nodded and freshened his drink. At this rate, he'd empty the bottle soon. Deciding that was the best idea he'd come up with in a long time, he abandoned his glass and grabbed the bottle around its neck then made his way over to one of the chairs for a sit. "Yeah, I saw him. Ugly bastard. All skin and bones, literally."

He barely repressed the shudder that tried to take his body at the memory of The Source lying on the rocks. "There is an issue."

Jara's eyes narrowed on him. "What's that?"

He took a swig from the bottle. "The bomb. We'll need extra time to get out of there after placing it."

"But you can do that, right?" Her blonde hair pushed away from her shoulders, a sure sign her anger was growing. When the sparks flew, he'd be a goner.

"Of course," he assured her. "It's just a pain to get in and out of there."

"Sergei," Jara called out.

Leo turned toward the door to the library, noticing for the first time they had company. *Damned bloodsucker.* They moved so quietly. You never knew when one lurked nearby. Hell, he'd almost missed the group that tracked him in the forest when he was hunting The Source. Luckily, just before he came to a river, he'd realized they were following him. He'd lost them in a cave which as it turned out inadvertently helped him to find The Source. Fate, it seemed, was with him today.

"I was just going to come get you." Jara crossed the floor, took the vampire's hand, and pulled him into the room. They sat on the settee.

Sergei appeared genuinely interested. "Why?"

"We have plans to make."

Jara spent thirty minutes selling her lies to Sergei and convincing him to accompany them to where The Source waited before she said, “So then, we are agreed. We shall leave this night. Why wait?”

Leo knew she wanted Sergei with them, so she could confirm that killing The Source immediately killed all other vampires. Like the proverbial canary in the coal mine, his death would signal death for others.

Sergei gave her a big smile and nodded. “I’d be happy to accompany you, Jara. I’ll go upstairs and change.”

Leo scrutinized the vampire as he ascended the stairs. Sergei seemed to agree a little too readily to come along. *Wonder what the bloodsucker has up his sleeve.* Leo silently vowed to keep an eye on the male.

“So, we’re all set,” Jara announced, clasping her hands together. “Leo go get the stuff we need for the expedition. The treasure awaits.”

****

Sergei materialized on the icy, snow-covered ground by the Siberian river. He’d pulled the location from Leo’s mind. Luckily, the demon had a knack for details, or he wouldn’t have been able to get here. Jara, Finn and Leo were a few steps ahead of him. His gaze fell to the white duffle bag Leo carried.

When the demon grabbed it at Jara’s home, Sergei’s preternatural sense of smell told him it contained explosives. Jara probably intended to use them to kill his sire and most likely him as well. He chuckled.

As if I’d allow that.

He didn’t doubt the treasure Jara referred to that waited for them would actually be his sire. If he bided his time, she'd lead him right to him. In the meantime, he'd continue to play dumb.

"Through here," Leo called before entering a cave.

One by one they bent at the waist to follow. When his eyes adjusted to the darkness, he realized they'd entered a long tunnel which smelled of musky earth. The rock walls were smooth as glass. It led to a large open area with a spring. Steam rose from the pool.

The group followed Leo around the hot spring to a long waterfall. It ran from the ceiling of the grotto down to the pool below, sending a fine mist over his skin.

"Back here," Leo announced, then disappeared behind the water.

Jara and Finn went next. Sergei wasn't used to being last, in fact, typically he led, but on this occasion, he reined in his natural tendencies and forced himself to stay back. Wait for the perfect moment.

He stepped behind the water to discover Leo pushing a large stone out of the way. *Another cave!*

Just how deep did this place go? How much farther until they found his sire? Anticipation tingled over his skin.

As if in answer to the unasked question, Leo stated, "In here."

When Sergei emerged through the opening, sparks shot from Jara's fingertips and ignited torches on the walls. Both Jara and Finn grabbed a torch from the sconces in which they rested and started down the rocky corridor. He noticed Leo refrained from holding one. It confirmed what Sergei already suspected, the white bag contained explosives.

"How much farther," Jara whined.

He barely kept from rolling his eyes.

"Only a little farther," Leo informed her, pushing on.

Sergei's heart rate increased. If his suppositions were correct, he'd be reunited with his sire in minutes, he felt sure of it. He fought to keep from showing his enthusiasm.

The corridor sloped downward. Water from the falls flowed around their feet and made the rock floor slick. The journey took longer than expected, but eventually, they arrived in what could best be described as a tomb.

The stone had been chipped away, leaving it rough and jagged. In the middle of the small room sat a dais, made from the rock in the grotto, and upon it lay a corpse in repose. The skeletal hands were crossed over its chest. Its flesh peeked out from holes in the rotting cloth. The pungent aroma of decomposition mixed with the mold on the rock. Knowing the decay was from his sire, the acerbic odor threatened to overwhelm him.

Sergei steeled himself against the stench. His sire needed him.

Jara approached, a malicious smile on her face. "I have a surprise for you."

After placing her torch in a sconce on the wall, she sauntered his way, coming to a stop just in front of him. Before he realized her intent, she snapped a set of handcuffs around both his wrists. White tendrils of smoke wafted from his skin where it burned from the contact with the titanium cuffs. A hiss of pain left his lips, and he bared his fangs at the bitch. He quickly snapped a mental barrier into place to block most of the pain.

"There. Now you can't go disappearing on me." She had the audacity to turn her back on him. "Finn, watch him while Leo and I get things ready."

Before the prick moved, Sergei pulled the gun from the pocket of his cargo pants and put his arms around Jara's head. The cuffs contained just enough slack to allow him to get one hand around her neck while the other held the gun pointed at her head.

She let out a scream that echoed in the room, and both her cohorts turned to face them with identical looks of horror on their faces.

"Don't move," Sergei growled, "or I'll kill her."

"You won't dare." Finn took a step toward them.

He tightened his grip on her neck and turned the weapon on Finn. "I could snap her neck and put a round between your eyes in the same instant."

Jara's form wavered in his grasp but did not disappear. "What the…"

"Trying to dematerialize, Jara?" He heard her gasp for air and loosened his grip just enough to allow her to breathe. He needed her alive, at least for a little while longer.

Leo wavered next but remained solidly where he stood. "Why can't we dematerialize?"

Was that panic in the demon's voice? *Good.*

"Did Jara forget to tell you? Or perhaps she didn't bother to read enough of the tome."

"What are you talking about?" Jara choked out.

"Your ancestors put a spell on this room. No one can materialize in or out. It was one of the protections they put in place to keep my sire locked away."

"You read the *Tome of Necromancy*?" Jara's tone sounded almost accusatory. "But how?"

"You can't keep secrets from me. Did you really think I'd let you kill my sire? I believe you call him The Source."

Jara stiffened.

"How did you figure out our plan?" Finn asked, the disbelief plain to see on his face.

Sergei wasn't going to waste time explaining things. He'd seen enough movies to know people's plans always went to shit when they started spouting at the mouth.

"Leo, put the bag down." He waved the gun in the large demon's general direction. "Slow and easy."

After Leo complied, Sergei moved to the body, taking Jara with him. He glanced down, laying eyes on Eldrick for the first time in centuries. Translucent skin clung to bones. Cheekbones and teeth pushed from his face. Once full and handsome, his sire's face now appeared drawn, skin taut against the skull. The thick muscles that used to cover his body were long gone. His flesh so pale, to describe it as ghostly did not quite do it justice. Eldrick's heart did not beat though Sergei was sure he was not dead.

His clothes lay over parts of his flesh with large holes from the decay. So little remained, Sergei could not tell exactly what he'd been wearing when he was brought here, but it appeared mostly black with a little tan.

Sergei's stomach twisted at the sight.

"Awaken him," Sergei demanded, giving Jara a shake.

"I can't. I don't know how."

"You lie!" Sergei turned the gun toward her face. "Awaken him or I'll kill you."

"Then how would you reverse the spell? You need me."

"I'll have one of them do it." Sergei gestured at Leo, then Finn with the weapon.

"Only I'm powerful enough to break this spell. They can't do it."

Her voice sounded calm, and Sergei couldn't help but be a little impressed at her composure. "Very well, do it, and I'll let you live."

"You expect me to believe you'll let me walk out of here, just like that, if I awaken the Source?"

As if I'd ever allow that. "I give you my word."

He shoved Jara's head directly over his sire's and placed the gun to the back of her head. "Do it, now!"

****

Jara braced her hands on either side of the corpse's skull as the barrel of the gun jabbed painfully against her head. She couldn't dematerialize. She certainly couldn't fight her way out of this. The two demons with her were no help. They just stood there, staring.

She had no choice. She'd have to bring the monster back to life. She could only hope that he'd be too weak to do any harm before she found a way to kill him.

"Fine," she capitulated. "But I need your blood."

Sergei released the hold on the back of her neck and stepped away. Jara straightened and turned to discover his gun pointed squarely at her chest.

"Take these cuffs off me."

"The key is in Leo's bag."

"Fine," Sergei ground out between clenched teeth. "Leo, unzip the bag, slowly, and bring Jara the key."

After the sound of the zipper sliding open and some rustling, Leo pushed the key into her hand.

"Careful," he whispered.

Oh, she'd be careful all right, careful to make sure this bastard died along with his sire when this ended.

After removing the cuffs from his wrists, she handed them and the key to Leo. "There, happy?"

"Not yet," Sergei replied, twirling one wrist. "Now, get to it."

"I need your blood."

"How much?" Sergei stepped back slightly but kept the gun trained on her head.

"Enough to fill his mouth."

Together, they strolled back to the body. Jara stood on one side while the vampire stood on the other. Sergei scored his wrist with his fangs, then placed it over The Source's mouth. In seconds, the wounds healed.

"That's not enough," Jara informed the bloodsucker.

"I know." Sergei again bit into his wrist.

The vampire repeated the process multiple times as his wrist continued to heal. It gave her immense pleasure to watch him maul himself over and over in order to get enough blood in The Source's mouth.

Before their eyes, the corpse became less translucent. His body remained skeletally thin, but his skin became less like tissue paper and more the consistency of newsprint. His eyes no longer protruded but melded back into their sockets, and his cheeks pushed away from his teeth.

"Awaken him," demanded Sergei. Excitement lit his eyes. "Do it. Do it now!"

When Jara hesitated, Sergei backhanded her face with his gun hand. The butt of the weapon opened a gash on her cheek, sending searing pain through her body. Her hand covered the wound, and she fought to rein in the anger at the blow.

Energy within built, thrumming through her body. The tips of her fingers tingled from the current. Her hair pushed away from her head, the roots standing on end.

Sergei leveled the gun at her face, squarely between her eyes. "Don't even think about zapping me."

Jara fought her body, willing the angry energy to calm, telling herself she'd get the chance later to evaporate this bloodsucker and, if she was lucky, his sire too. She took several deep breaths until at last the thrumming settled to a dull tingle throughout her body, and her hair settled over her shoulders.

"Stand back," Jara commanded.

"I don't think so," Sergei growled.

"I can't think with you hovering over me, threatening me."

Sergei took a small step back. "Awaken him."

Awaken him, awaken him. Her mind taunted her by mimicking his words. Could the bloodsucker think of nothing else to say?

She could stall no longer. She must do the spell. Jara hoped afterward she'd have an opportunity to right this wrong. To unleash The Source on the world would be a travesty too grave to contemplate. But for now, she saw no other options.

"White is the color of bone and ash. I speak to the dead to break the fast. Red is the color of blood and death." She ran her hands over the body. "I rub the bones and give them breath. Black is the color of crypt and womb. I bid you now, rise from this tomb."

No one moved. It was as if everyone forgot to breathe.

When The Source didn't stir, Sergei leaned closer and peered down on the body. "What happened? Why isn't he awake?"

Jara shrugged and shook her head. "I don't know."

"Maybe he needs more blood," Finn offered from across the room.

Sergei turned a hateful stare on Jara. "Maybe you didn't do the spell correctly."

Anger flared, making her cheeks red-hot. "I did the proper spell. I might have skimmed through the majority of the *Tome of Necromancy*, but I read the part with the spell multiple times. I recited it correctly. Maybe your blood isn't…"

The body on the dais rose in a fluid movement and stood next to Sergei. The Source reached out his arm and cupped Sergei's cheek. Time froze.

Jara blinked, and The Source disappeared.

A scream from behind her brought Jara out of her stupor. She turned in time to see Finn crumple. The Source followed his body to the floor, attached to his neck. In horror, Jara watched Finn become a shell. His body transformed to a husk of skin, the muscles and bones gone, as The Source drained him not only of blood but of his very marrow.

The Source's head snapped up; blood dripped from his mouth. His body filled out before her eyes. No longer skin over bones, he now sported muscles, defined muscles that flexed while he stood. His blood-red eyes locked on Jara, and she experienced true horror for the first time.

Her heart kicked up. She forgot how to breathe and

stood paralyzed whether from terror or a nefarious source she couldn't be sure which. It didn't matter. She wasn't going anywhere.

Leo turned on his heels and ran for the corridor. In a blur, The Source landed on his back and wrapped his body around the demon. The bloodsucker latched onto Leo's neck, and Jara closed her eyes.

The slurping and gnawing noises grated on her ears. She didn't want to chance a glance at Leo. She assumed his was a similar fate to Finn's. Only when the noise stopped did she open her eyes.

Leo's empty body lay lifeless on the ground. The Source stood over him, wiping Leo from his mouth with the back of his hand. His body now appeared whole. Defined muscles peeked through the holes in his clothes. They rippled under creamy skin when he carefully flexed and stretched each one as if trying them on for size. His crimson eyes alighted on her. A shiver skated down her spine. Panic lodged in her belly twisting it until bile rose in her throat.

Sergei took a knee, his forearm resting on the bended knee, his head bowed reverently. "Sire, I await your command."

Jara's mind raced. Her eyes darted from Sergei to The Source. The old human saying came to mind. "If you can't beat them, join them."

Jara dropped to one knee, mimicking Sergei's stance. "I too await your command."

As The Source approached, evil permeated the space. It engulfed her with its oily presence. She fought the urge to run, to look up, instead she forced her body to remain motionless, waiting to see what he would do.

In the corner of her vision, she witnessed his hand

pet Sergei's head. "My dear Sergei."

Jara expected his voice to sound gravelly, misused. Instead, it sounded deep and rich, like a velvet purr. It wrapped around her, enveloping her in its seductiveness. She wanted to lean into it, touch it. Let it touch and caress her. Let *him* take her, use her.

The man wasn't exactly ugly to look at. He sported a handsome appearance, with high Slavic cheekbones and a thick neck that led to broad shoulders. His black hair, a bit stringy from centuries of not being washed, hung to his waist, swaying when he walked in a hypnotic way that made her want to reach out and touch it.

The next second all longing for the creature subsided as he lifted Sergei from the hard ground with one hand around his neck. Sergei's toes dangled in the air.

"Master! Sire, please," the vampire choked out. To his credit, he hung limp in his sire's grip. He didn't struggle or fight the deadly hold. Jara couldn't imagine the self-control it took to accomplish that. He must have realized any struggling from him would meet with swift retribution.

"How could you allow them to do that to me?" The Source demanded.

Sergei tried to respond, but without air, the words did not come. The Source released his grip, dropping the vampire to the ground. Sergei immediately resumed the submissive position.

Bowing his head, he replied, "For centuries, I searched high and low. I killed and tortured countless people trying to find you. I did everything possible. But I didn't know her kind had done this to you."

Jara's blood ran cold. The sonuvabitch just threw her under the bus. She felt a hot stare on her. *What should I do? What can I say to come out of this alive?*

"I can give you an army," she blurted out desperately.

Oh hell. Now I've *done it.*

She didn't have an army. In fact, Finn and Leo had been her last two guards. She risked a glance at The Source to see if he seemed interested. Curiosity stared back in his eyes.

"You think I have need of an army, pretty one?"

Pretty? Jara keyed in on the word immediately.

Did he find her attractive? She'd used her looks before to get her way. Could she do so now to get out of this situation?

"I-I…" Jara swallowed the stammer and cleared her dry throat. "I only meant a being of your greatness must intend to rule the world. I could help you achieve that."

His finger hooked her chin, forcing her to tip her head back and meet his eyes. He gave her face a thorough perusal before speaking.

"Stand," he commanded, lifting her from the ground with his finger still under her chin.

She complied, the memory of Sergei dangling from his hand playing in her mind. He looked upon her, taking his time to circle her body as his eyes traversed every inch of her. They burned a hot path over her skin.

She stood stone still, allowing him to look his fill. He stopped in front of her and clutched her chin in a firm grip. His touch repulsed and excited her at the same time. He was evil incarnate. It radiated off him to coat her skin, but he was also the most powerful being she'd ever encountered, and one thing that attracted her was power.

His head bent to hers, his lips heading for her cheek. His tongue laved over the wound Sergei caused, and she trembled.

"Delicious." He pulled back.

"Sire, this woman—"

The Source lifted his hand and placed his palm out in the universal sign for stop.

The being slammed into her mind with such force only his will kept her standing. He raped her memories, brutally sorting through them, discarding the less interesting ones. He plundered all her innermost secrets, exposing them, ripping through them one by one. Images of Varrick's training, the demon tomes, scripture, and stories told to her as a child, all were his to take.

He witnessed the deaths, the births, and all the times she lied. He left nothing hidden, exposing her every desire and want as the pressure in her head built until she believed she would die.

Instead of death, it was The Source who released her. When he pulled from her mind, her body sank to the ground. Unable to hold herself up, she lay on the cool rocky surface, breathing hard from the excruciating pain in her head.

What would he do now that he'd seen her deceptive ways? Would he kill her, suck her bones like the guards?

Too weak to speak, she did the only thing she could, lie there waiting for him to do something. She didn't have to wait long.

"Sergei, help Jara up. We have work to do."

"But, sire. Surely, you don't mean to bring her with us."

"She has many skills which will come in handy."

"I brought her for your sustenance, your use."

He brought me? Has Sergei been playing me this whole time?

Jara's heartbeat raced. Her palms became sweaty. If only she possessed the strength, she'd zap the bloodsucker.

"And use her I shall." The Source ran his hand down her hair.

Chapter 17

Pain ripped through Natasha's back like a sword slicing through her flesh. She cried out, as her hand flew to her lower back. She breathed through the agony, air puffing through her lips in thick exhales.

"What's wrong?" Julie asked.

"It's nothing," Tasha lied, not wanting to alarm Julie. She rubbed her back. "I must have slept wrong. It's just some more back pain."

"I didn't know vampires could get back pain."

They stood in Nicholai's spacious kitchen surrounded by Italian maple cabinets. Natasha leaned forward on the wide island, resting her forearms on the marble countertops.

Julie pulled a pitcher of orange juice from the stainless-steel refrigerator and poured them both a glass. As she handed one to Tasha, her phone rang. Natasha glanced at the caller ID before she answered.

"Hi, Harleigh."

"Natasha, I'm so glad you answered. Are you okay?"

"I'm fine why?"

"You aren't in any pain?"

Male voices carried over the line in the background. Though she could not make out exactly what they said, they sounded hurried, anxious.

"Who's with you?" Natasha asked.

Julie straightened her shoulders, a concerned look took her face. Natasha smiled to reassure her sister-in-law.

"Just my cousin and a few…you didn't answer me. Are you all right?"

Her back spasmed, making her gasp. Julie's lips pursed with her concern.

"Do you want to lie down?" Julie whispered, worry audible in her voice.

Natasha decided if she had to be stuck in hiding, there were much worse people she could be stuck with. Julie's kind, honey-brown eyes radiated a genuine warmth. Her brother was fortunate to have found someone as sweet and pretty as Julie.

Natasha shook her head at her sister-in-law. Between Harleigh and Juliette, she felt like the only patient in a hospital. "Harleigh, I am—"

The pain that struck her back took her voice and dropped her to her knees on the hard marble floor.

"Tasha? Tasha?" Harleigh called through the phone as Julie ran around the island to her side.

Nicholai's mate knelt next to Natasha, put her arm around her shoulders. "Natasha, is it your back again?"

"Natasha? Tasha answer me? Hello?"

When the pain finally started to subside, Natasha raised the phone back to her ear and looked at Julie when she spoke. "I-I don't know what's wrong."

"Have you been having these pains long?" Harleigh asked.

"Since last night."

Julie helped her stand. She leaned on the counter for support as yet another wave washed over her.

"Are they coming more frequently?" Harleigh

inquired.

Natasha breathed through the pain, unable to speak.

Julie pulled Natasha's arm around her shoulders. "You need to lie down."

"Tasha, are the pains coming more frequently?" Harleigh asked again when Natasha didn't respond.

"Yes, they are."

"How many minutes apart?"

Julie steered them for the stairs.

"Every few minutes now."

"Natasha, I think you are having the baby," Harleigh said.

"What do you mean? This isn't contractions, Harleigh."

"Have you never heard of back labor?"

Natasha's foot did not quite lift high enough to clear the next stair, and she stumbled. "No. Besides, he's not due yet."

The alarm in her voice made Julie's eyes snap to her.

"You're having the baby?" Julie asked, having obviously heard enough of the conversation to piece together what Harleigh said. "We have to let Nicholai and Vladimir know."

"Don't you dare say anything to Nicholai. I'm not having the baby. It's too soon. I'm not due for another two months."

They continued their ascension.

"Natasha," Harleigh said, "I really think you are in labor."

"My back hurts, not my stomach. I can't be in labor."

"You may be having back labor," Julie commented

as they stepped onto the second-floor landing. "When my friend Penny had her baby, the pain radiated in her back."

Natasha grimaced. Apparently, everyone knew about back labor except for her.

"Tasha, hang on. I'm on my way." Harleigh announced in an authoritative tone.

"I'm not in Australia," Natasha informed her friend.

"Neither am I. I'll be right there."

The line went dead. Before Natasha could wonder what Harleigh meant, she materialized next to her and Julie. Both women screamed when the petite woman with elfin features and bright purple hair solidified.

Natasha sent her senses out to discover what Harleigh was. When she sensed a blank spot, she recoiled in fright.

"You're a demon." Natasha flung the harsh accusation at the woman she'd thought of as a friend.

Harleigh put up her hands as if surrendering. "I know. It's okay."

Tasha moved, standing between Harleigh and her sister-in-law. If Harleigh wanted to hurt them, she'd have to go through Natasha to get to Julie.

"What do you mean 'it's okay'? It's not okay. You're a *demon.*" Understanding dawned, and Natasha's eyes narrowed on her supposed friend. "Wait. You know what I am."

Harleigh nodded. "I know you are a vampire."

"Were you the one following me?"

"What are you talking about?"

"I sensed a demon. It was stalking me. *You* were stalking me."

"What?" Harleigh shook her head. "I never stalked you."

Natasha's mind replayed the events of the past few weeks, and she realized that most of the time Harleigh had been with her when she sensed the blank spots. They couldn't have been Harleigh, but what if she'd been working with another demon?

"If you weren't stalking me, then who was?"

Harleigh's eyebrows narrowed. "I don't know what you mean."

Understanding clicked into place like the buckle of a carnival safety bar. "You are working with that wolf I kept seeing!"

Harleigh staggered back as if the accusation struck a physical blow, shaking her head. "I swear to you, Tasha, I am not plotting against you. I admit knowing the wolf you kept seeing, but I didn't realize you thought he was stalking you. He's actually a decent enough guy who was hanging around to make sure *I* was safe. He wasn't there to harm…"

Another sharp pain stole Natasha's breath. Julie stepped around to her side. "We don't have time for this, ladies. Natasha needs to lie down."

"You're having the child," Harleigh informed her. "I can help."

Natasha's hand protectively covered her stomach. "Stay away from my baby. We know what the demons have been doing to vampires. I know what your kind did to my cousin. Get out of my brother's house before I summon him to kill you."

Tears welled in Harleigh's eyes. "Natasha, I don't know what you are talking about. What have demons been doing to vampires? What do you mean? I'd never hurt you or the baby. I just want to help. You are my friend."

"I don't believe you."

Demons had done terrible things to Demetri, unspeakable things. She just wanted to live in peace, have this baby in peace.

"You can trust me, Tasha."

The look in Harleigh's eyes bespoke of love and genuine concern. For now, it was enough to convince Natasha of her authenticity, but before Natasha could voice her acceptance, another pain struck her, and her knees went weak.

Harleigh rushed to her other side, and together she and Julie helped her into the nearest bedroom. The room was a winter wonderland of cream, white, and celadon. The colors were used interchangeably in the romantic room, anchored by a custom velvet sleigh bed. Not the best place to birth a child, but Natasha definitely needed a place to lie down at the moment.

"Breathe like this," Harleigh commanded after they got her onto the bed. Harleigh made a series of *hee* sounds as short breaths hissed from between her teeth.

Natasha mimicked the breathing, grateful when her pain began to subside. Julie disappeared, returning shortly with a handful of towels.

"Do you have a doctor?" Harleigh asked.

Julie placed the stack on the bed. "Who should we call?"

"No one. I have no specific doctor. I intended to find one, but I haven't had time."

Harleigh looked at Juliette. "Then I guess it's up to us." She rolled up the sleeves of her striped shirt.

"Do I need to boil some water?" Julie asked.

"No," Natasha informed her. "Vampire, remember. No problem with infections. No reason to boil anything."

She did the short pants again when another round of pain lanced across her back.

"The baby is coming fast." Harleigh started to remove Tasha's clothes. "Get me a sheet we can use as a drape and a blanket to wrap the baby in."

Julie ran from the room like fire chased her.

Natasha grabbed Harleigh's wrists and looked deep into her eyes. "Why are you helping me?"

"You are my friend, Tasha."

"But you are a demon."

"And you are a vampire. So what?"

"So, demons hate vampires."

"Well, this demon doesn't."

It went against everything she'd heard from Demetri and Nicholai. Demons were supposed to despise vampires. They tortured Demetri and caused countless deaths of others of her breed, but Tasha could not deny the sincerity in Harleigh's eyes.

"Are you really here to help me?"

"Of course. You're my best mate. You don't think I'd let you have this baby without me, do you?"

Natasha relaxed her hold, and Harleigh resumed helping her disrobe. "It's early. My baby will be small."

"But he'll live." The conviction in Harleigh's voice made Tasha's eyes snap to hers.

"How do you know that?"

"The same way I knew you were in labor." Harleigh pulled Natasha's slacks from her legs. "I had a vision."

Slightly out of breath, Juliette returned, holding an

arm full of cloth. “I wasn’t sure how many sheets and blankets, so I brought all I found.”

Harleigh smiled. “Those should be enough.”

She grabbed a sheet and draped it over Natasha just as another contraction hit. Tasha’s vision blurred. This was bad, much stronger than the previous pains. Something was wrong.

“The baby,” Tasha cried.

Harleigh took her hand and lowered her face right above Natasha’s, forcing her to stare into her eyes. “I swear to you your baby will be fine. I’ve seen it. He survives the birth.”

Julie maneuvered around to the opposite side of the bed and put a bowl on the bedside table. After wringing out the washcloth within, she patted Natasha’s head. The cool, gentle touch of the cloth calmed her, and Tasha found herself believing Harleigh. Of course, their son would be fine. He had Vlad’s genes after all.

“What else did you see, Harleigh?” Julie placed the washcloth back in the basin.

Harleigh straightened and glanced nervously between Julie and Tasha. “Let’s just concentrate on having this baby for now.”

Natasha anchored Harleigh’s wrist in a firm grip. “What else did you see?”

Harleigh tried to pull away, but Natasha refused to allow it.

“Tell me, Harleigh,” she gritted out between clenched teeth as the next contraction hit.

“I saw you pushing for all you’re worth. Now let’s get to it.”

****

Vladimir wound between the trees, staying behind

the group. Stephan, Demetri, Tatiana, and Nicholai trekked ahead, while he and Desmond brought up the rear. They headed toward the grotto to see if they could pick up any trace of the demon. Loud cuffing drew his attention.

Hello, dear Mishka, Vlad sent into the mind of the head of the pride. The tigers stalked behind them, ready to assist the group if need be. *Be watchful, my friend. We may have need of you.*

Vlad sensed the reply from Mishka. They were willing to help the Alphas hunt. In fact, anticipation from the pride flowed over him. They enjoyed the hunt, wanted a fight. Their front teeth contained sensors which could detect a pulse and help them locate a main artery in their prey. They wanted to use those sensors, feel the beat of a strong pulse before sinking their teeth into fresh meat.

Vlad noted how similar their longing was to his. He'd love nothing better than to be sinking his teeth into his mate as he sank into the heat of her body, but that would have to wait. His duty to his breed, to the Alphas, must come first tonight. There would be plenty of time to indulge in his personal fantasies later.

The snow-covered ground crunched under their booted feet, and the chilled breeze stung his exposed face. The temperature had dropped significantly. A deep inhale of the night air brought information. The scent of the pines mixed with that of his fellow Alphas and the tigers. Each unique smell was a familiar reminder of the friends, places, and animals he cared about.

When they crested the hill, Nicholai stopped suddenly. The expression on his face told Vlad something must be wrong long before he spoke.

"It is Natasha," he announced to the group, turning to face Vlad. "Julie just informed me my sister is having the babe."

Tasha, Vladimir sent over their link. *You are in labor? It is too early.*

The force of her pain came across their mindlink, making him nauseous.

Our son is like his father. Everything on his time, not others.

He must be with her, be there for the birth of his child, duty be damned. *I'm coming.*

The next contraction came across their link, this one lasting longer than the last. It buckled his legs, and he landed on the cold ground. His hand rested on his bent knees to support his weight. He concentrated hard and bore as much of the pain as Tasha would allow, wanting to spare her from feeling the brunt of it. As soon as the contraction eased, he'd dematerialize to Nicholai's home.

As the pain started to recede, his world spun. Colors around him blurred and shifted, changing from snow-white to cave-dark.

Ah Vlad, my son. I see you have come to join us for our family reunion. His sire's voice oozed through his mind leaving a noxious, oily film. With his mind fragmented by Natasha's pain and communicating through two mindlinks at the same time, Vlad could not stop Sergei from delving into his memories.

So good of you to join us and just when you are going to add a son to our ranks.

Sergei rifled through more memories. *Ahhhh, a mate. Congratulations, Vladimir. Too bad she won't be able to join us, but your son will make a nice addition to our group.*

Don't listen to him, Vlad, Natasha sent.

My dearest Vladimir, I am your sire. You must obey me.

No longer! Vladimir sent back. *I no longer serve you.*

We'll see. Especially when I hold the life of your mate and your child in my hands once more.

Rage filled his body, his hand fisted on his knees, nails digging into his flesh until the smell of his own blood filled his nose. Never again would the bastard who sired him have the opportunity to harm those he loved.

Sheer determination forced his legs to hold his weight when he rose to his full height. Just as his form started to waver, the sight of three people emerging from the grotto stayed his attempt to dematerialize to Natasha.

"Who the hell is that?" Stephan asked.

Vlad recognized one of the people immediately. "The male with the short brown hair and beady eyes in back is Sergei Mitrović."

"Your sire?" Stephan asked.

As the leader of the Alphas, Stephan was the one person Vlad confided in regarding his history. It was part of the requirement for being recruited. Stephan demanded access to each person's memories before inviting them to be on the Alpha Council.

Vladimir nodded. "I must kill him. He has threatened Natasha and our child. I cannot allow him to escape."

"He knows where to find her?" Nicholai shot Vlad

a concerned glance.

Demetri moved between his mate and the threat below. “Be cautious. The woman is a demon.”

“You mean the one who kidnapped and tortured you?” Tatiana pushed around Demetri. “Let’s get them.”

Demetri stepped in front of her, took her by the shoulders, and the look on his face told Vlad they were having an in-depth conversation through their mindlink. But he couldn’t care less about the personal dynamics between the two. Tatiana shouldn’t be going into battle for she was a female, a treasured member of their society, and no doubt, Demetri believed the same.

Vlad would never allow Natasha to put herself in harm’s way. He’d do anything to make sure she remained safe—including missing the birth of his child to ensure her safety.

“Nicholai, will you go home and be with your sister until I can get there?” Vlad asked.

Nicholai turned to face him. “What are you going to do?”

“I’m going to kill my sire and the people with him.”

Nicholai’s amber eyes narrowed, looking very much like his sister’s. “I want to stay and fight.”

“Vlad is right, cousin. Someone should go and protect Natasha and Juliette. We will take care of the threat here, then Vladimir can join you in time to see his son born, for we should be able to take out these three easily.”

“Five against three hardly seems like a fair fight,” Desmond chimed in with his thick British accent.

Nicholai’s eyes darted to the woman and two men

below then back at Vladimir. A nod of his head was his only reply before his form coalesced in on itself and he disappeared.

Tasha, Nicholai is coming.

He's here, Vlad. Where are you? When will you be here?

I must take care of something first. But I will see you soon.

*You better make it very soon if you want to see the birth of your...*The rest of her thought stopped when another contraction came across the link. Vlad again absorbed as much of it as possible to ease her pain. Perspiration broke out on his forehead.

Sergei was older, stronger. He'd need to be at his full strength and concentration to finish things between them once and for all. As much as he'd like to keep the link with his mate open and shoulder her pain, he needed to close it off for now, so he could concentrate on the upcoming battle.

I understand, Vlad. Go kill the murderer. The pain isn't so bad. I can take it.

I'll come to you as soon as it is over to help you through the labor.

I know you'll be here soon. It's okay. Don't worry. I've got this. Go. Take care of Sergei so our baby will be safe. I love you.

His heart swelled in his chest at her words. He sensed the truth behind them as she sent her love through their link. It gave him strength, filled him with purpose.

He closed off their link, sliding a mental barrier firmly in place to shield them both.

His eyes met Stephan's. The Alpha stood in his

black camo pants, his long black hair pulled back in a leather thong, looking very much like a male used to being in charge. But as far as Vlad was concerned, this was *his* fight. If the other Alphas wanted to join in, fine, but they better stay out of his way because he was gunning for one man and no one better interfere.

Stephan stepped toward the group. "Demetri, you and I will take the male with the stringy hair, Desmond and Vlad, take Sergei, and Tatiana, that leaves the woman to you."

"I've been wanting to kick that demon's ass ever since we found Demetri." A grin took Tatiana's face as she punched a fist into the opposite hand. "I can't wait to kill that bitch."

Demetri turned. "You will not—"

"Do not finish that sentence, Romanoff, or it will be your ass I kick instead of that demon's."

"We are wasting time."

Vlad didn't wait to find out how Demetri would handle his mate. With blurring speed, he rushed over the crest of the hill and materialized right behind the threesome just as a large male Vlad didn't know, with blond hair, red eyes, and a five o'clock shadow materialized next to him.

The man was large, taller than Vlad by about an inch, and thicker. He carried himself with an air of arrogance.

"Who the hell are you?" Vlad asked.

"Varrick?" the female demon called out.

The stranger looked in her direction. "Jara, I see you've made some new friends."

Sergei rounded on Vlad, an evil grin played over his thin lips. "So, you have come to meet your grandfather."

"What are you talking about?" Vlad asked.

"Why, Eldrick, of course."

"Varrick, you must leave. This is The Source," the female demon sputtered.

The large male with stringy, black hair turned toward Vlad. The weight of his stare settled over the warrior. Immediately, pressure squeezed his chest, robbing his lungs of oxygen. The male's power tingled over Vlad's skin in stinging bites.

The man called Varrick pulsed with his own power. His eyes became a deeper red. His blond hair stood away from his thick face that had become more beast-like. A corona of blue light glowed around him as he gathered energy.

In the next second, all hell broke loose. Varrick and Eldrick let their power flow at the same instant. The waves met in the middle of the group in an explosion that sent all but the two who released the power to the ground.

Energy poured over the group. Vlad's skin burned from the contact. Another man materialized. He sensed three blank spots and realized not only were Jara and Varrick demons, but this new male was one as well.

Stephan, Desmond, Demetri, and Tatiana lay on the ground. Tatiana was out cold with Demetri trying to revive her. Desmond helped Stephan to his feet then stuck out a hand to Vlad.

His eyes traveled between Varrick and Eldrick. They seemed evenly matched, and both were more powerful than anyone he'd ever come up against.

Impressive, isn't he? Sergei sent through their mindlink. *You should bow at his feet, so he might let you live.*

I'll never bow to him.

Pity. I never stopped loving you, Vladimir. Never stopped wanting you.

Sergei left Eldrick's side and circled Vlad. The Alpha made sure to follow, never allowing Sergei out of his line of vision as Stephan and Desmond went after Eldrick. His focus on Sergei, Vlad barely noticed when Varrick and the other demon attacked Jara.

The world narrowed to just his sire. Vlad focused, waiting for the opportunity to strike. A loud roar flowed over the land. Sergei looked in the direction from which it came. It was the opportunity Vlad needed.

He leapt forward, his fist connected hard with Sergei's jaw. The blow snapped his head to the side. Vlad's other fist landed solidly in his sire's abdominals, bending him at the waist as the punch forced the air from his lungs.

A body flew between them. Demetri's. His fellow Alpha hit the ground hard and rolled to his feet in a fighting stance. He leapt over Sergei and rejoined the battle.

Sergei launched and caught Vlad in a fierce bear-hug. His ribs cracked under the pressure. One punctured his right lung, and he struggled for breath. Pain blurred his vision for a moment. Arms trapped to his side, Vlad only had one option. The warrior amassed all the power he could, reared his head back, and hit Sergei's nose with his forehead. It was enough to lessen his sire's grip. Vlad broke free of Sergei's hold, then staggered away. Blood streamed down his sire's face, his eyes immediately swelled black and blue.

"You'll pay for that." Sergei wiped the blood from

his face with the back of his hand, leaving a red smear.

"Not if you pay first." Vlad kicked out and swiped Sergei's legs out from under him.

When the bastard landed on the frozen ground, Vlad fell on him, his knees landing on either side of Sergei's stomach. Vlad pummeled the vampire, throwing blow after blow until his face was so badly crushed, it no longer appeared human. Only the shock of the intense sting that struck his back stopped the blows.

Vlad bowed under the excruciating pain. It seared his body, burning white-hot. He lifted from his sire, held suspended in midair by an unseen force that wrapped around him in a suffocating grip. With audible cracks, his bones snapped from the pressure. Something poured from his nostrils, his tongue darted out to discover blood.

Pressure built in his ears until they burst. The world muted. Something warm oozed down the sides of his face. Higher and higher he rose until suddenly the throttling pain left, and with it, so too did the energy. He plummeted to the ground and bounced twice from the force of the fall. Multiple bones shattered, his arm dislocated. Pain flooded from his ankles to his back as his legs collapsed under the pressure of his body hitting the frozen ground feet first.

"Thank you, Master." Sergei called out before he hobbled over to where Vlad lay panting from his pain.

"This will hurt me more than it will you, my son." Sergei stood over him, the dagger in his hands poised over Vlad's heart. "Well, on second thought, maybe not."

Sergei plunged the dagger into Vlad's chest.

Chapter 18

Horror gripped Desmond's throat when Vlad's sire pushed a dagger into his heart. The sound of splashing water drew his gaze from the gruesome sight. The Alpha turned to see a pride of tigers swimming toward the mêlée, ready to join the battle. The chaotic scene erupted in a flurry of movement.

As the tigers emerged from the river, Tatiana revived. With her safety assured, Demetri turned to help Stephan engage Eldrick. Desmond knew he and Demetri could take on the large vampire. Stephan's healing abilities, however, were needed elsewhere.

"Stephan, Vlad needs your help," he yelled and ran toward Demetri.

The female demon was surrounded by her kind. Two male demons circled her with clenched fists. Her hair pushed away from her head, and short streams of blue electricity crackled from her fingertips.

"Jara, don't you dar—" The large demon's comment was hushed by Tatiana joining the fight against Jara. She tackled the female from behind, took her to the ground while the two males closed in. The tigers surrounded the group of demons, and Desmond had only a second to spare of concern for Tatiana's safety before he reached Eldrick.

Just as he threw a right hook, Demetri jumped on Eldrick's back, wrapping his arms and legs around the vampire's body. He grabbed the male's head and wrenched it to the side. The large male dematerialized out of Demetri's grasp, then reappeared next to the demonic huddle.

He sent his energy out in a powerful blast. Tatiana, Varrick, and the other male demon went flying. The tigers tumbled over the ground in a mass of white fur and paws.

"Cyrus," the large demon called, just as Demetri yelled, "Tatiana!"

Both men rushed to the sides of their fallen partners as Stephan reached Vladimir to aid him. Desmond turned on Eldrick. The vampire helped the female demon to stand. Desmond took a step toward the pair, gathering his power to him. A wicked grin came over Eldrick's face, and he wrapped an arm around the female demon. She appeared weary, scared. A pained scream left her lips as their forms melted together then shrank in on themselves. They vanished in a blink.

Astonishment widened his eyes. He'd never seen anything like it. Had Eldrick dematerialized with the demon? He didn't know of any vampire who could force another to dematerialize.

He turned in time to witness Stephan grab Sergei by the head. The Alpha pulled him from Vlad, then ripped his head from his shoulders. The rending of sinew and flesh sounded in the night air. His body slumped to the side, then fell lifelessly to the ground. The tigers encircled the body as a unit, hunger in their eyes.

A violent scream poured from Vlad's open mouth. His face contorted as if his soul had been ripped from his body. Desmond surmised the end of his maker caused the outburst. *Poor bugger, to experience that pain on top of all those injuries.* Desmond wouldn't wish that on his worst enemy.

It spurred Stephan into action. He returned to Vladimir and ran his hands over his wounds. A yellow light radiated from his palms. Vlad turned away from the light. His gaze locked with Desmond's.

"Go to Natasha. Make sure she is all right."

Desmond stepped closer. Blood covered the ground below Vlad's body, staining the pure snow crimson. "You're going to go to her. Stephan will fix you up good as new."

Vlad's heartbeat stuttered. The wounded man shook his head from side to side. His voice sounded weaker when next he spoke. "I must know she is all right. I don't have the strength to forge a mindlink. I've lost too much blood."

"Don't waste your breath talking," Stephan admonished. "Shut up so I can concentrate. You have so many damned injuries."

His hands glowed brighter.

Desmond glanced over at Demetri and Tatiana who stood talking to the two male demons. They did not seem to be in any danger at the moment. Vlad grunted as his hand shot out to wrap around Desmond's ankle in a weak grip. Their eyes met, Vlad's silent request on his face

"I'll go. I'll go."

Their gaze held for an instant before Vladimir's lids closed, and a heavy sigh left his slack mouth. Desmond heard Stephan utter a string of curses before he dematerialized.

Desmond materialized on the fir-patterned parquet

floor in the foyer of Nicholai's home. A deep woof echoed in the space. Desmond glanced in the direction of the noise in time to see Juliette's dog, Connor, trotting toward him, tail wagging.

Kneeling down, he took the Irish wolfhound's huge head between his hands and gave it a shake. "Long time no see, my good man."

Connor's tongue darted out and slobbered a wet kiss from chin to scalp.

"Ugh!" the Alpha groaned, then wiped away the spit. "I'm going to have a see if Julie will teach you some manners. Speaking of your owner, where is she, boy?"

Desmond rose and looked up the double winding staircase spread before him. A feminine yell echoed through the halls. Crystals shivered in the chandelier above his head.

With Connor hot on his heels, Desmond took the stairs two at a time, following the sound of excited voices down a long hall. He paused before an open door to observe the chaos within while Connor barreled in and lay beside the bed.

His friend Julie sat next to Natasha on the bed, holding her hand. Nicholai stood on the opposite side, wearing a track in the plush carpet. His hand scrubbed down his ashen face.

Natasha lay on the bed, a sheet draped over her raised knees. A tiny slip of a woman knelt between her legs. Her purple hair stuck out from her head like she'd put her finger in a light socket. Blood soaked the bed, surrounded the woman kneeling in it.

"Push," she commanded.

Natasha crunched her body, her head moving

toward her knees. A look of determination mixed with pain contorted her face. Her eyes scrunched closed, and her lips turned blue from the strain.

"That's it, keep going, Natasha," the purple-haired woman coached in a thick Australian accent. "I can see the head. Just a little longer."

Natasha collapsed back onto the pillow. Her black hair lay matted against her head from perspiration. An anguished wail left her dry lips.

Nicholai froze and turned to his sister. "No! Tasha, no!"

Tears fell from her eyes. "Vlad's dying, Nikko."

Nicholai's gazed darted to Desmond. He nodded slightly in confirmation, concerned to say anything aloud for fear Natasha might hear.

"Stephan is there, Natasha," Desmond assured her. "He's trying to save him."

The purple-haired woman turned. Time froze when their eyes met. Her elfin features, small nose, and prominent cheekbones made a beautiful combination. Somehow her wild hair complemented her pretty face rather than detract from it. Her petite body shifted under his stare, giving him a nice view of the way her tight striped T-shirt hugged her full breasts. She was a vision.

A demon! he realized when he sent his senses out. Desmond stormed into the room.

"Get away from her," he commanded, advancing on the woman.

Nicholai met him and rested a staying hand on his shoulder. "She is Natasha's friend."

"And midwife," the tiny woman informed him. "Now, if you don't mind."

She turned back to Natasha just as she crunched her body and gave another push.

"That's it, Natasha." Julie slid an arm around Natasha's back to support her position. "You can do it. Keep pushing. Harleigh, you ready?"

"Of course, I am." The female demon smiled, and Desmond's breath left his lungs. "This is it. Push! Push!"

Natasha let out a scream to wake the dead. Desmond adverted his eyes. After a brief pause, a baby's cry filled the room.

"Good on ya, Tasha." Harleigh finished wrapping the infant in a blanket. "I knew you had it in ya. He's a handsome little fellow."

She placed the baby on Natasha's chest. The new mother stroked his cheek. Tears streamed down her face as she gazed lovingly at the infant.

"My life is now complete," she cooed to the newborn with a smile.

Julie stroked his head, and a tear rolled down her cheek. Nicholai moved back to the bed and sat beside his mate. He wrapped an arm around her, then reached out to the baby.

It gripped his finger in its tiny hand.

"He likes you already, Nicholai," Natasha whispered in a weak voice.

Harleigh ran to get more towels when Natasha's face went ghostly white.

"What is it?" Nicholai asked. His eyes met his sister's. "No, Natasha. It cannot be true."

"Oh, Nicholai," Julie wailed, turning into his chest.

Natasha's body convulsed. Harleigh knelt in the pool of blood, working over Vlad's mate furiously.

"Nicholai, I want you and Julie to raise the baby." The wish left Natasha in a breathy sigh.

Juliette gasped. Hard sobs shook her body, making Nicholai move in unison.

"What's going on?" Desmond asked, unable to keep quiet for another minute. It was obvious he was the only one in the room that didn't understand why not only the women were crying, but even Nicholai had tears in his eyes.

Then he heard it. Natasha's heart beat erratically. It skipped a beat, two. Natasha was slipping away, fading quickly.

"Tasha, I forbid it! You may not follow Vladimir into the Great Beyond." Nicholai loomed over his sister.

Her legs fell open, arms went slack around the child. More blood flowed about the demon on the bed. Connor rose from the floor. The pooch laid his head on the bed and let out a sorrowful whimper.

Nicholai gently took the infant from his sister's chest and handed him to Julie. "Tasha, no! You will not leave me. Will not leave your child!"

Natasha steady stare moved from her child to her brother. "Promise me you and Julie will raise him. Love him."

"I will promise no such thing, sister mine," his sentence broke on a sob, "because you will be here to raise him yourself."

With the last of her strength, Natasha's eyes pinned Julie's. The expression on her face appeared much fiercer than her small voice when she squeaked, "Promise me."

Julie glanced down on Nicholai's sister with tears

streaming over both cheeks. She covered Tasha's hand with her own. Her voice was but a whisper when she made her vow. "I promise."

Natasha's eyes closed, and Harleigh yelled, "Natasha, don't you dare leave us!"

Chapter 19

The last thing Vladimir Starikovich felt before the nothingness took him was Stephan's healing energy radiating through his chest, but his friend should have saved the effort. Vlad could have told him his sire's dagger struck true. The instant it pierced his heart, he'd recognized it as a fatal blow.

Pain. So much pain. Every broken bone, each torn ligament from the fall ached with a fiery burn, but nothing compared to the thought of leaving Natasha. Then the darkness came to wash away the pain. He no longer felt his physical wounds, but the loss of his heartmate—that he felt with an intensity that would have stolen his breath if he'd been breathing.

Not breathing. His mind stumbled at the thought. He wasn't breathing. He pushed his awareness out. Nothing. He reached for Tasha's mind. Nothing.

I'm dead.

It was the only explanation. His heart did not beat here, his lungs took in no air, though he still seemed to have a body, or at least it felt like he did. The darkness made it difficult to tell.

This is what death is like?

An eternity of darkness, with only your thoughts to entertain you, or haunt you as in his case. He'd spend his eternity thinking of her. Their child.

I love you. The last thing she'd said before he'd

blocked their mindlink in his mind. Why hadn't he said those three little words back? Now he'd never get the chance. He'd regret it for the rest of his…

Life was no longer the correct word to end the saying. He'd have eternity to regret his decisions, all of them. From allowing his sire to slaughter his human family, to waiting so long to follow the pull of his heart and claim his heartmate. So much to regret. So many sins to pay for.

Perhaps that was the reason for the darkness. Instead of the Great Beyond, he'd gone to purgatory to await judgment. And he'd no doubt be condemned.

A faint light appeared in the distance. The Alpha watched it expand, pushing away the shadows. When his vision cleared, he realized a thick blanket of fog covered the ground. He glanced down his body. It appeared whole. He wore a white, pristine suit. Next, Vlad examined his hands, flipping them over several times when he realized they were not swollen or bloody from pummeling Sergei.

He stood alone. Nothing else could be seen, no other people, just a great expanse of bright light and the cloud-like fog, so thick his feet disappeared beneath.

Now what?

His mind went to Natasha. Had the baby been born? Had it survived? He prayed it would. Having a child to care for would give her a reason to live. As much as he wanted to be with her, he didn't want this for her. This nothingness. This void.

He wanted her to continue to be with her family and friends, most especially their child. He wanted her to *live*.

"But what about what *I* want?"

Vlad whirled around at the sound of Natasha's voice, and his eyes drank her in. Adorned in a flowing white gown, his mate glowed with a radiance only possible in the hereafter. Gone were the colored strands of her hair, leaving it a natural obsidian color. The surrounding light glistened on the lustrous strands. It looked so soft falling about her shoulders. He couldn't believe she was real. Maybe she wasn't. She looked like an angel standing before him…perhaps she was.

She glided toward him, her dress flowing behind her body. The instant her arms wrapped around him, he knew. She was his heartmate. This was Natasha. Through the connection between them, his body recognized hers. His very soul recognized hers.

Vlad wrapped his arms around her and squeezed her to him in a tight embrace. Suddenly, eternity didn't seem so grim. Not if he got to spend it with her.

"Oh, Vlad," she whispered in his ear. "I was so afraid."

"I know, *milenky*, I know. But you are now safe. I'll never allow anything to hurt you."

His fingers laced in her silky tresses to hold her against his neck. She nuzzled in like a child wanting to be soothed after a bad dream.

Their child!

His gut clenched. Fear crept up his spine. His eyes darted around the great expanse. Where was their child?

He put his mate away from him and turned in a complete circle to make sure the babe had not joined them.

"He's not here." Tasha laced her fingers with his.

"How did you know who I was looking for?"

She gave him a sad smile. "I'm still in your mind.

In fact, here I don't even have to use our mental path. I just seem to know what you are thinking."

Vlad reached for her other hand. "So, our son lives?"

Tasha nodded. "He does. He is very strong, like his father."

"But he was born early. He must be so tiny."

"Yes, but he will survive. Harleigh said she saw it in a vision."

"Your friend is psychic?"

"Yes, and a demon."

Shock straightened Vlad's spine. Natasha tightened her grip on his hands to keep him from releasing her as she relayed the tale of how she discovered her good friend was not only a demon but also a midwife. With each detail she relayed, his concerns eased, until at last, they abated entirely. It seemed they owed the life of their child to the demon's knowledge and actions. He'd be eternally grateful.

"So, Nicholai and Juliette will raise the boy?"

"I hope you agree they were a good choice."

"If we cannot be there for him, then at least he will have your brother and Juliette."

"I know they will be great parents. You should have seen the way Julie looked at our son when she held him for the first time. Love radiated through the room, Vlad. She's going to make an amazing mother."

"And your brother? He agreed to care for our child?"

Vlad knew the answer before she spoke it. Of course, Nicholai would agree. He loved his sister dearly, would do anything for her. And the Alpha would make sure to bring their son up in the ways of their breed, help him become a strong and noble warrior. It reassured Vlad, but his heart still grieved for the child he would never know. However, if they couldn't live together as a family, at least he'd be with his heartmate in the Great Beyond.

"I feel the same way." Tasha squeezed his hand as her eyes misted with unshed tears. "At least we have each other and can keep watch over him as he grows."

Vlad took her in his arms and pressed his lips to her forehead. "I love you." His breath ghosted across her skin just as a strange pull pulsed through his body.

****

Tearing her eyes away from the sight of the tigers eating Sergei's body, Tatiana watched her heartmate donate blood to Stephan. The Alpha leader appeared ghostly pale. His face etched with lines from the strain. He'd been working over Vladimir for an hour, refusing to let the male go into the Great Beyond. But it didn't look good. For all his efforts, Stephan only managed to act like a life-support system by keeping Vlad's blood circulating and his lungs breathing as the Alpha leader's healing energy flowed through Vlad's body.

At her insistence, the two male demons remained so she might talk to them as Stephan worked to heal the Alpha. The demons looked on in awe at the curative light which emanated from Stephan's palms.

"The vampire is healing him?" the larger blond asked.

Tatiana refused to answer any questions. The last thing their enemies needed to know was anything about their powers.

"Your Majesty, don't you think we should leave?" the other demon whispered, obviously not realizing vampires possessed extraordinary hearing.

"Your Majesty?" Tatiana's eyebrow rose. "Mind explaining that?"

The demons exchanged glances. The thickly muscled male scrubbed his fingers over his five o'clock shadow.

"Well," Tatiana prompted when he didn't answer right away.

"I am the king of all demons."

He paused as if expecting a reaction, but he'd wait a long time for one from her. She'd spent hundreds of years keeping her feelings bottled deep inside. She never reacted emotionally, always kept herself in check. It was one of the reasons she'd been asked to join the Alpha Council, she remained as cool under pressure as any of the males on the team.

"So, *king,* what's your name?"

"Varrick," he responded easily.

His stance appeared relaxed, hands held loosely down at his sides, but Tatiana sensed the coil of power within. This male was a warrior, ready for battle. She understood why he was king.

"So, tell me, Varrick"—she refused to give him any respect by using his title—"did you order the kidnapping and torture of my mate?"

Because if so, she'd take his head from his shoulders.

The other demon blanched, then his body tensed.

"Easy, Cyrus," Varrick murmured. His red eyes pinned her under their hard stare. "I do not answer to vampires, even pretty ones."

Her hands clenched into fists at his insolent tone. His lack of response was as good as a confirmation as far as she was concerned. Her muscles tensed, body readied to pounce.

Calm yourself, kotik kisa, *do not attack him. He was not one of my captors.*

But, Demetri, he probably ordered you to be taken.

Stephan does not want you to attack. Keep them talking. He wants to know why they helped us fight.

Fine, she'd get Stephan his answers, then kick the demon's ass for his part in her mate's abduction. Her heartmate's chuckle played through her mind.

"So, Varrick. What brought you to our woods?"

"I have a female who is out of control, needs to be reined in."

Tatiana knew instantly to whom he referred. "You mean that bitch with the blue sparklers for fingers?"

A half smile lifted one corner of his mouth. "That would be her."

Tatiana, her name is Jara.

I know. I ran into her the night we found you. She was one of your captors.

One of my torturers.

The reminder heated her blood with a fiery need for revenge. "We have something in common, Varrick. You want to rein her in. I want to get my hands on her."

"It would seem we have a mutual goal," the demon king agreed.

"But, sir—" the other demon cut in. The lift of the king's hand stilled the remainder of his sentence in his throat.

"Perhaps there is a way we might work together to achieve our goals"—Varrick's eyes darted over to where Stephan worked over Vladimir—"since we have a common interest."

****

Desmond and Nicholai materialized next to one another in the white bedroom, each holding handfuls of herbs. Julie, cradling the tiny infant in her arms, closed Connor outside the room, then made her way over to stand beside the bed. The petite demon headed toward the Alphas with due haste.

"Give me those," Harleigh demanded, reaching for the plants. "What took you two so long?"

Desmond handed her the pile. When their fingers brushed, a jolt coursed through his body. "You gave us quite a list."

"So what! Do you think bringing someone back from the brink is an easy spell? The only thing keeping Natasha's soul from completely leaving this world is her child. A part of her still wants to be with the boy, and that's what we will use to call her back."

Harleigh went to work mixing the herbs in the bowl Julie had used to wet Tasha's face as she'd labored. In no time, her delicate hands mixed the greenery into a gummy paste.

Nicholai moved around the bed. "What can I do to help?"

"Put this on her stomach, as it absorbs it will help heal whatever went wrong. I think her uterus tore in the birth, but I can't be sure. All I know is there's way more blood than there should be. Hurry, if you want to save your sister."

Desmond adverted his eyes when Nicholai pulled the sheet from Tasha's naked body. He focused on the demon instead. She brushed the back of her hand across her forehead, leaving a greenish-brown stain from the vegetation. If the situation wasn't so dire, he'd have teased her.

"I'm done," Nicholai announced and covered his sister with the sheet. "What do I do next?"

"Nothing more you can do," Harleigh informed him. "Give me a minute, then I'll start."

She closed her eyes and folded her hands in front of her chest in prayer. For several seconds, no one spoke or moved. All eyes remained on the woman, waiting to see what she'd do next.

The air changed. Energy filled the room, not the tingling energy of a person drawing power to them, but a warm, soothing energy. It flowed around Desmond's body in waves, bringing a sense of peace and tranquility. His muscles relaxed, and he noticed so too did the others in the room. Everyone seemed affected by the extraordinary sensation.

A soft, almost contented sigh left Harleigh's full lips. "There. Now I can begin."

She laid one hand on Natasha's head and the other on the infant's. "I need a focal point." Her eyes found Desmond's briefly before darting across the room to settle on a table. "The flowers will do. They are natural, enticing."

At her comment, Desmond noticed for the first time fresh flowers occupied a vase on the desk. His attention quickly returned to Harleigh when she began to chant.

Her violet eyes went vacant as her angelic voice lifted to the sky. A lilting melody filled the room, wrapping them in its precious notes.

"Divine Mother Goddess, divine Father God, blessed Spirit, I come to you this day with love and respect and ask of you to bring your divine healing energy in this sacred space," she sang. "May you send your healing energy to this person. I implore you, to assist me in holding her to this world. Empower us. Strengthen us. And support us as we walk her back to the blessed path of life."

Chapter 20

Vlad took Tasha into his arms. Even here, her warmth radiated through him. She snuggled against him, wrapped her arms about his waist in a tight hug. A tear wet his shirt.

Vlad ran his fingers through her soft hair. "Why do you cry?"

"For our son." She pressed against him harder, melting against his body. "He'll never know his mother and father. Orphaned from birth."

Vlad nodded. His gut twisted, but determined to sooth his heartmate he whispered, "He will have Nicholai and Juliette. They will do right by him. See he is brought up to be a fine man."

"I know." Her body shook.

"And we will have each other."

His fingers splayed in her hair, drawing her head back so he could gaze upon her beautiful, tear-streaked face. The sight tore his heart in two. Vlad bent to kiss away her tears, pressing his lips to one cheek, then the other, until at long last the tears ceased.

"Better now?" Hope lightened his heart.

She gave a small shrug. "As well as I can be without our child."

Vlad pinned her with his intense stare, willing her to believe his sincerity. "Natasha, you are my other half, my heart, the very air I breathe. You give me a reason to exist whether as flesh and blood or in the afterlife. Without you, there is only darkness and emptiness for me. Just because I am strong, does not mean I cannot feel utter despair and loneliness. Your love keeps me warm, keeps the cold away.

"Even here, in the Great Beyond, no light, no warmth came until you arrived. I stood in total darkness, completely void of any feeling other than desolation and hopelessness. Then you arrived, bringing light, love. You changed everything with your presence."

"Oh, Vlad," she whispered, then laid her head on his shoulder.

"I know you grieve for our son, for the loss of being a parent to him. I do as well. I know the joy of raising children, remember it well, and I wish you had been able to experience it. But know this, Natasha, I will spend eternity trying to make up the loss of him to you. I may never be enough, but as the Fates are my witness, I will never leave you wanting for love."

"I know, Vladimir. Being with you for eternity is the only thing making the separation from our son bearable. Being here in your arms, knowing we can be together, it soothes my heartache, calms my mind." She shifted, glancing up at him. Tears once more pushed into her eyes. "I will always mourn the loss of the time with our son, but I know in my heart Nicholai and Juliette will do right by him. He will be loved and cared for. As long as you are with me, I can face anything."

Vlad gave a weak smile. It did not reach his eyes. "I will try to be enough for you."

Concern narrowed her dark brows. "But you are enough! You are my reason to go on. Your love for me lifts me up, will carry me through this time. If we cannot have a life together in the world, then at least we will have our eternity together here in the Great Beyond."

A large tree sprouted up from the fog next to them. From the thick trunk, limbs branched out. Green leaves and long bunches of delicate pink blossoms dripped from the boughs. The tiny blooms cascaded from the tree in three-foot lengths. Behind the tree more foliage sprouted in Technicolor shades of burgundy, lilac, and azure. Light showed through the thick florae, playing with the color, making it take on subtle hues that added to the beauty.

Tasha gasped. "Did you make that?"

"No. I thought you created it."

"What could it mean?"

A strange pulling sensation formed in his stomach, something between nausea and a cramp. He pushed the sensation down. "I don't know."

"It's so beautiful, like Heaven." She turned her wide gaze on him. "Do you think it might be? Heaven, I mean."

"It certainly seems like Heaven."

Tasha's face twisted before she pulled away from him and wrapped an arm around her waist. "I don't feel right."

Vlad reached for her. "What's wrong?"

"My stomach," she grunted, doubling over.

He laid a hand on the small of her back. "It will pass. I experienced it a moment ago myself."

"I…I don't think this will pass, Vlad. Something is wrong. Something is happening." Her form wavered slightly. If he hadn't been staring directly at her, he'd have missed it.

"Tasha." He grabbed her shoulders and helped her stand upright. "Look at me. Use me to focus. Push the feeling away."

"It's pulling me. Like something is calling to my spirit, wanting me to leave."

"Don't you dare go!" Panic made the order come out harsher than he'd intended.

She couldn't leave. He would not survive eternity without her. Had he been judged for his transgressions on Earth? Was an eternity without his heartmate to be his punishment? He couldn't bear it. His fingers tangled with hers in an effort to hold her to him. "You must stay here with me, Tasha. Fight this."

Her body became translucent. "I can't, Vlad." Her ethereal voice barely reached his ears. "I'm trying, but I can't."

Desperation knotted his stomach. The cramping returned.

"You must! Don't you leave me here all alone!" His voice echoed in the vast space. The beautiful foliage started to wither as if tied somehow to her.

Her mouth worked, but no sound came out. As she faded completely from sight, he just made out the words, I love you.

In a blast of light that would have blinded an angel, Natasha disappeared. Ripped from him. The sensation of her fingers around his remained. Vlad looked down on his empty hand, turning it over in disbelief.

His eyes darted frantically, searching for some sign of his beloved. Vlad's legs refused to support his weight. He knelt on the ground, surrounded by the dense fog. It rolled over him, covering his lower body as the plants disappeared, leaving only him and the haze.

Despair flowed over Vlad in a suffocating wave. The darkness pushed in, stamping out the light. Natasha left, taking Heaven with her. He had nothing, literally nothing as the last of the light faded.

"What have I done?" he called out to the Fates. "Do I really deserve this? This hell?"

If he did, at least Tasha wouldn't suffer it with him. No matter what lay ahead, at least she would not be tormented too. He might be going to Hell, but hopefully her goodness, her kindness earned her Heaven. Vlad just wished he told her he loved her before she'd been taken from him. He'd let yet another opportunity to declare his love for her pass, and he'd regret it for all eternity.

****

Natasha's eyes fluttered open. Light poured in, making them tear. Pain radiated from her stomach like knives piercing her flesh. "My stomach's on fire."

"I know, sister mine. We are getting you something for the pain."

Nicholai's voice startled her. She'd expected to hear Vlad. Attempting to clear her vision, she blinked several times. Her gaze roamed the room. Nicholai sat next to her on the white bed. Juliette stood nearby, still cradling Vlad's son. Desmond remained stone-still at the end of the bed with an expression that appeared to be a mixture of disbelief and awe. Natasha's eyes tracked to where he looked. She found Harleigh standing next to the bed.

Sweat dotted her forehead, and dark circles encompassed her tired eyes. She appeared weary; her body swayed. Just as she started to collapse, Desmond caught her in a blur of movement. He lifted her in his arms. Harleigh's head lolled against his shoulder, then her eyes closed.

"Take her to the next room," Nicholai ordered. "See to her while we see to Natasha."

"No." Harleigh's voice came out in a whispered hush. "I want to stay here with Tasha."

The demon's eyes opened, falling on Natasha with a concerned stare.

"I'm okay, Harleigh."

"Natasha's right. Or at least she will be with a little blood," Desmond adjusted the demon in his arms.

Harleigh did not struggle against the hold. The fact she remained limp against his body showed Natasha just how exhausted her friend must be. She wondered what happened to cause such a thing.

Before she voiced the question, Nicholai's wrist lay over her mouth, and his ancient blood trickled onto her tongue.

The crimson goodness left a coppery tang on her taste buds as the rich scent filled her nose. Her stomach gurgled with joy. Hunger pangs twisted her gut. She greedily lapped at the wrist, taking the healing blood inside. Her eyes closed of their own volition at the delectable taste, and her hand clamped around his forearm to keep it to her.

Nicholai ran his fingers through her hair, pulling it back from her face. "Easy, sister. I am not going anywhere. Drink your fill."

Tell me what happened, Nicholai, she sent over their link.

"I am not exactly sure what happened. It would

seem your friend saved your life, but I do not know how she managed to do it."

"I almost didn't do it," Harleigh added, sounding a little stronger. "The spell took a lot out of me."

Desmond turned his body so the woman in his arms could see Tasha. "Harleigh was amazing. She brought you back from the brink of death with a bunch of herbs and some hocus-pocus."

"Not hocus-pocus, you big lug. A special chant, one very old and not well-known. If I hadn't spent so much time reading in the Room of Tomes, I wouldn't have known it existed."

"What's the Room of Tomes?" Julie inquired as she rocked Tasha's baby.

"A place in my cousin's home that is filled with books. All kinds, so many that the shelves cannot contain them all. You should see all the stacks that are piled higher than me all around the floor."

Nicholai's stare left Natasha's face and flew to Harleigh. "Let me understand this. You are saying in a demon's home, there is a book which contained a spell to keep people from dying."

Harleigh nodded, and Tasha instantly sensed the reaction in her brother. His anger flowed through the room, building until the lamp next to the bed shook with his power. Natasha held firm to his arm.

What is it, Nicholai?

Demetri suffered for nothing!

What do you mean? I don't understand.

The demon just said there is a book that contained a spell to heal people. When the demons abducted Demetri, they claimed they did it to try to discover how to keep their breed from dying. They claimed they were trying to find out how we vampires heal so easily. Yet all the time, they had a way to save their race. His suffering and the deaths of the ones taken before him were for nothing!

Natasha closed the wounds on Nicholai's wrist with a flick of her tongue, then released his arm. If she didn't intercede, her brother might turn his wrath on Harleigh. With the pain in her belly abated, she wrapped the sheet around her body and eased herself into a seated position, then rested her back against the headboard.

Natasha reached for Vlad over their mindlink, needing his strength and support, the instinct to connect with him as automatic as breathing. Darkness, nothingness met her attempt. Grief swamped her, pushing in, sucking the air from her lungs.

Vlad was dead. Images of their time in the Great Beyond flooded her mind, but the sound of crying brought her out of the reverie. Her heartmate was gone, and if she didn't do something, her best friend would be too.

"Nicholai calm yourself." When he didn't comply, she cupped his cheek with her hand. "For the baby, calm yourself. You are upsetting him."

Her brother glanced quickly between Julie and Harleigh, then finally his gaze landed on her. Tasha forced what she hoped would be a reassuring smile. The expression on Nicholai's face informed her he found it sad rather than reassuring. "Let Harleigh explain. Perhaps there is a reason why she knew of the spell when the others didn't."

"Well, demon? Care to explain yourself?"

"What are you talking about?" Fire leapt into

Harleigh's eyes, and she squirmed out of Desmond's arms.

"I'm talking about why your kind saw fit to abduct, torture, and kill vampires under the guise of needing to discover the reason behind our ability to heal when you had a spell that brought people back from the brink of death."

Harleigh's hands fisted on her hips in pique, her hair pushed away from her head. Power emanated from her tiny body. Her violet eyes glowed a strange reddish color like they were changing behind a purple lens.

"Are you wearing contacts?" Natasha asked.

Harleigh ignored the question, her focus squarely on Nicholai. "I don't know anything about demons killing or torturing vampires. I have no idea what you are going on about."

"Both of you stop right now. You are scaring the baby. If you have to flex your power, do it away from him or so help me, I will make you both regret hurting him."

That defused the situation instantly. Harleigh's hair settled around her skull. Nicholai's power receded.

"Demons abducted and tortured our cousin, supposedly to discover why we are immune to illness."

Shock widened Harleigh's eyes. "I didn't know. I'm sorry. But my spell only brings people back from the brink of death. It can't heal them. Natasha's body healed itself."

Juliette quietly walked over and placed the baby in Natasha's arms. He felt so small and light. She looked down on his tiny face, still red from crying. Tears streaked his flushed cheeks but did not detract from his features. His bright eyes were black as coal, nose long and straight. His Siberian heritage proudly showed. Even his chin reminded her of a tiny version of his father's. He was the spitting image of Vladimir. Suddenly nothing else mattered, only her son. Vlad's son.

The babe settled immediately, but though no tears fell, his tiny body jerked with silent sobs left over from his incensed cry.

"It is okay, little one," Natasha cooed, running a finger down his cheek. He turned into the touch. "Uncle Nicholai and Auntie Harleigh did not mean to scare you."

"Of course, I didn't," Harleigh assured in a soft voice. "I'm so sorry."

"I am most sorry as well." Nicholai had the decency to look properly chastised. "I did not think about the baby."

"This is a time for joy, Nicholai. The baby survived the early birth, and Harleigh brought Natasha back to us." Juliette placed a reassuring hand on her mate's shoulder. "Do not demand answers Harleigh may not have. There will be time for questions later. Now is a time to rejoice in the miracles Harleigh brought to us."

Nicholai laid his hand over Julie's. "Of course, you are correct, my *lastochka*. We should be grateful for the blessings we received this day."

Desmond cleared his throat, drawing everyone's attention. "It would seem a discussion is in order. A calm, rational discussion. I shall contact Stephan and encourage him to bring here the demons that showed up to fight with us so we might hash all this out. In the meantime, I think Harleigh and I should go, leave the Peterhofs to have some time to themselves."

He took Harleigh by the shoulders and began to escort her out of the room. She put on the brakes just before they reached the door, then turned to flash a large grin at Natasha over her shoulder.

"Thank you, Harleigh." Natasha smiled back at her friend. "Thank you for saving my life and giving me a chance to watch my child grow."

"I'd do anything for you, Tasha. You know that."

"I know." She tipped her chin toward Harleigh in acknowledgment. "Now go rest up. I have a feeling we'll all need our strength for what's to come."

After the couple left the room, Natasha turned her full attention on her brother and his heartmate. "I owe the two of you my thanks as well."

"We didn't do anything," Julie protested.

"Yes, you did. You agreed to raise my child, care for him, love him. I can never tell you how much it meant to me."

"We will still be here for him, for you as well," Julie offered. "Stay with us. Raise him here where he'll be surrounded with love. Nicholai will spoil him rotten, but it will be done with love."

Tasha smiled. The idea of her brother spoiling anyone other than Julie seemed laughable, and yet the sentiment sent a warmth through her cold body straight to her heart. The heat spread slowly, warming her from the inside out until she felt comforted, protected by the sensation.

Demetri's presence flooded her mind. *Natasha, he lives.*

Nicholai's eye's widened. "Tasha!"

"I know," she replied. "Vlad is alive!"

Rapture poured over her as she reached for her

mate with her mind.

Chapter 21

Natasha cradled the tiny infant in her arms, rocking back and forth in the antique chair Nicholai had brought to her bedroom. She stared down into the tiny face, seeing Vlad in their child. Though covered with baby fat, the outline of his strong cheekbones displayed proudly. She traced down his straight nose with one finger and tapped his ruby lips. As he opened his mouth, his dark eyes stared into hers, misty from drying tears.

"Shhhh, little one. No more crying," she soothed as she sent the chair rocking. "It's all right. *Mamachka* has you. No reason to cry just because you woke up."

The doorknob turned, drawing both of their attentions across the room. Vlad pushed through the door. Though dressed in a dark gray suit with a crimson tie, he appeared more back-alley than debonair. Lines creased his forehead from the pain he still bore. His eyes, dull and weary, took in the room. Tasha knew his body still contained evidence of the recent battle, even though he'd spent the past two nights having healing sessions with Stephan. Demetri and Nicholai generously donated blood to him and their ancient power now flowed within him helping to heal him, but it would take another night or two for him to reach his full strength.

In the meantime, he'd been a doting father and

mate, barely letting Natasha or their child out of his sight. He refused to rest, seeing to their every need, and she found it endeared him to her all the more for it.

"I heard him cry. Is everything all right?" Vlad crossed the room and knelt in front of them.

Natasha gave him a reassuring smile. "Of course. He simply awoke from his nap crying as most babies do."

Vlad's brows furrowed deeply over his obsidian eyes. "Is he hungry? Does he need to be changed?"

"He is fine. Look, he wanted his *batya*."

Vlad's shaking hand wrapped around the small one reaching for him from the swaddling blanket. Realization dawned on her heartmate's face. "Is he not advanced? I do not remember other children being so aware at only a few days old."

"Who is the last vampire baby you spent any time with?"

Vlad shifted slightly as if kneeling had become uncomfortable. "I don't recall ever being around a vampiric child."

"Please sit, Vlad. You are hurting." Natasha started to rise from the rocking chair.

Before she shifted fully forward, Vlad laid a stilling hand on her shoulder. "Don't you dare get up on my account. You need to rest far more than I do. You gave birth only two days ago and almost died in the process."

"But I'm fine. You aren't the only one Stephan has healed. Between sessions with him and donations from the Alphas, I am perfectly fine." Her gaze roamed over her heartmate's body. "But you are not yet at one hundred percent."

An inelegant snort burst from Vlad's throat. "I am fine. My only concern is for you and the baby."

He cupped her cheek in his large palm. "You look beautiful, by the way."

Tasha smiled. She'd chosen a crimson gown that matched the color of Vlad's tie perfectly. Nicholai gave the satin creation to her as a gift in celebration of the event about to take place. She'd toned down her hair and makeup. Gone were the multi-colored strands. She'd dyed her hair back to its original dark color, and Julie had gathered it on top of her head in a loose chignon. Instead of the usual thick eyeliner, she'd opted for subtle natural eyeshadow and some mascara. Today her usual Goth look and spiked choker would not do, but she knew tomorrow she'd be putting it back on.

A soft knock sounded on the door.

"Come in, Marcus." Vlad's deep voice startled the baby, making him jump in her arms. His little lip began to quiver.

She patted his back, cradling him against her breast, and sent her love to surround him. He settled immediately as Marcus crossed the room. "Hey there, Boris and Natasha, it's about time for the G and G."

Tasha giggled, and Vlad shot his fellow Alpha a look which clearly stated he didn't appreciate being called Boris even in jest.

"What is G and G?" Vladimir gingerly rose to his full height.

"A grip and grin." Marcus reached for the child. "Let me have a turn with the little man."

Natasha transferred the baby to Marcus, making sure to support his head with her hand. Marcus held him like a football, cradled in the crook of one arm. He tickled the baby's tummy with a thick finger. Natasha had to admit, he looked rather at ease with their son. She wondered if he had much experience with children. His brown eyes were full of love as he gazed down on the boy. The black suit he wore complemented his large frame and chestnut hair, making him look more like a runway model than a battle-hardened fighter. Tasha loved how he joked and played, even though he was an Alpha.

"And what's a grip and grin?" Vlad crossed his thick arms over his chest.

Marcus graced them with a wide smile. "A grip and grin. You know, taking a picture."

"Oh, like when you wrap an arm around someone to take a picture with them." Tasha stood.

"Exactly, Natasha." Marcus glanced from the baby to her. "Now let's go. Everyone is waiting downstairs. Stephan sent me up to get you…and him."

Marcus bounced their little bundle of joy in his arms.

"You go ahead," Vlad suggested, then reached for her hand. "We'll be down in just a second."

Marcus left the room, giving them some time alone. It was the first time they'd been truly alone since the baby had been born. Vlad took her in his strong embrace, crushing her to him as if he wanted to lose himself in the softness of her body. She wrapped her arms around his narrow waist, reveling in the hard planes of his body pressed against hers. She felt protected, loved.

You are those things and so much more, he sent over their mindlink.

I could stay like this forever.

Me too, Natasha. But I think our presence is required downstairs.

Natasha snuggled closer, allowing the strength of his arms to surround her. *Just another minute.*

His deep chuckle came from low in his chest, and she knew he would indulge her. Her mind wandered back to two nights ago.

When Harleigh brought her back from the Beyond, she'd thought she'd lost Vlad. She'd been alone and scared. Only the love for her child kept her from seeking a way to join him. Then he'd come back to her, and suddenly her world felt complete again.

A smile played on her lips as a contented sigh pushed through. Vlad pulled back slightly and took her chin between his finger and thumb. He tilted her head before he placed a kiss on her lips that curled her toes. It began as a gentle caress, barely a touch, but quickly turned urgent.

His mouth pushed against hers, his tongue slid along the seam of her lips, bidding entry. She welcomed him into her mouth. His passion flowed over their link, feeding her own. Tasha's breath left her lungs in short bursts, and she moaned. He tasted of mint. The delicious flavor combined with his masculine, woodsy scent to drive her wild.

Two days, two long days of not making love. Their bodies craved one another, longed for each other. Tasha covered his racing heart with her hand, enjoying the way his muscle flexed beneath her palm.

Laughter drifted up from below to infiltrate their moment. The interruption calmed her like nothing else could have. She pulled back from his embrace to gaze up into his handsome face.

"We need to get downstairs."

"I intend to finish this later." Vlad's eyes sparkled with promise. His deep, guttural voice sent a shiver of anticipation down her spine.

"I certainly hope so," she replied with a wink and a mischievous grin.

Vlad took her hand and led her through Nicholai's estate to the music room. Her heartmate pushed the door open with a grand sweep of his arm to bid her entrance. The room looked beautiful with its tan-colored walls and decorative white molding. The carpet complemented the paint with its intricate patterns in reds and beige. It crushed beneath her high heels when she entered. Several chairs in various styles sat scattered around the room, each padded with velvet tan fabric. In one corner stood a baby grand piano with a beautiful flower arrangement on the top.

A fine feast spread over a long table against one wall, no doubt provided from Nicholai's restaurant, The Cold Shoulder. The enticing aroma filled the air, making Tasha's stomach growl in anticipation.

All the Alphas were in attendance as were their mates. Juliette stood off to one side talking to Katrina, Stephan's heartmate. Both women wore strapless gowns. Julie's was gathered under the bosom with an empire waist, no doubt to hide the womanly curves she seemed embarrassed of. Though why she didn't like her figure, Natasha would never know. Nicholai seemed to love it.

Much more form fitted, Kat's gown clung to her lithe body. The blue-gray color perfectly matched her eyes and complemented her long blonde hair.

Across the room, Marcus stood next to his mate,

Christina. The green dress she wore accented her emerald eyes and red hair. Alex stood with them, looking handsome. The suit he sported had a thin pin-stripe pattern that matched the blue of his eyes. He pushed a hand through his blond hair, messing it as all eyes turned to Natasha and Vladimir.

Demetri crossed the large room to receive them. After grasping Vlad's forearms in greeting, he turned to embrace Natasha in a bear of a hug.

"My little cousin, you have made a strapping child." Tasha smiled as he continued. "The babe is strong, a survivor. But then I would expect no less from our bloodline."

Tatiana joined them dressed in black slacks and a loose-fitting blouse, not as formal as the other women, but none the less attractive. Her fingers laced with Demetri's when she spoke. "What Demetri means to say is congratulations."

Her cousin rolled his eyes. "Natasha knows what I mean."

Yes, I do. She'd read his emotions through their mindlink. Demetri loved their son. In fact, the Alpha was already quite smitten with the tiny boy. He presented with a gruff exterior, but inside Demetri was a softy, at least when it came to children. He'd make a great father one day, Tasha mused.

Not any time soon, I hope. Vlad sent over their link. *He's arrogant enough without having fathered a child. What was that about* his *bloodline being the reason for our child's strength? I believe my bloodline played no small part in his survival.*

Of course, it did, Tasha reassured her mate, not wanting male egos to ruin this special occasion. It seemed to appease Vlad, for she sensed the tension leave his body.

The group gathered around the couple, and Natasha reclaimed her son from Marcus' arms.

"So, what have you decided to name him?" Desmond asked in his proper British accent.

"Wait, don't tell us, let us guess," Marcus suggested, wide-eyed. "I'll go first. Colby-Jack."

The ridiculous name earned a laugh from the group.

Alex clapped Marcus on the back. "Good try, but I'm betting they picked Tom Collins."

"No, no," Desmond broke in. "I'm betting they named him Baby Guinness."

"Or how about Rob Roy," Marcus chimed in, laughing. "No better yet, Fuzzy Navel or White Russian."

The quips earned a growl from Vlad, who braced his feet wide and crossed his arms over his chest. His disapproving stance made Katrina, Julie, and Christina obviously uncomfortable, for the three of them stopped laughing and donned wide-eyed stares as if scared he would go berserk.

Natasha joined the Alphas in their laughter and shook her head. While the others were no doubt laughing at the baby names, she found it ridiculous how scary Vlad could be. Little did those women know he was just a big teddy bear. Well, maybe not exactly a teddy bear, more like a Siberian brown bear with a good heart. But, nevertheless, the women had nothing to fear from Vlad. Natasha made a mental note to reassure them after the ceremony.

As the laughter died down, Tatiana stepped

forward. "Don't you boys ever think about anything other than drinks?"

"Hey, I guessed a cheese," Marcus whined.

Tatiana shook her head, sending her black hair swirling around her head. "All kidding aside. I bet they named him Nicholai or maybe Demetri."

"I would never do that to a child," Vlad said, earning scrutinizing looks from both of Natasha's relatives. It wasn't until her heartmate laughed, her family realized he'd been joking.

"How about calling him Boris?" Marcus suggested with a smile.

Christina smacked her mate hard on the shoulder. "Enough joking. Tell us his name."

Natasha exchanged a glance with Vlad. They had decided on a name last night. "Viktor," she announced.

Silence settled over the crowd while they absorbed the name, then Connor barked his approval from the side of the room which triggered a round of congratulatory hugs and pats on the shoulders. Everyone seemed to agree Viktor was a fitting name for their son.

"I believe it is time to officially welcome Viktor into our fold." Stephan reached for the baby.

Natasha handed him the child. They all took a seat for the naming ceremony, except Stephan who stood with the child in the center of the room.

As the leader of the Alphas, it was his right to preside over the ritual. His large frame stood tall and proud in his designer suit. A leather thong tied his hair back from his face. Dark, sapphire eyes roamed over the infant before he addressed the crowd. A slight smile played on his lips, making him appear as if he enjoyed this moment almost as much as Natasha.

"We are gathered here today to welcome Viktor Starikovich into our world. We give thanks for this tiny miracle. May he grow to live a long and honorable life. Everyone present will promise to guide him, instruct him in our ways. His care is entrusted to each of us, and we will do no less than offer our protection to him. Each one of us will vow today to teach him, watch over him. Do those present promise to help Viktor grow and learn our ways?

"We do," the chorus of voices answered.

Viktor let out a yelp of surprise and began to cry. Stephan looked stricken, as his eyes darted to Natasha. She rose from her chair to rescue the big, bad Alpha leader. She settled her son on her shoulder and rocked her body side to side, all the while singing a soft lullaby to him. He quieted instantly at his mother's voice.

"That's a beautiful song." Juliette rose. "It reminds me of another I know."

Christina nodded her head. "I know the one you mean."

The redhead grabbed Julie by the hand and led her to the piano. Connor joined them, circling three times before laying down under the instrument, and Christina began to play an intricate introduction. Julie's beautiful voice filled the room when she sang. Natasha didn't know the song the duet performed, but she appreciated the sentiment. This was not the first time she'd heard them perform together, and she hoped it wouldn't be the last. Their music made every celebration special.

Vlad wrapped an arm about her shoulder and tucked her to his side. He kissed her temple. "I love you," he whispered against her skin.

"I love you too," she replied, gazing up into his eyes. A happiness the like of which she'd never seen before lit the dark eyes.

Nicholai approached them and held out a drink to Vlad which he accepted gratefully. Her brother placed a quick kiss on both her cheeks. "Congratulations, sister mine. You have a beautiful baby, and I am ever so grateful you and your heartmate are with us to raise him."

"Thank you." Vlad shifted his weight between his feet. "I understand you and Juliette were going to raise Viktor if Natasha and I…"

Nicholai raised a hand to quell the remainder of his sentence. "No need to finish that. The two of you made it through."

"Thanks to Stephan." Vlad lifted his chin in the Alpha leader's direction in acknowledgment.

"It's been quite a couple of days," Demetri commented, joining the group. "First, your sire shows up, bringing with him a crazy demon and a…a…I'm not sure what the creature was."

"He was no vampire or demon that is for sure. His abilities were incredible," Nicholai said.

"Varrick called him The Source, whatever that means," Tatiana volunteered as she settled beside Demetri.

Demetri put an arm around his mate's waist. "I believe Stephan has summoned Varrick. Perhaps when the King of the Demons arrives, he can enlighten us about this Source."

"That doesn't sound good." Natasha worried her lower lips between her teeth. "This Varrick is coming here?"

"Do not worry, my sister. He would not be stupid enough to try anything. All of the Council will be in attendance when the two meet."

Vlad gave her shoulder a squeeze. "I'd never let anything happen to the two of you."

The sincerity in his voice rang out. And by the softening of her brother's and cousin's eyes, they recognized it as well.

"I think it is about time we ate," Nicholai stated, changing the subject before things got any mushier. "My chef outdid himself. Come, let us fill our stomachs."

"Sounds good to me." Tatiana led Demetri by the hand toward the table.

"Are you hungry?" Vlad asked.

"Yes," Natasha admitted with a sheepish grin as her stomach rumbled its response to his question.

"You remain here. I'll bring you a plate."

While Vlad and Nicholai headed for the buffet, Tasha gazed down upon Viktor and smiled at her little man. He'd fallen asleep while they talked. Viktor's long lashes lay like two dark crescents against his pale skin. Viktor.

It was the perfect name, strong, sure. It spoke to what he would become. Their son would be raised with pride and love. He'd grow into his name. He'd become a victor. How could he not with Vladimir as a father?

Gazing at the small bundle nestled in her arms, it was easy to forget how tough and invincible he'd be one day. How courageous and bold being exposed to his father and the Alphas would make him. In just a few years, Viktor would be old enough to start honing his skills. In the blink of an eye, he'd be full grown, ready to take his place on the Alpha Council. But for now, he was just a babe in his mother's arms.

He appeared so peaceful. She wished the calm would remain, but with the so-called Source on the loose and the King of the Demons coming to call, she doubted the serenity would last. Natasha let out a deep sigh and looked around the room at her family and friends. For tonight, she'd allow herself to be at peace. She and her son were safe surrounded by the love of good friends and family. For tonight, all was right with the world, and she intended to enjoy it while it lasted.

Epilogue

Alex stood in the back of the room, leaning a shoulder against the wall. Stephan chose to receive Varrick and his entourage in Nicholai's reading room. In the attached conservatory, Desmond and a female demon, who was Natasha's friend, stood talking while Desmond absently rubbed Julie's Irish wolfhound on its head. Behind them, the soothing sound of running water came from the fountain in the middle of the small room. Surrounding them on all sides sat lush green plants, giving the illusion of summer as Alex looked out through the circular dome of windows onto a scalped hedge garden.

In the reading room, Stephan and Varrick faced each other in the high-back leather chairs. The king brought a second demon with him. The unexpected visitor caused a moment's commotion on their arrival, but Stephan welcomed both men inside.

Alex gave Cyrus an assessing stare. According to Nicholai, who stood next to him, the demon had skills. Nicholai witnessed his fighting prowess on the battlefield. The fair-haired male, who kept glancing over at Desmond and Harleigh, looked rather effeminate with his blond hair and blue eyes. But the Alpha knew looks could be deceiving, and they most definitely were in this case. Those blue eyes were colored contacts. The vampires now knew all demons had red eyes. They also had preternatural powers though the king had been rather close-lipped about them so far.

Tatiana and Demetri stood behind Stephan's chair in obvious support. The warriors looked ready to pounce at the slightest provocation. Vlad remained off to one side, his feet braced wide, arms crossed over his chest. He smelled of smoke and outdoors from taking a cigarette break.

The fact he hadn't given up the habit since the birth of his child surprised Alex. Well, if he knew Natasha, she'd be getting onto him pretty soon about doing just that. A smile tugged at his lips as his gaze traveled to Marcus. His comrades had certainly been falling like dominoes. One after the other found his mate. Only he and Desmond remained footloose and fancy-free.

And didn't that just suck!

He wouldn't be finding a heartmate anytime soon, not with what Stephan had in mind.

His stare briefly flickered over Nicholai, who maneuvered within striking distance of Cyrus and Varrick, before returning to Desmond. He and Harleigh seemed to be deep in discussion. Stephan's deep voice drowned out their low conversation, and Alex quickly focused back on what was important—the Alpha leader's confab with the King of the Demons.

"So, Varrick, we are agreed then. We have a truce."

The demon nodded his thick head, sending his blond hair over his red eyes. He hadn't bothered to wear any contacts, and it added to the menacing look about the thickly muscled male. "An alliance, I believe would be a more fitting word. We agree to work together to hunt and destroy the threat to our world."

"Correct." Stephan steepled his fingers. "We will pool our resources, our…skills to see our common goal is achieved."

"And what of his sister?" Tatiana asked, clearly agitated. "She tortured Demetri and killed our kind. What will happen to her? Will you kill your own sister, Varrick?"

Cyrus shifted closer to his king, reading the threat in Tatiana's harsh tone. Varrick lifted a meaty hand to still the guard's movement and turned his intense gaze on the female Alpha. "My sister fell out of favor the day she went rogue. You want her, have her. All I ask is that you finish the job, or I will do it for you."

Tatiana didn't look convinced.

Stephan cleared his throat. "Since we have come to an understanding, I propose an exchange. I suggest you allow one of my Alphas to stay with you at your compound in Mason's Bluff. As an ambassador of sorts."

An affronted expression took Varrick's face. "I can't allow that. Vampires carry diseases which could kill us."

"No, we don't," Stephan assured him. "We possess a natural immunity."

"But you still carry disease."

"No, we don't. We don't get ill. We don't carry diseases. There is no reason not to allow one of us to stay with you."

Varrick's eyes narrowed. "You are pushing rather hard. Do you want to send someone to spy on me?"

"No, nothing like that," Stephan assured him. "I simply thought if I had a trusted liaison staying with you, he might help facilitate communication between us."

"Communication will be difficult." Varrick crossed a muscular leg, resting his ankle on the opposite knee. "We do not have much technology in the compound. The rock doesn't allow for it."

Stephan smiled. Alex had seen that smile before, a mixture of triumph and cunning. "Then I have the perfect man for the job. Alex is top rate with all things electronic. He's an expert in computers and satellite communications. He can stay at your compound and help bring you into the twenty-first century—technologically speaking."

Varrick's intense stare landed on Alex, and he straightened under the scrutiny, pushing away from the wall. "You can do that?"

Alex nodded once. "Yeah, I can wire anything, even a rock."

Varrick turned his attention back on Stephan. "And if I agree to have the male stay with me, I assume I can send you a demon in return?"

"Of course," Stephan answered easily.

"Very well, then Harleigh shall stay here with you."

Cyrus and Harleigh both made a noise of protest which died immediately when Varrick's head snapped in their direction. Cyrus' face reddened. His body shook with the effort to contain his anger. He obviously didn't approve of his king's choice.

"But, Varrick, don't you think there is someone better suited?" Harleigh asked.

"I think you are perfect. You are already acquainted with several of these vampires. You are good friends with that one's mate." The king gestured at Vlad, whose hands fisted at the mention of his heartmate. "You are familiar with this home, and no doubt, they can find a room for you."

"We will be moving our operation to Savannah," Stephan informed the demon.

"You mean to the plantation house?" Cyrus asked, making Alex wonder just how the demon knew of Marcus' place.

Before he could ask, Stephan continued, "The plantation in Savannah is more conducive to our needs."

Alex agreed it made an excellent choice. Marcus had recently built a top-notch training facility with an indoor pool, a weight room, and more than enough bedrooms for all the Alphas. Too bad he wouldn't be joining them.

Varrick rose from his chair and stuck out his hand to Stephan. "So, we have an agreement. Harleigh will remain with you, while Alex shall come with me."

Stephan rose to shake the king's hand, and Alex knew his life would never be the same.

A word about the author...

Born in Virginia, Brenda Sparks now resides in the Sunshine State with her incredibly supportive husband and their beloved son. Balancing her professional commitment to the local school district with her writing is challenging at times, but writing suspenseful paranormal romances is a passion that won't be denied.

Her idea of a perfect day is one spent in front of a computer with a hot cup of coffee, her fingers flying over the keys to send her characters off on their latest adventure.

Brenda loves to connect with readers. Please visit her at:

www.brenda-sparks.com

Thank you for purchasing
this publication of The Wild Rose Press, Inc.

For questions or more information
contact us at
info@thewildrosepress.com.

The Wild Rose Press, Inc.
www.thewildrosepress.com

www.ingramcontent.com/pod-product-compliance
Lightning Source LLC
Chambersburg PA
CBHW051539260626
47170CB00003B/1010